WHY YOU SHOULD NEVER KISS YOUR ENEMY

ERIN NICHOLAS

THE SERIES

Why You Should Never...

ABOUT THE BOOK...

The last thing single dad and surgeon Nate Sullivan needs is more stress and distraction in his life.

That makes his best friend's gorgeous, mouthy, doesn't-t-respect-schedules, hates-authority, has-no-boundaries sister a huge threat to his carefully balanced life.

Nate is the kind of guy Emma Dixon hates: buttoned-up, rigid, his-way-or-the-highway. So why is he the guy she can't quit thinking about and who she most loves sparring with?

They're like oil and water. But when they're thrown together on opposites sides of a "project"--Nate trying to keep his son from falling for the wrong girl and Emma playing cupid for the couple– they find they're more like gasoline and a match.

CHAPTER
ONE

"SO, why don't you ever ask me to take my clothes off?"

Nate Sullivan didn't miss a beat. He didn't act surprised, or amused or—most of all—interested. "Because X-rays can see *through* clothes." He also didn't lift his head from whatever he was putting into her medical record on the handheld computer.

Emma Dixon sighed. Nate was the one man in the world who looked at her with only exasperation. When he looked at her at all. She *hated* that she was attracted to him. "But it seems that you're passing up a great opportunity."

"Well, seeing women naked *is* why I went into medicine in the first place," he said, dragging the pad of his index finger over the screen. "But then shattered bones won my heart and that's the only thing I want to look at all day long now."

And that bugged the crap out of her, Emma could admit. Not that she believed Nate didn't like looking at naked women, but that he didn't want to see *her* without her clothes. She wasn't sure what to do with that. Men always wanted to see her without her clothes on.

"I know you're not gay. You have Michael, after all," she said, referring to Nate's eighteen-year-old son. "Do you have trouble getting it up?"

Nate didn't even blink as he continued tapping on the screen. He also didn't look up.

Okay, that was low. Childish even. He just brought out the worst in her. She became this sad attention-seeking-low-self-esteem-over-compensating hormonal teenage girl that she hated when she was around him. She wanted to get a reaction from him. Always. Any time they were together.

"I even wore my pretty bra, in case you wanted to see me in one of those skimpy gowns," she said, in spite of knowing she would not be proud of whatever came out of her mouth at that point.

Finally, he looked up and handed her a piece of paper. "Here's a refill on the pain meds and no sex for six more weeks." He completely ignored all of her attempts to rile him.

Bastard.

Emma looked at the prescription in her hand, then frowned at her surgeon. "You actually wrote that on the prescription?"

"Makes it official. This way, if you do it anyway and then come back in here complaining about how bad your hip hurts, I can officially say 'told you so'."

Emma resisted the urge to growl at him. Barely. "Seriously? It's already been twelve weeks."

He raised an eyebrow, in that very irritating you're-acting-like-a-four-year-old way he had. She swore he only gave that look to her.

"Six more weeks."

Nate Sullivan was cocky. Full of himself. Had a God complex. The whole nine yards. And he was completely and utterly immune to her charms. That made him more unique than the fact that he could put anyone back together again, no matter the trauma. It was thanks to him that she was now in one piece after the car accident and that she was walking again.

Unfortunately.

Knowing that she owed the guy who could make her bat-shit-crazy in under two minutes, made her...bat-shit-crazy.

"My physical therapist says that it's ridiculous to still have a sex limitation after this long," she said, folding the script and putting it in her pocket. She would fricking follow the damned thing because she would rather chew glass than hear "I told you so" from Dr. Sullivan.

"Does he?" Nate didn't seem concerned. He was sliding her X-rays back into their envelope.

"He says that I won't know what I can do until I try it."

"You sure he was talking about sex and not jogging?"

"You said no jogging yet either."

"Right."

"He says that part of his job is to help me try the things that might be a challenge at first. You know, the whole *physical therapy* thing. He says I can try the new things out with him."

That got Nate to look up. "Jogging, right?"

She leaned back, bracing her hands on the exam table behind her. Damn, there was something about him in that long lab coat and tie. She never saw him like that. He played football on the same amateur team as her brother, the Omaha Hawks, and he hung out with the guys afterward down at their favorite bar, Trudy's, so she always saw him in uniform or jeans. And he looked very fine in both. But once he'd become her doctor—not that she'd had any say in that, having been unconscious and all at the time—she'd seen him dressed up and in charge. And damned if it didn't make her tingle every time.

"Do you *really* think I need to wait six more weeks?"

"To jog?"

She allowed a long pause before saying, "Sure. Jogging."

He narrowed his eyes. "Yes. I think you need to wait six more weeks to...jog."

She had no desire to jog. She hadn't been a big fan of it before her accident and, frankly, the idea of landing on her hip and pelvis like that made her shudder. It didn't hurt much anymore but it seemed she always expected it to.

Nate started to turn away, then stopped. She followed his gaze to what had caught his attention. Her cane.

"What's that?"

"You walk around here like a know-it-all but you've never seen one of those?" she asked, her stomach knotting. She knew what he was going to say. It was the same thing her therapist had been saying for four weeks. She didn't need the cane anymore.

And when they broke their pelvises, they could toss the cane after eight weeks if they wanted to. This was *her* recovery.

Instead of grilling or lecturing her, however, Nate pulled his phone from his jacket pocket, dialed and lifted it to his ear, all the while watching her. "This is Dr. Sullivan. I need to talk to Bruce."

Her physical therapist. Great.

He didn't even bother to greet Bruce. "Why is Emma Dixon still walking with a cane?"

He paused to listen, then said, "Get her off of it," and hung up. He pocketed the phone and turned away, adding something to her medical record.

"Seriously? You don't want to talk to *me* about it?"

"Bruce told me what I needed to know, and I told him what he needed to know," Nate said without looking up.

She felt the knot of tension tighten. "What did he say?"

"You know better than anyone what he said, Emma."

She felt her tummy flip at his use of her name. It was so stupid, but he rarely called her Emma, and never called her Em like everyone else did, so when he used her name, it always startled her. "He told you that he tried to get me off of it, but I won't do it, right?"

"Right."

"I don't want to get rid of it yet. Why isn't that okay?"

"Because it's ridiculous. You can't expect to make progress if you aren't willing to try."

"It's okay for me to not have sex for six more weeks, but I can't keep the cane?"

"Right."

"Why?"

"Because in my professional opinion, that's what needs to happen."

God, he was frustrating. He was so damned bossy. She'd seen him yell and get riled up on the football field, but most of the rest of the time he seemed—stuck up. Conservative. Uptight. Something. She loved to try to rile him simply because it was so interesting to see him get worked up. She seemed to be the only one who could really get him going. He'd argue with her, when he'd shrug at everyone else who disagreed with him. She always loved sparring with him.

But she hadn't imagined such a dominant, I'm-the-boss side of him.

And she certainly hadn't imagined liking it.

"I'm not ready to get by without the cane yet," she said. She could be equally stubborn. Ask any of her siblings.

"But you are ready for sex?"

Something about the way he said it, or was looking at her, or something, made her need to take a deep breath. "Maybe."

"Is there someone that you're dying to get back in bed with?"

No.

But that was neither here nor there. Nor was it any of his business anyway. She didn't have anyone she wanted to sleep with, but that didn't mean she wanted to be ordered *not* to sleep with anyone by her annoying, I-know-better-than-everyone-else-in-the-world doctor.

She didn't care if he did know better than everyone else in the world about her injury and its repair.

It was so strange, looking at him now, to think that he'd seen parts of her body that no one ever had and, god-willing, no one else ever would. That he'd had his hands inside her, putting her back together, was strangely intimate.

Or stupid.

It was definitely that.

"Why do you want to know?" she asked. Did Nate truly care who she was sleeping with? Surely not.

"I would not be pleased to know that one of the physical therapists I refer to the most is having an inappropriate relationship with one of his patients."

Oh.

She frowned. "I'm not sleeping with Bruce."

Nate seemed satisfied with that simple answer. Which also irritated her. If he cared, he didn't care much.

"No sleeping with anyone for six weeks. At least," Nate said.

She tipped her head, watching him, hating him for looking so good in a tie, hating herself for liking him in a tie. She didn't go for guys in ties generally. She liked blue-collar guys, guys who worked with their hands. Her attention dropped to Nate's hands and she had to swallow hard. He worked with his hands. He'd had his hands all over her. He'd worked for hours to make sure she was okay. Her *life* had been in his hands.

And she'd been unconscious for the whole thing.

And that disappointed her.

Which she freaking *hated*.

She'd been in a car accident. She'd been bloody and broken. He'd cut her open, for God's sake. There wasn't one damned thing about it that was sexy or hot. She needed to get a grip.

This was all a product of Nate being the one guy she couldn't seduce. He could resist her. More, he could make her feel stupid and silly. She hated that more than anything else.

She slid off the table and slipped her sandals back on her feet. "I'm tired of *that* topic and I have my paper for more drugs, so I'm gonna head out."

She pulled the hem of her top down—the top that Nate definitely did not want her to take off—and ran a hand through her hair. But as she twisted the doorknob, Nate again used her name.

"Emma."

Schooling her features before she turned, she gave him a bored look. "What?"

"Behave."

She hadn't behaved since she was six. "See that's where this doctor-patient thing stops working," she told him, pulling the door open. "You can control my medication and you can bully my physical therapist. You can even keep me from all of my favorite workouts. But *nobody* has the power to make me behave." She pulled the door shut behind her and headed to the front of the clinic to check out.

There was something stupidly satisfying about having the last word with Nate Sullivan.

It wasn't right to sleep with a woman just to shut her up.

Nate knew that. And he wasn't going to do it. Probably.

But *damn*. Emma Dixon made him want to...teach her a lesson.

That was what it was. He wanted one night to show her she wasn't quite as smart as she thought she was.

God, she got under his skin. Made him feel irritated. Like he had an itch he couldn't quite reach.

She thought she had him pegged. That drove him crazy. But lots of people made assumptions about him, and it never bothered him with anyone else.

Emma poked at him whenever they were together. From the first moment he'd met her, Nate knew Emma was absolutely the last woman in Trudy's Tavern he should flirt with, or dance with, or drink with. He shouldn't laugh with her or kiss her or run his hands through her hair or...anything. He shouldn't do *anything* with her. Because he was nothing if not intelligent and capable of learning from past mistakes. And he had made those with women who weren't half as much trouble as Emma Dixon.

Still, whenever he spent time with her—like the fifteen minutes they'd been together in the exam room—and she did her I-know-I-can-get-to-you thing, he wanted to strip her down and surprise the hell out of her.

She was seductive and flirtatious with him—when she wasn't being sassy and sarcastic—but it was so blatant that he knew she thought he wasn't interested.

That was one of the many things about him that she didn't know.

She also didn't know that he liked her trying hard to get his attention.

She didn't try that hard with any other guy. She didn't need to. But she was almost desperate in her attempts to get Nate to respond to her. And it amused him, in a way. He knew he was an anomaly in Emma Dixon's world. He had a penis but wasn't trying to get her up close and personal with it.

But when he wasn't as riled up, he hated it. He hated not being able to tell her that she was gorgeous and funny and sexy as hell and smelled like heaven.

She didn't need his attention. She didn't really want his attention. She just hated that he seemingly didn't notice her and fall at her feet. That helped him keep his distance. Because if he *noticed* her in all the ways he wanted to, neither of them would ever be the same again.

Nate shook off all the crazy thoughts of Emma Dixon and headed for his office. He had ten minutes until his next patient and he wasn't going to spend all of his down time thinking about the last woman he should come within twenty feet of.

He swiped across his phone and noticed a voice message from his son, Michael.

Nate hit the button for his voicemail as he walked toward his office.

"Dad, hey, I'm taking Shannon out tonight for her birthday.

There's this…thing, she wants to do and… I don't want to fight about this, okay? It's her birthday and I'm her boyfriend, so I'm taking her out. I'll be home. Eventually."

As his son spoke, Nate felt his jaw and neck getting tighter and tighter.

Michael was an atypical teenager in many ways. He was exceptionally bright and clever and funny. He'd spent a lot of his childhood around adults. Adults who talked about the theater and politics and world events. He hadn't watched a lot of cartoons, hadn't played in the sandbox, hadn't dressed up like a super hero. He'd had a nanny who read to him and took him to the park and to museums and music lessons and play dates with other kids who spent time with books and in museums.

He'd had the best of everything and he'd been mature and responsible and well-mannered and cooperative from a young age. Nate and Michael's relationship had always been strong.

But he was a typical teenager in one very important way—as he got older, he got more independent. His thoughts and beliefs and opinions were influenced by people other than Nate and Nate's grandfather, the other significant adult in Michael's upbringing. He wanted to try new things and he'd gotten rebellious when Nate disagreed with his choices.

They'd started arguing lately. A lot. About what was important in life and goal setting and keeping focus on the future. Michael wanted nothing to do with medicine, his family's legacy. He wasn't even entirely sure he wanted to go to college. He had already started building a small business—something with computers that Nate didn't entirely understand—and he wasn't convinced that college had anything to offer him.

Nate didn't necessarily want Michael to become a physician—though he'd be the first in four generations not to. But why couldn't he get an MBA before starting his own business? Or even a computer science degree. Surely Michael didn't actually believe he knew *everything* there was to know about computers. Michael might have the brains and talent to do whatever he wanted, but a degree would open more doors, would show potential employers or investors that Michael had discipline and drive, that he was committed to doing things right and that he was worth taking a risk on.

Frankly, Nate wanted Michael to get a degree because *he* would like to see his son's discipline and drive and to see that he was committed to doing things right. He wanted Michael to be successful, but he wanted him to work for it so he would appreciate it.

It had taken Nate a long time to get to that point himself.

He'd been an orphan before he even knew his parents—his mother had been diagnosed with cancer while pregnant with Nate and succumbed when he was only eight months old, and his father drank himself to death after that—so he'd been raised by a grandfather who had far more money than patience and who parented with elaborate gifts, high expectations and little else.

Nate had been a single, teenage father, but he'd had nannies to take care of the middle of the night feedings and the colicky moments.

He'd gone to medical school, but getting in had taken nothing more than putting his last name on the application to the school where three generations of Sullivans had gone and where the medical school library was named after his great-grandfather.

Medical school itself had been as tough for Nate as for anyone, but he'd had his pick of residencies and been assured a job at the hospital where his great-grandfather, grandfather and father had worked.

Money and influence had created an easy path for Nate and it had taken him a long time to truly appreciate—and enjoy—what he had.

He wanted Michael to be more appreciative and humble than he had been. He wanted Michael to be a harder worker than he had been. He really just wanted Michael to be a better man than Nate had been.

And on top of all of their disagreements about college and his future, Michael was in love for the first time. Very much in love. With Shannon Watson. The recently-turned-eighteen-year-old daughter of Emma Dixon's best friend.

Not only was Shannon Michael's first love—and everyone knew how stupid love made a guy—but she was beautiful, popular, vibrant, and loved to go out. Nate had only been around Shannon for fifteen minutes before thinking that if he didn't know better, he'd assume she was Emma's daughter.

Nate gritted his teeth as he dialed his son's number.

Of course this most recent and gigantic pain in his ass had something to do with Emma Dixon.

Michael had met Shannon at a Hawks football game. Nate had played defensive back for the Hawks for the past two years and Michael never missed a game. Neither did Emma, their quarterback's sister. Emma had brought Shannon and her mom, Dena, to a game last fall and Michael had fallen head over heels in the space of an afternoon.

Michael's phone rang. And rang. Then went to voice mail.

Nate swore and disconnected, then called again. Michael was screening his calls, knowing that Nate was going to yell.

Nate could admit that he wasn't crazy about Michael's preoccupation with the young Miss Watson. She'd been distracting him for months from his schoolwork and other responsibilities— like spending time with his father.

But Nate especially wasn't crazy about walking in on Michael and Shannon naked in Michael's bed one afternoon when they should have been in school. Or finding out there were no contraceptives being used. Or realizing that Dena wasn't at all concerned. Dena's approach to parenting was incredibly laid back. She was more like an older sister to Shannon than a mother, as far as he could tell. And not a responsible, concerned older sister like Emma's sister Amanda.

Michael's phone rang and rang again.

Finally, Michael answered. "*Dad.*"

"You will not be going out tonight without providing a lot more information to me and having a *discussion* about it first," Nate said. Since the afternoon he'd found them skipping school and skipping the condoms, he'd grounded Michael.

Or tried to.

Michael had turned eighteen two months ago, but he was also still living under Nate's roof and on Nate's tab. Which meant that they argued on a daily basis now.

"What information do you need to have?" Michael asked. "You're going to say no to whatever I say."

"I am willing to listen," Nate said, working to keep his voice calm. "Because it's a special occasion, I will *consider* suspending your grounding for one night. But I need to know where you're going, who you're going to be with and what you will be doing." Maybe if he was reasonable and willing to compromise, Michael would be too.

For instance, if Nate said yes to Michael taking Shannon out, perhaps Michael would agree to buy and *use* a box of condoms.

Nate forced himself to unclench his teeth and relax his shoulders.

He also very much wanted his son to be more responsible than he had been. Nate had been used to doing whatever he wanted and having his grandfather bail him out of trouble. Consequences simply hadn't been a part of Nate's reality. Which was why he hadn't paused for one second to think about a condom when Stacie Franklin—his high school sweetheart and Michael's mother—had slipped off her panties in the backseat of his car.

He wanted Michael to understand consequences and being responsible. But he had no idea if he was handling this well. He'd never had to ground Michael before. The rebellions and the disrespect were new. Nate knew, on some level, that they were normal, but they'd started almost overnight and he was adjusting too. He also knew that his role model, his grandfather, would have never been in the running for Father of the Year, but Nate didn't have a lot of other examples.

At least if Michael was grounded, he was safe.

Of course, grounding an eighteen-year-old was nearly impossible.

"I'm taking her out. Dad, you need to trust me."

"I did. You messed up. Now you need to earn back my trust, Michael."

"How can I do that if you never let me do anything?"

"How can I let you do anything when all I can think about is you skipping school to have unprotected sex in your bed in *my* house?"

"Is that what you're upset about?" Michael demanded. "That we did it in *your* house? Which, by the way, I thought was also *my* house."

"It's the house you live in," Nate said tightly. "But I believe I make the payments."

"So that *is* what bothers you most?" Michael sounded amazed.

"No." Though it did bother Nate that his son would be so brazen as to bring his young girlfriend to the house like that. "What bothers me is that you were irresponsible on so many levels—skipping school, having sex in the first place, having sex without a condom or any other protection. You're going to be leaving home soon and I have to know that you're able to make the right decisions."

"Yes, I'll be leaving home soon," Michael repeated. "Thank God." And he hung up.

Nate gritted his teeth and squeezed his phone tightly, resisting the urge to hurl it against the wall. Fine. He'd had his say. He'd expressed his concern. Michael was eighteen. Nate couldn't babysit him.

Nate paced to his desk and tried to concentrate on his work messages, but his mind kept going to Michael. He was directly defying Nate. That had never happened before. Nate wasn't sure what Michael expected to happen now. Did he think that Nate would respect his honesty and let him go? Did he think that Nate would realize it was pointless to try to curtail his legally-an-adult son's activities? Right. Probably more the latter.

While it was true that he couldn't send the cops to retrieve his son or anything, that didn't mean he had to roll over and let this happen. Michael needed to understand that Nate was still in charge here and while he knew Michael had a lot going for him, the kid still needed guidance.

He needed to find Michael and talk to him.

After jerking his lab coat off and loosening his tie, Nate punched the button that would connect him with his receptionist.

"Shelby, I need Dr. Chapman to cover the rest of my patients or I need them rescheduled if he can't see them."

Chapman was a new resident. He likely had room in his schedule and could easily take care of the surgical follow-ups Nate had scheduled that afternoon.

"I'll take care of it, Dr. Sullivan," Shelby said.

And that was why he always got her very expensive Christmas gifts.

"Thank you."

Tucking his wallet into his pocket, Nate strode to the door.

He knew exactly where to start his search for his wayward son.

That was definitely not Dena's big-assed silver crew cab pickup sitting in front of her place.

Emma pulled up to the curb and shut her car off. Not only did Dena not have enough money to even make a down payment on that truck, Dena would never buy that truck. Dena was more a classic Volkswagen Beetle—a used, beat up, bright yellow classic Beetle—kind of girl. Cheap, compact and fun.

Emma glanced at the beat up, bright yellow classic Beetle in Dena's driveway in front of the truck and grinned. Dena had come up with the "cheap, compact and fun" phrase herself the day she bought that car. Eight years ago.

Emma looked back at the truck and shook her head. She wished that the truck belonged to a new boyfriend who had come into Dena's life to sweep her off her feet and shower her in lavish gifts.

But she knew exactly whose truck that was. And he was no Prince Charming.

Emma sighed and pulled her purse out of the passenger seat.

Nate Sullivan was here.

This couldn't be good.

Emma made her way up the walk, reflecting on the last conversation between Dena and Nate.

He'd caught the kids in bed.

Nate had stormed over to Dena's place, convinced that she would be equally concerned and angry and that they could form a united front when talking to Shannon and Michael about the risks they were taking.

But Nate didn't know Dena.

It took a lot to get her friend upset. Dena was laid-back, probably too much so when it came to Shannon, frankly. Emma loved her but she didn't always agree with her parenting style. Emma had been stepping in to give Shannon advice and to admonish her as needed since Shannon had been two years old.

Shannon had two parents—in every way that counted. Dena was the easy one. The one who praised her and thought she walked on water and told her she could do anything she set her mind to. Emma was the one that reminded her that "anything she set her mind to" would require a college degree and some money. Emma and Dena were a good team. When Shannon was upset or hurt or sad, Dena was the shoulder she cried on. When she got into trouble or had a decision to make, Emma was her rock.

It worked for them. Had been working for the sixteen years Emma had known the Watson girls.

But Nate didn't know that. Dena was Shannon's mother and he insisted that she take responsibility and discipline her daughter.

Discipline wasn't really Dena's thing.

Emma let herself in through the kitchen door and immediately heard the raised voices.

"You are telling me you have *no idea* where your daughter is right now?" Nate said, frustration clear in every word.

"I know *exactly* where she is," Dena shot back. "She's with Michael. And that's all I need to know."

Emma sighed. This was going to be fun.

She tossed her purse on the table and propped her cane against the wall as she glanced into the living room. Dena was in the recliner where Emma had left her that morning before her appointment with Nate. Dena had been throwing up since one a.m. and Shannon had called her to ask if she could bring some crackers and tea over.

Nate stood a few feet inside the front door. He looked pissed off.

"You don't care that our children are out doing God-knows-what, without even telling us where they are going to be or who they are going to be with?"

"I trust my daughter," Dena told him.

"Then you're naïve."

Oh, boy. Emma hung back. If Michael and Shannon were going to get serious—and she suspected they were on a direct path to very serious even now—Nate and Dena would have further reasons to interact. Emma couldn't jump in every time. She leaned against the counter and gripped the edge to keep herself in place.

Dena wasn't a fighter and Nate was...Nate. But she'd give them another minute.

"I know my daughter. Shannon is a good girl and I'm thrilled that she met Michael. He's so good for her," Dena said. "I'm happy any time she's with him."

Yeah, Dena felt very strongly about that. Since Michael had stolen her heart, Shannon was considering staying closer to home for college, was smiling a lot more and was feeling more confident and sure of herself. Michael *was* good for her. Getting Dena on the let's-break-the-kids-up bandwagon was never gonna happen.

"We can't ignore that they're too young and have too much ahead of them," he said, clearly exasperated.

It was nice to know someone else could get that same you're-making-me-nuts tone from him.

"They're potentially fucking up their future!" he added loudly.

And that was her cue.

"Imagine my delight at getting to see you twice in one day, doc," Emma said as she came into the room and crossed to where Dena sat. Her friend looked like hell.

Nate scowled at her. "What are you doing here?"

"I'm here every day," she said. "But especially when my friend is sick and being yelled at."

He had the decency to look sheepish. "I need to find Michael."

Emma gathered up the two empty cups by Dena and gave her friend a smile. Emma would handle Nate. Nate was used to telling people what to do and having them jump to do it. He was used to people caring about his opinion and following his instructions.

Emma didn't really do that.

"I thought he was taking Shannon out for her birthday," Emma said easily, moving to the kitchen to deposit the cups in the sink.

"He's not supposed to be going out."

Emma looked at Nate through the doorway. Even though they were in two different rooms, they were maybe forty feet apart. "What do you mean?"

"He's grounded."

Emma laughed. "How do you ground an eighteen-year-old?"

"You tell him he's grounded," Nate said tightly.

"And I can see that it's working like a dream." She didn't miss Nate's glare before she turned to fill the teakettle with water. She set it on the stove, then said, "What's the problem exactly? He's taking his girlfriend out. They're here in the city. There are no plans for elopement. I don't think you need to worry."

She turned, startled to find Nate had crossed the room and now stood towering over her. He was a lot bigger than she was. She knew his stats from the football team. He was six-two, two hundred and twenty-five pounds. She was five-six, one hundred and sixteen—give or take two pounds depending on how the weekend had gone.

"You know where they are."

He said it in an accusatory tone.

She met his gaze. "Yes. They're fine."

"Where are they?"

She raised an eyebrow. "You're going to go wherever they are and drag Michael out of there?"

"Yes."

She raised the other brow. "You're kidding, right? You wouldn't actually go storming in somewhere and yank your eighteen-year-old son out in front of his friends and girlfriend?"

"He's with friends? Somewhere public?" Nate asked, not at all answering any of *her* questions.

Emma crossed her arms. "If you think I'm going to tell you that, you're nuts."

"I'll pay you."

"I'll punch you in the face."

He looked taken aback at that. Good. If he thought he could *pay* her to squeal on the kids he was more than nuts…he was a jackass. And thought she was too.

"Then what do you want?"

They were in the middle of an argument and her mind still went to very inappropriate places with that question. She shook her head. "Nothing. I'm not going to tell you. If Michael wanted you to know, he would have told you."

She, on the other hand, knew every detail. She'd helped Shannon pick out her clothes and had lectured her about safe sex. She'd even given Shannon condoms. Not that she thought that would placate Nate.

Most of the night would be innocent. Michael was taking Shannon to see some obscure band she loved that was playing a very small show in an old theater downtown. Then there was some party at a friend's house.

But Emma also knew there were plans to spend the night at another friend's house. Together.

She'd almost said no on that one. But that wasn't her place. Dena knew about the sleepover plans too, but was unconcerned. She was perfectly fine with her daughter being intimate with Michael. He was a great guy who made her daughter very happy. They were both adults. New adults, sure, but adults nonetheless.

In many ways, Dena had been waiting for that day for eighteen years. She loved Shannon and had done a good job raising her, for the most part. But it had been tough. Dena was the first to admit that having Shannon out on her own, hopefully settled with a great guy who could give her stability and a great future, was Dena's idea of a dream come true. She'd always welcomed Emma's willingness to share the load, and having a good guy able and willing to step in to help Shannon emotionally, physically and financially had been Dena's prayer for years.

It was all out of love for Shannon. But yes, if Shannon and Michael got serious, Dena was all for it. Emma knew that even an early pregnancy that would bond them together forever wouldn't be a disappointment to Dena.

Emma understood where her friend was coming from. But Emma did fall more on Nate's side of the argument. Michael might do the right thing and marry Shannon if there was an unexpected baby in the picture, but that was not the ideal way to get stability and security. Not at all.

Not that she'd admit to agreeing with Nate on anything.

"Emma." Nate's voice dropped low and he moved in close, backing her up against the refrigerator.

Damn, this close she was unable to ignore how gorgeous his dark green eyes were. And that mouth… She had to want the guy she couldn't have, didn't she?

"I need you to tell me where they are."

His hand came to rest on her hip and she took a shaky little breath. He was going to *seduce* the information out of her?

He leaned in, his mouth near her ear. "Please, it's important." He paused, then pulled in a breath. "Dammit, you smell good."

Okay, the seduction thing might work.

Crap.

She closed her eyes. Maybe that would help. She put her hands up on his chest, to hold him back. Because that mouth this close was dangerous.

Not that touching him helped. He was warm and solid and smelled damned good himself.

"Nate—"

His hand slid around to her butt and he pulled her closer. "How about a hint?" he asked. "I want to be sure he's okay."

Emma tried to shake her head, but she wasn't sure she pulled it off. "Shannon trusted me. This night means a lot to her."

"Then you leave me no choice," he said huskily.

Oh, boy. What was he going to try next? She almost couldn't wait to find out. If he kissed her, or pulled her more firmly against him, or slid his hand to her breast…she'd tell him anything. Even that she'd been attracted to him for a good year and a half now.

The next thing she felt, though, was her phone sliding out of her back pocket.

Her eyes flew open as Nate stepped back.

"Seriously?" she groaned. "That was low."

And she'd fallen for it. Completely.

He gave her a smug grin. "And you fell for it. Completely."

Dammit. He now had something far more important than her phone—the knowledge that he could affect her. She had a feeling that was going to be a bad, bad thing.

He held the phone up to her face to get past her lock screen, then started swiping and she knew he was looking for messages from Shannon. Which he would definitely find if he kept going. Emma grabbed for the phone, but he lifted it up out of her reach.

"Nate. You can't go through my phone."

"Afraid I'll call all your lovers and tell them about the six-weeks-no-sex rule?"

She made a grab for the phone again. And missed. "No. I'm afraid you're going to ruin the relationship that your son is building with this girl he cares about a lot—and maybe even his relationship with *you*."

She saw the change in his face. He hated that idea.

She could work with that.

This night was a big deal to Shannon. Even more, Michael was a big deal to Shannon. She was in love for the first time and it was with a guy who Emma thought was terrific. As a weird big-sister-mom-friend combo to the girl, Emma knew Michael was exactly the kind of guy she would have chosen for Shannon.

Until Shannon met Michael, her plan had been to go to college as far away from home as she could get. She wanted to get a psychology degree and counsel at-risk teens.

The idea that Shannon would go off to college in some far away city and fall in love with a guy that Emma would meet for the first time when he proposed and they came home for

Christmas made her stomach cramp. She'd never once told Shannon to stay home or that she couldn't do exactly what she wanted. But she'd wanted to. She was going to miss that kid severely.

Now Shannon was thinking of staying closer to home.

Emma loved that. Emma loved Michael for that.

Because of Michael, Emma could selfishly celebrate that Shannon might still be close enough for lunch dates and sleepovers.

Nate sighed heavily. "I will listen to suggestions. As long as they *don't* include the words 'leave them alone'."

That had been her exact suggestion. She frowned. "You can't go barging into wherever they are, and Michael's not answering your calls, so what are you going to do? Spy on them?"

Nate's face brightened immediately.

Emma groaned. "*No.* You can't spy on your son."

"The hell if I can't. That accomplishes all of the objectives," he said. "It helps me know where they are and what they're doing, but it's not barging in or dragging him away from his friends—or whatever."

"Nate, seriously. You can't stalk your son. That's…creepy."

He shrugged. "Don't care. My job is to protect him, whether he likes it or not, by whatever means necessary."

He was serious. Part of her admired how strongly he felt about his role and how protective he was. Part of her thought he was in need of a prescription or two from his friendly neighborhood psychiatrist.

"You're not going to be able to figure out where they are," she said, feigning cockiness.

"Shannon didn't text you about how to get to the Washburn Theater downtown?" he asked.

Dammit.

"That might be for something else."

"*I wish you could come with us tomorrow night. You'd love the band,*" Nate read from her screen. He looked at her. "She sent it yesterday. Which makes tomorrow night tonight."

Emma sighed. "Michael's taking her to see this band she loves. She was amazed they were coming through Omaha. It's a one-night show."

"What's the Washburn Theater?" Nate asked.

"An old building down on Tenth Street," she said. "It used to be a restaurant or a club back in the twenties. They have a stage and this big open area with room for tables and dancing and stuff. They produce little plays and have comedians and live music and stuff." She shrugged. "It's harmless, Nate. They card at the door. The kids can get in underage but they're given a different colored wristband so they can't get served at the bar. The band plays for a couple of hours in front of an audience of like two hundred. This is small-time stuff."

"Thank you." He handed her the phone and started for the front door.

Oh, no. No way. She ran after him, slipping around him and blocking his path. "You're not going down there."

"You're moving fast for a chick who uses a cane."

Dammit. She frowned. "I don't need it all the time." She didn't. It was for long distances and for when she got tired. Her hip was sore today, but her concern for Shannon had easily over-ridden her achiness. Of course it had to happen in front of Nate.

"Clearly." He moved to open the door.

"You're not going down there," she repeated firmly.

"I am."

"You can't seriously want to hear this band play for two hours. You'll hate it."

"Not as much as I'll hate being a grandfather already."

Emma felt her mouth drop open.

He scowled at her. "What?"

"Overreact much?" she asked.

"Get out of my way."

"No."

He put both hands on her upper arms and started to move her. "There's no way you can physically keep me from going down there."

Emma thought fast. He was going down there. This had disaster written all over it. She shrugged off his grasp. "Fine."

He let her go and stepped around her.

She headed for the kitchen, grabbed her purse and cane, called, "I'll text you" to Dena and was out the door, down the steps and beside Nate before he got to the truck.

He looked at her as he reached for the door. "What are you doing?"

"If you think I'm going to let you go after Shannon by yourself, you're nuts."

Nate sighed, that familiar put-upon expression on his face as he regarded her. He didn't seem particularly surprised. He seemed annoyed.

She could live with that. Nate was pretty much perpetually annoyed with her and she'd survived this long.

"Besides," she said, opening the passenger side door. "You're going to make an ass out of yourself and I *must* have a front row seat for that."

CHAPTER
TWO

HE SHOULD HAVE LIED to her.

The thought wouldn't leave Nate alone as they drove toward downtown Omaha. Emma was little and his truck was big, but she seemed to take up a lot of space.

"Nice truck," she commented, settling into the seat as if she was getting comfortable in her favorite easy chair. She leaned back and stretched her legs out, propping her feet on the dash and causing the short cotton skirt she wore to hike to mid-thigh. One shoulder of the nearly see-through T-shirt she wore kept slipping down, exposing the strap of the fitted tank underneath that molded to her breasts and flat stomach. "Ah," she sighed, as the cool air from the vent hit her skin. "I love getting sweaty, but I'm a big fan of the AC too."

Jesus.

The smooth, tanned skin drew Nate's attention and he couldn't look away. She had to use a tanning bed. It was early June and hot today, but it hadn't been warm enough to lie by the pool and get a tan like that. Besides, she had to be naturally pale.

All four of the Dixon girls were blond and fair. Emma's skin was much more golden than any of the others.

She shifted again, crossing one ankle over the other, and toeing off her ridiculously high-heeled sandals. Her feet were beautifully arched, with sexy crimson toenails.

Beautifully arched? Sexy toenails? Nate rubbed a hand over his face. He needed to get a grip. He'd never noticed a woman's feet before and had definitely not found them particularly sexy. Nor had he made note of the color of their toenail polish.

"What's wrong with you?" Emma asked.

They'd been alone in close proximity for more than five minutes today. That was what was wrong with him. That didn't happen. On purpose.

"Tanning beds are bad for you."

She gave him a funny look then said, "One of my friends owns a massage and tanning place. I let her take free yoga classes in exchange for free massages and *spray* tans."

He focused on the road instead of on the woman beside him. He shouldn't have played with her in the kitchen. He'd wanted her phone, but getting that close, smelling her, putting his hand on her ass? Not the brightest move if he wanted to *stop* feeling like he'd very much love to grip that ass while thrusting into her against the nearest wall.

She wiggled again and her scent filled the air around him.

Dammit. He shifted and thought about rolling down a window to dispel the teasing aroma.

"I walked into the convenience store after school one day to buy a pack of gum and there was a new girl working. She was sitting behind the counter with a little girl on her lap, reading her a book."

Nate looked at Emma. She looked like she was making herself right at home. She held a water bottle and a bag of M&M's, presumably that she'd taken from her purse, and was reclining as if she'd never been more comfortable.

"What are you doing?"

"Telling you a story."

"Why?"

"Because I want to," she said.

"Because you're completely incapable of being *quiet* for a few minutes?"

"Based on past experience, I'm pretty sure *you* don't have anything to say that *I* will find interesting, so I might as well be the one talking." She held her bag of M&M's out.

He ignored the candy. "And being *quiet* is out of the question."

"If I'm quiet, you won't hear this story."

"Exactly."

"Exactly." She poured four of the M&M's into her palm and went on. "I asked the girl her name and she said Dena and that her daughter's name was Shannon. Then something out the window caught her eye and she swore. She looked like she was about to be sick. She handed Shannon over to me just as this guy got out of his car. It was her boss and if he found out she had her kid at the store while she was working she was going to get fired. When he walked in, I pretended that Shannon was my little sister and I kept her occupied while Dena talked to her boss. We looked around the store, I bought a package of cookies and then we went outside and around the corner of the building. We sat there and ate cookies and I told her stories and we sang songs until the guy left and Dena came out to get her."

Nate couldn't help it. He was intrigued. Dammit.

It wasn't the story of Dena and Shannon as much as it was the look on Emma's face as she told it. She had a small smile on her face and her voice held an obvious affection. He wasn't sure he'd ever seen Emma so...soft. She was sexy, she was fun, she was flirtatious. She was energetic and in-your-face and loved the spotlight. And with him she was sarcastic and annoying. But when she talked about meeting her friend and her daughter, she looked almost sweet.

"She gave me a free root beer float after he left as a thank you." Emma shot him a smile and wink. "I was twelve, so that was a big deal."

That wink.

Nate scowled.

That wink made him want to kiss her.

The story she was telling made him want to sink his fingers into her hair, tip her head and hold her in his control while he possessed her mouth.

God, that mouth. He'd heard her say the sassiest things at the bar, swear like a sailor at football games, and laugh a laugh that always hit him deep in the gut. But it was this story about how she'd met her best friend that made him want to do very dirty things to that mouth.

Maybe there was something wrong with him.

He propped his elbow on the edge of the window next to him and resigned himself to hearing this. There was enough traffic that they couldn't pick up much speed and the stoplights seemed to sense him coming, making sure he hit every red. If he couldn't shut her up, he figured he could enjoy watching her— her *mouth*—as she kept talking.

Emma was always talking.

"The next day I showed up and Shannon was with her again. She had toys and was playing behind the counter. She was being good and quiet, but I felt sorry for her. I mean, she was two. She needed to run and play and be loud."

"And you told Dena that, I would guess."

Emma told everyone what she thought all the time. It wouldn't surprise him at all to find out she'd done so even at age twelve.

"Sure." Emma shrugged. "I told her I thought she should let me babysit while she worked. We lived about four blocks away."

"And Dena went for that? A little girl she'd met the day before, basically off the street?"

Emma frowned at him. "No. She turned me down. But then I went home and got my mom and she came back with me to talk to Dena. Mom felt bad for Dena too. Mom told her that she should talk to the other family I'd babysat for as a reference. And Mom told her that we would provide food, snacks, diapers, whatever Shannon needed during the time she was with us. And *then* she told her I would do it for free. I wasn't so crazy about that part."

Emma gave a little laugh and Nate had to grit his teeth. That laugh—why did it always make him want to grab her?

"But Mom could tell Dena needed help, so Mom wore her down. Mom's good at that. She can always get everyone to do things her way eventually."

Clearly Emma took after her mother in that regard, Nate thought.

"Dena finally agreed, and I started watching Shannon after school five days a week. We'd feed her and play and read, and we'd give her a bath and she'd go to sleep in my bed with me. Dena would pick her up at midnight and take her home."

"How old was Dena?" Nate heard himself ask. Why was he engaging in this conversation? He wanted some quiet where he could think about Michael and what he was going to do about this new relationship that was screwing with his son's head.

"She was eighteen when we met. She had Shannon when she was sixteen."

"And you became friends?"

Emma nodded. "Slowly. I mean, she was six years older than me and I spent most of the time with Shannon, not Dena. But she wore makeup and had her own car and had her ears pierced —*three times*."

She said it with an emphasis that made Nate smile in spite of himself. "That was cool?"

Emma widened her eyes. "Very. I thought she was awesome. I looked up to her, I guess. We started hanging out some too. Like, she'd take me along when she took Shannon to the zoo, and she took me along when she drove to see her grandparents in Kansas City for a weekend. That kind of stuff.

Then as I got older, she'd go shopping with me and I'd talk to her about boys and about drama with my sisters and my friends and my parents." She gave another soft laugh. "I had a lot of drama."

"Hard to imagine."

Emma was all about drama.

She nodded, looking at the M&M bag instead of him. "I guess we really first became friends when my dad died. I was thirteen and our house was incredibly sad. I could go to Dena's house and get away."

Nate stared at her. But thankfully, Emma kept talking—and when had he ever thought *that* was a good thing?—because he had no idea what to say.

"She let me watch movies my mother never would have approved of and let me listen to hard rock with swear words and she talked to me about *her* boyfriends and…looking back, I'm not sure that our friendship was all that appropriate. She was the one who pierced my ears the first time, the one to let me try smoking, and who gave me my first taste of liquor—tequila, by the way—and who was honest with me about sex."

Emma shifted to sit sideways in the seat, the movement pulling her skirt higher and making Nate swallow hard. A minute ago he'd been on the verge of reaching over to hold her hand and in a blink he was thinking about running his hand up her leg and wondering about the panties she was wearing.

Letting her come along tonight was a bad idea.

"I mean, I knew the basics," she went on. "Mom had that talk with us, and we'd watched the film in school."

She gave him a grin that his body took as naughty, whether it was truly meant that way or not.

"But Dena told me the truth."

"The truth?" Nate hated that his voice sounded gravelly. Hated even more that he wanted to talk about sex with Emma Dixon. *All* about sex. Like what positions she liked and which ones she didn't—so he could work on changing her mind.

"That sex was awesome. About orgasms. About oral sex. About all of it."

Nate gaped at her. Holy hell.

Hearing Emma say orgasms, made him feel...*hungry*.

Which was stupid. Emma was the most openly sexual woman he'd ever met. Emma said the word orgasm like a weatherman said precipitation.

Still, Nate felt like he hadn't eaten in days and she was a double decker bacon cheeseburger.

Maybe when comparing a woman to food it was best to compare her to something rich and decadent and classy. Maybe she should remind him of filet mignon or crème brulee. But dammit, Emma Dixon was definitely a cheeseburger—his weakness, the thing he most tried to avoid, the thing that combined all the things that were so bad for him but were too fucking hard to say no to when put on a platter right in front of him.

And he wanted to dive right in with both hands.

He shook his head.

Letting her come along tonight was a *really* bad idea.

"She told you all about that stuff when you were *thirteen*?" he demanded, trying to work up some ire to override the sudden lust.

Emma laughed.

Which didn't help the lust thing at all.

"No. Not that young. But as I got older. She was like this cool older sister. I could ask her anything, say anything to her."

"You had an older sister," Nate pointed out.

"But Amanda's only a year older than me," Emma said. "She didn't know all the things Dena did."

"And your mom was okay with you hanging out with Dena?" He might find Emma's wild side sexy as hell, but he could never totally shake the parent in him.

"Mom thought of Dena as Shannon's mom. My mother took Shannon into her life like she was her grandma. She loved—loves—that kid. Mom overlooked a lot of Dena's...flaws. Or maybe she didn't know about the parties and the boys and the inappropriate things Dena introduced me to." Emma shrugged. "Anyway, it wasn't all wild and crazy. I made Dena stop smoking, she chewed my ass hard and long when she found me at a party with drugs. I didn't speak to her for a week when she missed one of Shannon's parent-teacher conferences, she literally pulled me out of bed with a guy who was no good. We've had each other's backs."

Nate sat, stoically not looking at the woman beside him.

She made him nuts. Plain and simple.

Usually it was because she was mouthy and cocky. And because, around her, he felt constantly turned on and frustrated.

Now she was showing him another side...and it wasn't helping the turned-on thing at all.

"Why are you telling me all of this?" he asked irritably.

"Because I wanted you to know that I care about Shannon," Emma said, her voice harder now. "And that I care how this night goes down."

He knew she meant it. And he knew that she was going to make this all very difficult for him.

He sighed. "How's it going to go down, exactly?"

"I'm going to be right there with you, whatever happens. And you can deal with your son, but you won't say anything or do anything to Shannon."

He looked over. She sounded riled and, as always, part of him—the part that wasn't a mature, responsible, professional man—wanted to get her *really* worked up.

"What is it that you think I might do to Shannon?"

"Embarrass her. Make her feel bad. Make her feel like she's not good enough for Michael."

Nate scowled at that. "It has nothing to do with her being good enough or not good enough."

Emma scowled right back at him. "Good. Remember that. And don't say or do anything stupid."

They turned onto Tenth Street and Nate let the comment go

as he turned his attention to their surroundings. He'd simply prove to Emma that he didn't say and do stupid things. Ever.

The Washburn Theater was on the left. Nate moved the truck over to the curb in front of the building and shifted into park.

"Whoa," Emma said. "You can't pull up in front. Keep driving."

Nate frowned. There was no parking lot at the Washburn. All that was available was street parking up and down the part-residential/part-business streets of the neighborhood. Nate looked around. There were no spots close. Surely they had a valet. "Why not?"

"You're going to pull up in front of this little old theater, where some no-one's-ever-heard-of-them band is playing to a crowd of teenagers, in your big old fancy pick up, get out in your suit and tie and walk in and blend?" she asked.

He opened his mouth to reply that no one had said anything about blending when she went on right over top of him.

"You are going to *try* to blend. You're going to go in there, not make a big deal out of anything, check the place out, reassure yourself that everything is fine and you're going to..." She trailed off, studying him. Her gaze went from his hair to his shoes. "Be cool."

Unfortunately, there was nothing sexual about the look she was giving him. It was more like she was sizing him up—and finding him lacking.

Which was *fortunate*, Nate insisted. It was fine. Neither one of them needed to be looking at the other with anything sexual in mind.

His gaze still went to her breasts, displayed perfectly by the scoop-neck, spaghetti-strapped tank top she wore under the too-big T-shirt that kept sliding around.

"Yes, I do look fine," she said to him, pulling his attention back to her face. She gave him a knowing look. "I'll blend in perfectly, thank you."

Nate wanted to laugh at that. One thing Emma Dixon did not do was blend in.

"What do you suggest?" he asked, hating that she had a point. He had no doubt that he would, indeed, be conspicuous at the Washburn.

"Pull down the street a couple of blocks," she said. "We'll walk."

He found a spot nearly six blocks from the front of the theater. He put the truck into park and shut it off. "Ready?" he asked, turning toward her.

"Almost. We need a few adjustments here first." She reached for him and Nate froze, anticipating her touch.

As she leaned in, her scent wafted up to him again and the neckline of her shirt gapped. The swell of her breasts teased him and all he could think about was that she clearly didn't have a bra on. All he'd have to do was pull one side of the top down slightly and he could run his thumb over her nipple.

He was so focused that he didn't realize what she was doing until she'd run her hand through his hair and tousled it.

Satisfied that she'd messed it up enough, she started to pull back, but her gaze caught on his and she stopped.

His attention went to her lips and her tongue darted out to wet them.

He watched her swallow. Then she lifted her hands to his throat to loosen his tie. It struck him as stupidly seductive. When she slid the tie from around his neck, he noticed she went nice and slow. Was she imagining this in a much more conducive environment where they could leisurely undress one another, absorbing every inch they bared, anticipating the next one?

There was something about Emma, though, that made him think if he was in a more conducive environment, there would be nothing slow or leisurely...or even nice...about it. He'd want to tear her clothes off, throw them to the side and plunge into her body without letting her catch her breath and not worrying about breathing himself until he had every inch of her against and around and under every inch of him.

She seemed like the clothes-tearing-not-breathing type too. But as her fingers freed the top two buttons on his shirt, they were trembling.

Emma met his eyes. Her hands went to his waist and she tugged on his shirt, pulling it from his pants. Lastly, she undid the buttons at his wrists and rolled the sleeves up to his elbows.

"That's the best we can do, I guess," she said, not moving back, but taking her hands off of him.

He was immediately relieved and then instantly wanted them back.

"I'm presentable now?" he asked with a wry smile.

She pulled in a breath and then gave him a smile. "Presentable enough," she said. "But it's not your clothes that are the biggest problem, you know."

"Oh?" He wanted to grab her. She was right *there*. He wanted to run his hand over her bare arm, and put his tongue against the pulse point in her neck, and kiss her. And kiss her. And kiss her.

Dammit.

"Your attitude is what's going to make it hard to blend in."

"My attitude?"

"That holier-than-thou thing you have going on. All the time."

And the urge to grab her should have diminished right then and there. This was the scrapping they did all the time. But there was a part of him that wanted to show her he didn't just *think* he was better than all the other guys—he could back it up.

"I need to be cool," he said, feeling heavy as he said the words.

Michael had always thought Nate was cool. They skied and traveled and went white water rafting and zip lining and snorkeling. Michael had all the best computer equipment, they had a regular pizza night and Nate had taught Michael everything from how to tie his shoes to how to play—and win—at poker. Michael had always told Nate he was cool.

Until the last year or so.

Sure, Nate hadn't been thrilled when Michael wanted to start his own tiny company. He'd known it meant that Michael was thinking he didn't need college and they'd argued. And no, Nate hadn't been happy when Michael met Shannon. Not that she wasn't a nice girl. But Michael was just finishing high school. It was a time for focus and goal setting. He'd had his eye on Harvard at one time, but if he had a girlfriend in Omaha, the chances of him moving to Boston were significantly decreased. So they'd argued about that.

It seemed over the past several months, they'd argued a lot.

Which was very common between teens and their parents. But it wasn't common for him and Michael.

"Yes, you need to be cool," Emma said, breaking into his thoughts.

"Anything specific?"

She looked at him thoughtfully. "No looking at people like you're a thousand times smarter than them and no talking like you're a dad and…maybe no talking, period."

"I'm not going to talk. At all?" he asked, raising an eyebrow.

This was interesting. And insulting. Of course, this was also Emma critiquing him and giving him advice, so of course it was insulting.

"When you talk you *sound* like you're a thousand times smarter than everyone else."

"Thank you. I think."

"And you sound like you know it," she added. "In this crowd, that's not a good thing. Follow my lead and stand there and look…bored. Can you pull bored off?"

"Absolutely. If I can throw in irritated, I'm all set."

She rolled her eyes. "How about this—be the opposite of how you usually are."

"Great. No problem."

"Here." She dug in her purse and pulled out two small plastic bottles like the ones you would find in a minibar. She read each label, then handed him one.

"What's this?"

"Flavored vodkas. Olivia and I were going to try some new recipes."

"Tonight?"

She shrugged. "Sometime."

"And in the meantime, you're carrying the vodka around in your purse?"

She grinned. "You never know when you might need it."

"Pain pills and alcohol don't mix."

"I haven't had pain pills in three days."

There went that excuse. He read his bottle. Whipped cream flavored vodka. "You've got to be kidding."

"You want the cake flavored instead?" she asked holding hers out.

"What happened to vodka flavored vodka?"

"What do you make with it?" she asked, one eyebrow up.

"Vodka."

She twisted the cap off of her bottle and tapped it against his. "Cheers." Then she shot it back.

He sighed. A shot wasn't a bad idea, everything considered. He twisted his cap off and took the shot. And nearly choked. It was sweet and...*sweet*. And damned if it didn't taste like whipped cream.

The vodka warmed his throat, chest and stomach and he sighed. *That* wasn't all bad.

Emma grinned. "Ready?"

Probably not. Not even with three more of those little bottles.

Nate kept his back turned to Emma as she got out, not wanting to see how she managed it in that tiny skirt.

"Let's go."

When she stepped onto the sidewalk beside him, Nate realized she had her cane with her.

"Seriously?"

"What?"

"A hot young woman dressed like *that* but using a cane is not exactly inconspicuous, Emma."

She huffed out a breath. "I tweaked my hip in class this morning," she said. "I don't usually use the cane unless I'm walking long distances. But it's been hurting today."

He stood on the sidewalk staring at the woman who stirred up more feelings than any woman had in a very long time. She was usually making him grit his teeth because he was trying *not* to notice her or react to her when he did notice. She also made him grit his teeth when she didn't react the way he wanted her to. But there were moments since her accident where he felt something new—if he didn't know better he'd say it was protective.

He'd been there the night she and her sisters had been in the car accident. Their whole group of friends and all of Emma's sisters had been together earlier that evening. Nate and Cody had needed to pull their friends Conner and Shane apart after an argument and take them home, so they'd split up. The girls had stayed behind at the bar.

When Nate had gotten the call about the accident and that Emma was going into surgery, he'd gone directly to the hospital like everyone else. But where everyone else congregated in the waiting room, Nate had headed straight for the OR. He'd taken over her case and had done the surgery he'd performed a hundred times before almost on autopilot, holding back his emotions and not letting the realization that it was Emma on his table sink in until he'd closed her up.

As they'd wheeled her to recovery, he'd gone to the showers and let the sweating and shaking take over.

Her injury had been severe. He'd placed a lot of pins to hold her together. And he was damned good at his job.

But he couldn't stand the idea that the sassy, mischievous, vivacious woman he'd known and been resisting could be vulnerable—in any way. Watching her sweat through rehab had sucked too. Fortunately, she'd bitched and moaned and he'd been able to tease her and push her. That had saved his sanity as much as it had hers.

Like now. Her hip hurt. She wasn't fully recovered. No matter how much he'd love to tell them both that it was no big deal, it still jabbed him in the chest to think that he couldn't snap his fingers and command her to be better.

The common mantra to patients was "it takes time" and "keep up with the rehab". The poor physical therapists had to deal with the whining and pep talks.

Except that Emma was right here. In front of him, looking fine and sounding fine and being...not quite fine. And he wanted her to be fine. More than fine.

"Do you need me to carry you?" he asked her, putting a touch of exasperation in his tone.

He knew that he drove her crazy. Of course he knew that. And he'd noticed that no one could get thirty more reps of her exercises out of her as easily as he could, so he'd visited her rehab sessions more often than he did with any other patient.

She looked up at him. Slowly her mouth curled. "Over your shoulder with my ass in the air or Scarlett-O'Hara style?"

Both images made him think about climbing the stairs in his house to his bedroom.

"How about piggy back?"

"Oh, I get it. You want my legs wrapped around you. You don't have to pretend to be concerned. Just ask."

And there was the feistiness he hated—and couldn't seem to get enough of. Damned right he wanted her legs wrapped around him.

"Just ask—that's all a guy needs to do, huh? No romance needed? No sweet talk?"

She smiled. "I said that's all *you* need to do."

He didn't respond to that. That was the best approach. That was almost always the best approach when it came to him and

Emma. It was not the one he always used, but it was almost always the best one.

He took the cane from her fingers and tossed it into the backseat of the truck. "Let's go."

She opened her mouth to say something and he held out his elbow. "I'll help."

She closed her mouth, looked from his arm to his eyes. Then she stepped close, looped her arm through his, leaned into him slightly, and they headed for the theater.

It cost sixty bucks each to get them in, and when he balked at reaching for his wallet, Emma elbowed him in the side.

He handed over the cash, let the twenty-something—who was definitely pulling off the bored look—loop a bright blue band around his wrist and then followed Emma through the doors, up the three steps and through a set of interior double doors.

As they stepped into the dark on the other side of the doors, he felt Emma's hand slip into his. One of the two big guys on either side said, "Bracelets."

Emma lifted their joined hands, showing off the glow-in-the-dark blue bands.

"Have fun."

The guy stepped back to let Emma by, but Nate didn't miss the way both guys checked her out. The one closest to him met Nate's gaze and gave him a nod.

Nate felt a stupid surge of *hell yeah she's with me*.

She wasn't. Still, it didn't feel *bad* knowing those guys thought so.

The deep bump of the bass grew as they walked down a short hallway lit by soft sconces on the walls until they came to yet another set of doors.

"You ready?" Emma asked, her hand still in his.

"I've gotta see what's worth sixty bucks a head," Nate said.

She laughed and pulled the tall, heavy door open.

The noise hit him first. His eyes were already accustomed to the dark, so he could see that the room was about the size of a small gymnasium, with the same high ceiling and tall arched windows about three-fourths of the way up the walls. The windows were covered with black drapes at the moment, and an elaborate lighting set hung from the ceiling in front of them, pointing at the stage on the opposite end of the room, spot-lighting the band. There was also a second floor with a balcony that ran the length of three of the walls. People stood, leaning on the railing, watching the band and the people below them. There were no chairs, no bleachers, no theater seats on either level. The main room had a big, hardwood floor and the crowd stood, dancing, singing, and shouting to be heard over the music.

They moved fully into the room, Emma still by his side, and as he took in the details of the crowd, he admitted she was right. He definitely didn't fit it.

There was a mix of ages and styles—some in blue jeans and T-shirts, some in black leather. He saw a cluster of girls that couldn't have been more than fourteen and a group of guys and girls who were holding beers and hard lemonades. As they moved further into the crowd, Nate noticed that he wasn't the only thirty-something in attendance. There were a few even older, drinking and seemingly enjoying the music.

Emma stopped about a third of the way across the floor and turned to him. She had to get her mouth near his ear to be heard, but his body didn't care *why* she was pressed up against him. Without thinking, he moved his hand to her butt and leaned in so he could hear her. And smell her. And brush his lips very lightly over the skin of her neck. It would seem accidental to her, but getting even a small taste was an opportunity he couldn't pass up.

She shivered and he smiled a smug smile that she, thankfully, couldn't see.

"We should go up to the balcony. We can see better from there."

God, she smelled good.

"Fine. I'm with you," he said.

It took her a moment to step back and when she did, she met his eyes and licked her lips again.

He simply waited for her to move.

Finally, she turned and started for what he assumed to be the stairs to the balcony. There was a moment's reprieve from the noise as they stepped out of the main room into the stairwell and climbed, but neither of them said anything. Emma kept hold of his hand. He followed, unable to keep from noticing that she looked as great from behind as she did from the front, especially with the way the soft knit of her skirt molded to her curves.

They stepped out onto the second level after only sixteen steps. The second floor had other rooms as well, likely offices by the looks of them, but the huge arched doorway that led to the balcony was immediately to their left.

"Over there." She pointed to a space at the railing and started in that direction. She dropped his hand as she wove through the crowd but he kept his gaze on her.

She was halfway across the balcony when a guy turned suddenly and caught her shoulder with his elbow. His drink sloshed over the edge of his glass and he scowled at her, but Emma didn't notice as she was trying to catch her balance on her stupid high heels. Nate pushed around the guy in front of him and grabbed her, keeping her upright with one hand on her upper arm and one on her low back. With a sigh, he turned and steered her three steps until her back was against the balcony railing.

"You're an incident waiting to happen, aren't you?" he asked near her ear because of the noise level.

"Don't you mean accident?" she asked.

He pulled in a deep breath of her scent before saying, "Accidents are unintentional. And Emma, you are nothing if not intentional."

"You like women who are more subtle?"

"All women are more subtle than you," he told her.

"Meaning?"

The lighting up here was better than down on the floor and standing this close, he could see her face clearly. She braced her hands behind her on the railing and watched him carefully, like she was very interested in his answer.

"Meaning you say what you think, do what you want, and don't think more than two minutes into the future when it comes to consequences."

"Seems that you've given that—*me*—a lot of thought."

He chuckled. "I think everyone knows that about you."

"But I don't know many people who are so *annoyed* by it."

He looked at her for a long moment, debating whether to end the conversation there or to go ahead with it.

But he *was* annoyed by it. He was turned on by and drawn to her sassy nature. That who-cares-I'll-deal-with-the-fallout-later thing she did. He was jealous of it, honestly, and wanted it for himself.

She owned her own business, but it was a small yoga and exercise studio that's hours of operation revolved entirely around how Emma felt. She could stay out late and party because she didn't have classes starting until ten a.m. and that was only Monday, Wednesday and Friday.

He had a kid, a business and a surgery schedule. Surgery. He cut people open for a living. He couldn't say "fuck it" and do two more shots at the bar whenever he felt like it.

"Why do you care if I'm annoyed by it?" he finally asked.

"I don't know," she said. "Maybe I'd like to evoke an emotion other than irritation in you."

Oh, if she only knew.

"You annoy other people too," he pointed out.

She nodded. "I know. But I guess I don't want them to feel anything else for me."

He blinked at her. This was beyond stupid. This was why they didn't have more conversations alone.

"Enough." He turned her so her belly was against the railing and caged her in by placing his hands on the railing on either side of her. "Look for Michael and Shannon."

They stood like that, not moving, scanning the crowd for a few minutes. Eventually, she shifted off of her right leg, leaning onto her left.

He resisted the urge to put his hand on her hip, to rub it or… something. "You're that sore?"

"Stiff."

He barely heard her over the music and crowd. He put his mouth close to her ear. "What were you doing this morning that hurt it?"

She turned her face so her mouth was closer to his. "Trying some advanced yoga poses."

"You need to be careful not to push too fast." He had no problem with yoga. Emma's physical condition prior to the accident and surgery had given her the potential for full recovery. But some things simply took time.

"I'd be happy to show you what I was trying and you can tell me if it's too much."

There was something in her voice, even with the music thumping and the crowd noise rumbling around them that made his body react. He was sure Emma demonstrating *any* yoga poses would be too much—of something.

"I'll take your word for it."

"Chicken."

Very likely.

They didn't try to talk for a couple of minutes. Then he felt compelled to say, "It's normal, you know. To still be stiff and sore at times. And you're trying high level stuff." It was normal. And it was good for him to remember that too. He hadn't failed her. He'd put her back together and had done a hell of a job. She was healing. She was getting better. She was going to be fine.

He saw dozens of people every week in her same—and worse —condition. Their lingering aches and pains never bothered him.

But it bugged the hell out of him to think of Emma hurting.

"I know that, Nate." She sounded frustrated. "That doesn't make it not hurt. You say that to me all the time, and I'll bet you say it fifty times a day to other people. And then you don't see us for six weeks and by then it *is* better and you feel all great about yourself and what you did. But living with it day to day is different. So...shut up, okay?"

He wasn't sure how to respond to that. She was right, of course. So he did shut up.

They stood facing the stage and the floor below them. He was aware of every inch of her. Especially when she shifted again, this time to lean back against him slightly. He knew she might not even be aware of it. She was seeking a position that would take weight off her sore leg and leaning against a support would help with that. But the position, thanks to her heels, put her butt right against his fly.

He held his breath and tried to ignore it, making his mind focus on searching the crowd for his son.

Then she wiggled.

Whether she meant to or not, he couldn't handle that. He put his hands on her hips to stop her squirming and moved her an inch forward. That was all he needed. An inch of space between their bodies.

He felt the tension in her body immediately and assumed that meant she either hadn't intended the position to be what it was, or his hands made her stiffen up. Which could be good or bad.

After several seconds, he started to relax. But right when he thought maybe he was safe and again began his search for his son, Emma turned.

His hands skimmed over her body as she spun, and when she faced him, he wasn't inclined to remove them.

"You want to make both of us feel better?" she asked.

He could hear her, but he didn't want to miss anything. He

put his hand to the back of her head, holding her still, and leaned in. "Tell me."

She lifted onto her toes, her mouth right against his ear. "We try some of the high level things I want to do…together. Then you can see that it *is* actually hard for me and get off my ass about it…or you show me that it's fine and alleviate my fears and then I'll listen to all your instructions from here on out."

He worked on simply breathing. He wanted to press more firmly against the railing and test some of her hip range of motion right here and now. And he couldn't deny that the idea of her listening to all his instructions from here on out was really fucking tempting. "I'm guessing we're not talking about jogging now."

"I hate jogging."

"I don't know much about yoga."

"Then we'll stay away from the yoga."

He pulled back to look down at her. Dammit. He couldn't sleep with her, but there were so many reasons that he wanted to and with her standing so close, the dark and the music and her scent and her lips right there…the reasons why it was a bad idea were fuzzy.

Nate didn't do fuzzy. A woman who muddled his brain and distracted him so easily was the last person he should—and would—get involved with.

He liked to be in control in his relationships.

It came from a history of a controlling son-of-a-bitch grandfather and two women who had made choices, without his input, that had changed his life profoundly.

He was never going to be in a position again where someone else made decisions that affected his life and his loved ones.

Staring at Emma now, he shook his head. It was ironic, but he loved strong, independent women and knew that none of the women he was attracted to would put up with his chauvinistic, controlling tendencies in a full-blown relationship. Therefore, he kept women specifically compartmentalized to the bedroom. There they didn't seem to mind him being demanding.

Bringing Emma into his bedroom seemed inevitable. But he knew Emma Dixon would not *stay* compartmentalized. Keeping Emma to one part of his life would be like telling a tornado to only tear apart a room instead of taking the whole house. It would never work and he'd be left with a big mess to clean up afterward.

"You're thinking about it too hard," Emma told him.

She gripped the front of his shirt and pulled him down for a kiss.

The moment their lips met, as heat and desire and need swirled in him, Nate knew the tornado comparison was exactly right. And that it was futile to try to resist its force.

Nate had been fighting this for months. There had been opportunities before this. He could have had her before this; he knew that. But he'd fought it. Fought against his natural instincts. Fought against his body clamoring for hers whenever she was within a few feet of him. Fought because her brother, his teammate and a damned good guy, would want to kick his ass. Fought because there was no way they could make this more than a night. Or two. Maybe a long weekend.

Now it was happening, in spite of all that, and he couldn't fight anymore.

He was going to let the tornado sweep him away this one time. For just a moment.

He slanted his mouth on hers, taking over the kiss. One hand still held her head, the other gripped her ass and brought her fully against him. He stroked his tongue deep, tasting her mouth fully, reveling in the feel of her lips against his as she arched closer.

Her hands went from his shirt front to his neck, holding on tight and he backed her up the two inches to the railing, the firm support behind her enough that he could press his hips into hers.

He felt her groan more than heard it and he wanted to see her face, to see how he was affecting her. He held her face in both hands and pulled away.

Her lipstick was smudged, her lips swollen and parted as she breathed fast. Her cheeks were pink and her eyes opened slowly. When she did lift her gaze to his, she definitely looked dazed.

"Holy shit," she said. "We should have done that a long time ago."

"Emma—" But something caught his eye over her shoulder. Someone winding through the crowd on the first floor. He tried to peer closer, but the person—who looked very much like his son—moved out of view.

"Nate."

She moved her mouth to his again and for a moment he was lost. She tasted like cake. From the vodka. All at once, flavored vodka seemed like a hell of an idea.

Then he remembered seeing Michael. Or someone that looked like Michael.

He tore his mouth from hers. "Emma, stop."

She was breathing hard as she stared up at him.

"I think I saw Michael."

She closed her eyes and breathed deep. When she opened them again, she nodded. "Okay. Right."

She swiveled to look at the stage and the crowd below while Nate struggled to get his breathing, heart rate and the need to grab her and put his hands all over her under control.

The breathing and heart rate calmed. The need to have her didn't dissipate at all.

CHAPTER
THREE

EMMA TURNED BACK after a moment and said loudly, "They're not there anymore."

Nate sighed. "Okay." Fuck. Now what? Did Emma know more about their plans? Would she tell him? Should he check her phone again? He might as well. After all, it was a better reason to put his hands on her again than because he wanted to start taking her clothes off. "We need to…" Then her words sunk in. He scowled. "*Anymore*? You saw them."

She wrinkled her nose. "Dammit."

"Yeah, dammit." He took her by the upper arm and turned her toward the staircase.

As they headed for the truck, he worked on not yelling. Which resulted in him not speaking at all. She'd fucking kissed him to distract him so Michael and Shannon could sneak out.

That pissed him off way more than it should. It shouldn't have surprised him. Yet he found himself completely surprised and…hurt. No, not hurt. That was stupid and pathetic. He was… annoyed. Very annoyed.

Which obviously meant that he'd wanted the kissing to mean

more to her than it had and he was feeling offended—at least that was better than *hurt*—by the idea that it had all been nothing but a diversion.

She wisely didn't talk until they got in the truck.

Nate opened the door and nudged Emma in.

Once he'd climbed in and shut the door, he turned to her, careful to keep his voice even. "I don't like being manipulated."

"I know how that seemed, but—"

"Don't make it worse by lying," he cautioned. He'd shown her that she could get to him. Until now, he'd held the power because she'd thought he'd never cave. But he had.

She took a deep breath and turned to face him. "Full truth. I don't want you following Michael and Shannon tonight. But you already knew that. Yes, I saw them there. But I didn't know they were leaving and I didn't kiss you so you wouldn't see them. I didn't even mean to kiss you. We were talking about my hip."

"And then you made a smart-ass comment about trying out all the things you were worried about doing," he pointed out. "That wasn't supposed to distract me?"

"It was supposed to get your attention," she admitted. "The way you always talk about my hip like you know how it's feeling and how it's working makes me nuts."

"I put it back together," he said even while he acknowledged that it was dumb to defend himself like this. "I know your hip better than anyone."

"Not better than *me*," she insisted. "You might know how the pieces look and how many pins are in there, but you don't know how it *feels*."

In the time Nate had known Emma, he'd often had moments where he was torn between shaking her and kissing her. But up until tonight, he hadn't known what kissing her would be like. Now that he did, the urge to shut her up with his own mouth was nearly overpowering.

"And I thought," she went on, "that maybe if it affected you personally, it would make you more empathetic when your patients told you things were tough. That if you saw it up close and personal, it would help your bedside manner."

"Affect me personally?" he asked.

Emma braced her hand on the seat between them and leaned in, her voice dropping, her gaze on his lips. "You know, like if you were trying to get my leg up on your shoulder so you could thrust nice and deep, but it couldn't quite make it and you had to adjust."

And that was what he got when he let Emma Dixon run away with a conversation.

He shook his head as heat shot through his body. "Jesus, Emma."

She gave him a smug smile and leaned back, apparently satisfied with his reaction. Because of course he'd reacted to her *again*. After months of resisting reaction, he was sure as hell making up for it tonight.

"Anyway," she said, now lounging casually, her arms crossed. "I didn't mean to kiss you. But you were right there and once I started...holy hell, Nate, I forgot about everything else but kissing you some more." She looked at him and sighed. "Seriously, we should have been doing that for a long time now."

Fuck.

Nate closed his eyes and tipped his head back on the seat. "Where are Michael and Shannon?"

"We're not going to talk about it?"

"No."

"Right now or ever?"

"Ever."

"I think we should."

His head came up and he looked at her with a frown. "We shouldn't," he said firmly. "Trust me."

"You're telling me that you have absolutely no interest in doing it again?"

"Emma," he said, through gritted teeth. "We are *not* talking about this. Now or ever. Drop it."

She looked at him thoughtfully for several seconds. "Tell you what. You don't have to talk about it. But I don't think there's a way to keep *me* from talking about it."

He narrowed his eyes. If she started talking, he knew there was no way she was going to keep the topic only to the kiss they'd shared in the theater either. He'd never survive this. *This* was definitely part of the reason he'd never let on that she could get him worked up. Because Emma didn't know when to say when. She had no boundaries and no filter. She'd keep at him until she wore him down. And then she'd hate the result.

"Why do you want to talk about it anyway?" he asked, letting his irritation show.

"Because I want to do it again," she said, as if it should have been obvious. "And I want to do more than that."

But she didn't. Not really. Emma Dixon didn't know everything, in spite of what she thought, and getting into a relationship with him was something she would *not* enjoy.

"If I'm not around when you're talking, I guess it won't matter, will it?" he asked.

"You're taking me home?" she asked.

"That seems like the best choice."

"How are you going to find out where Michael and Shannon are?"

He'd planned on calling and texting his son increasingly horrible threats until Michael called back or came home. He frowned at Emma. "You know where they're going after this?"

"I might."

"Emma," he said in the voice he used in the ER when his staff wasn't moving fast enough. It always got a positive response. "Tell me where they are."

"Only if you keep me with you."

"Is it on your phone?"

She held her phone up, then tucked it under her skirt. "You're sure welcome to check."

He wanted to. Far too much. Bringing her along in the first place was a horrible idea.

And he'd think of her the next time he had cake or whipped cream. He was sure of it.

"Give me the address." Once he knew where the kids were, he could drop her off.

Which, of course, she realized. "Take a left on seventeenth."

"We're going to do it this way?" Nate asked, resigning himself. It was Emma. Of course they were going to do it the hard way.

"I'm not letting you loose on Shannon without backup," Emma said.

"I promise I don't need backup."

"Ha-ha. No dice, Doc," she said, tipping her water bottle back. "You're stuck with me tonight."

Yep, it looked like he was.

Fuck.

He took a nice long look at those tanned legs in the short skirt, then turned his attention out the windshield and worked on ignoring the woman that he'd never been able to ignore before. And that had been before he knew that her mouth fit his perfectly and that making her groan was the most fun he'd had in a long time.

Emma worked hard on not grinning.

Nate didn't want to want her. That was clear.

But he did want her.

Thank God. For one, Nate wasn't immune. He was damned good at hiding it, but he wasn't immune to her. For two, she'd finally kissed him and it had been everything she'd assumed it would be and then some.

Damn, the guy could kiss.

She wasn't nearly done with him yet.

No matter what he thought.

"It's the blue house on the right," she said as they pulled onto the street where the party was going on tonight. "But don't park right in front. We don't want them to see us."

They shouldn't even be on the block if they didn't want to be noticed. This neighborhood was made up entirely of older homes that were rented out to college students. No one here drove a big old truck like Nate's.

"Who lives here?" Nate asked.

"A friend of Shannon's who graduated high school last year," Emma told him. "She and her roommates are having a party tonight and Shannon mentioned that she and Michael would stop by." She swiveled in her seat. "Now what? You can't go up to the door and ask to be invited in and I'm not sure peeking in the windows is a good idea."

"His car is here," Nate said, pointing out the front window. "We'll wait here."

"If you want my opinion," she said. "I say you give all of this up and trust your son. I'd be happy to do what I can to take your mind off of things."

Nate looked at her with the weird combination of heat and resignation she'd already seen more than she liked tonight.

"If you're bored, you can feel free to get out."

"And go where?" she asked, looking around.

"You could call one of your sisters to come get you. Or a cab," Nate suggested. "I'll pay."

He'd love that. But now she knew that he wasn't simply frustrated with her. He was *sexually* frustrated. She couldn't contain her grin at that.

"If I leave, how will you find them when they take off from here?"

"I'll follow them," he said simply.

He was nuts. He was hot. But he was nuts.

Emma sighed. "We're going to have a stake out? Seriously?"

"This way I know where they are and when they leave and where they go next."

"You need a hobby."

"I can call a cab for you right now," he said, withdrawing his phone.

"Nate, you want me to stay." She kicked off her shoes, stretched her legs out and propped her heels on the opposite seat. "You're going to need a character witness when the neighbors call the cops to report the stalker in the truck."

He looked up and down the street. "I'm not thinking this street has a neighborhood watch, you know?"

She chuckled. "Fine. We'll stake the house out and stalk your son. Whatever. I didn't have anything else to do tonight."

He looked over. "Maybe *you* need a hobby."

"I have hobbies. But my doctor says I have to wait six more weeks to get back to them."

He pulled a long breath in through his nose and Emma bit her lip to keep her smile to herself. She wasn't nearly as promiscuous as she let on, but it seemed that comments about her reported wild sexual habits riled Nate up the easiest, so she made a point of mentioning her reputation whenever possible. The comments had the same effect on her brother, but that wasn't nearly as fun.

"We should get in the back seat," she said after a few moments of silence.

He looked suspicious. "I don't think so."

She glanced around the neighborhood. "Seriously. The back windows are tinted and back there it's harder to see us anyway. We can't just sit up here. We're not exactly inconspicuous," she added, using his word from earlier.

He glanced around too. Then he muttered, "Shit."

She grinned and started to climb into the back of the crew cab. A truck this size had a roomy back seat but she wasn't opposed to sitting closer to Nate.

"For God's sake," she heard, then felt his hand on her butt as he pushed her over the seat. "Nice view," he muttered.

She grinned even bigger, glad he'd noticed. Her short skirt didn't cover much even without things like climbing around in pickups.

She settled into the seat on the passenger's side and watched Nate get out of the truck and open the door to allow him to climb up into the backseat. Oh. That would have worked too, she supposed.

He didn't look happy as he slammed the door, shutting them in together again. But he didn't say a word. For five minutes. And he was clearly trying to keep his eyes on things outside of the truck.

Screw that. This neighborhood was *not* that interesting.

"Stalking your son is crazy, you know."

"I know."

Her eyes widened. "You do?"

"I'm sure this is an overreaction," he admitted.

Emma was impressed he realized that.

"But Michael is avoiding me. He hasn't eaten a meal at home and has answered only two phone calls from me since I found him in bed with Shannon."

"Oh. Yikes," Emma said quietly.

"If he isn't going to be responsible and mature about telling me where he's going and what he's doing, then I'll find out another way. If he doesn't want me to follow him, then he'll be frank with me. If he's not, he leaves me no other choice."

That wasn't entirely true, of course, but she could at least agree that Michael could be handling this better too. One thing she could say for Shannon—she didn't always make the best choices, but she was honest about what she chose.

A few more minutes ticked by and Emma felt herself growing restless.

They were clearly going to sit here for an unspecified amount of time. They could at least try to make it fun.

"Want to make out?" she asked.

"No."

And up until about two hours ago she would have believed that. But that hadn't been a banana in his pocket at the concert. Okay, she could play along. What else did she have to do?

"Want to talk about our hopes and dreams?"

He looked over with one eyebrow up. "No."

Good. What was she going to tell him? About that dirty dream she'd had about him a month ago? *That* would be a bad idea.

"Then it's Truth or Dare." Which also probably wasn't brilliant.

Nate rolled his eyes. "And if this was my thirteenth birthday party, I might think that was a great idea. But it's not. And I don't."

"Come on. We're just sitting here. What else are we going to do?"

"Sit and silently stew over the fact that my son is rebelling against everything I'm trying to do for him."

She stared at him. "Um. No. Truth or Dare."

"No."

"Then I'll play by myself," she said, thinking fast. "And I pick dare."

"Emma."

She ignored him. Staking out the house where Michael and Shannon were having a good time with their friends was ridiculous. And sitting this close to Nate after kissing him in the theater was making her want to take all of her clothes off.

She was well known for being bold and without boundaries. Time to put some of that to good use.

"Emma," she said. "I dare you to take the finger vibrator out of your purse and use it right here in the back of this truck."

There was a heartbeat of silence. Then she reached for her purse.

"No!"

The word was loud and firm and Emma instinctively pulled her hand back, turning wide eyes on Nate. He looked like he was in pain. And really mad.

"I have to. It's a dare."

Nate didn't scare her. He made her frustrated and horny... but not scared.

"If you take a finger vibrator out of your purse, I'll throw your ass out of this truck."

Her tummy flipped. Damn, there was something about that commanding tone of voice that made her get all hot and tingly.

"Oh, come on, Nate. You have to admit that there's a not-so-little part of you—" her gaze dropped to his lap, "—that wouldn't mind seeing this."

His eyes narrowed. "You pull a vibrator out and I will physically remove you from this truck and leave it up to you to find a way home."

Whether it was the expression on his face or the tone in his voice or both, she believed him.

She sighed and slumped back in her seat. She wasn't sure how far she would have gone with the vibrator. Honestly, with Nate sitting there watching her? All the way. No doubt. And it wouldn't have taken long to get *all the way* with his eyes on her.

"If you don't want me playing with myself..." she let the words, and their double meaning, hang in the air between them for a moment, "...you're going to have to play with me."

Not at all subtle, but she wasn't very good at subtle. She sat watching him.

His jaw tightened and she saw him clench a fist. Finally he said, "Fine." Though it clearly wasn't fine with him at all.

She pounced. "Were you in love with Michael's mom?"

He frowned at her. "I didn't say truth."

"You want dare?" she asked. She really wanted him to answer her question though. "'Cause I've got a good one."

And it was going to involve either him taking his shirt off or kissing her again. Or both.

He narrowed his eyes. "Fine, truth."

She wasn't sure if she was happy or disappointed. She did want the story of him and Michael's mom. But damn...that kiss was going to haunt her for a long time.

"Were you in love with Michael's mom?" she repeated, her fingers curling into her leg where her hand rested on her lap.

There was a long moment of silence. Then he said, "Yes."

It was incredibly stupid that his answer bothered her.

"What happened?" she asked.

"One answer per truth. I know the rules," he said, pinning her with his gaze. "My turn. Truth or dare?"

This was usually easy for her. She always took the dares. And she wanted to know what Nate might dare her to do. But it might involve walking home or sitting and not talking for an hour or something. "Truth."

He paused, as if that wasn't what he'd been expecting. Hmm, what had he wanted her to do? Did it involve the mini vibrator? Maybe she should change her answer.

"What's with the need to constantly shock and awe?"

She sat up straighter. That was an honest-to-goodness truth-type question. It wasn't some flippant thing like *do you prefer chocolate or caramel sauce spread all over your body?*

"Uh..." Did she answer truthfully? Of course. She'd never fudged on a truth or a dare in her life. She took a deep breath. She knew herself. She could answer this. Even if she wasn't sure why Nate was asking. "My dad died when I was thirteen. Amanda was fourteen, Isabelle was twelve and Olivia was eleven. It was completely overwhelming for my mom."

"I thought Conner stepped in to help," Nate said.

This was going to be a conversation? Interesting. She nodded. Everyone knew that her brother Conner, older than Amanda by three years, had assumed the role of father figure to his sisters. A role he still took seriously. Which made things interesting for his friends, Ryan and Shane, who had fallen in love with two of Conner's sisters.

"He did. But he was seventeen. A kid himself. At first he threw himself into things like figuring out the finances, repairing the roof and getting a job." Her dad's death had been unexpected and he'd been young, so things were definitely in disarray. She went on, "That first summer we were all signed up to do different things. But Mom and Conner couldn't handle us going in four different directions. To make things easier, they sent us all to the same summer camp."

"But you didn't want to go."

"No. Camp isn't my thing." She'd planned to spend her summer hanging out with Dena, going to the mall and flirting at the pool.

"I'm shocked."

She ignored that. "Not only did we all go to camp together, but we were known as the Dixon girls. We were always lumped together. No one ever figured out our individual names. They'd call me by one of my sisters' names all the time. Finally, I got sick of it. We were playing sand volleyball and one of the boys called me Amanda. I went under the net, tackled him and rubbed sand in his face until he'd repeated my name ten times."

Nate's eyes slowly widened. She grinned. "No one forgot who *I* was after that. From there I kept working to stand out. I snuck out of my cabin at night and got caught kissing that same boy I'd tackled in volleyball. I started a protest against lima beans in the cafeteria. All kinds of stuff. By the end of the three weeks, everyone knew who I was."

"And you've never stopped."

She shook her head. "I love my sisters, I'm proud of them, but I don't want to *be* any of them. I want everyone to know *me*. And I still love kissing and I still hate lima beans."

Nate sat watching her and Emma let him. There was something in the way he was studying her that made her squirm—in a good way.

"Your turn," he finally said.

Yes. This was great. "Truth or dare?" she asked. *Please pick truth, please pick truth.* Though she did have a great dare in mind…

"Truth."

"What happened with Michael's mom?"

She knew he'd been expecting the question. He took a breath, then said, "I was head over heels. Stacie and I met when we were sixteen. We dated for a year. When she got pregnant, I thought it would be fine, we'd get married, it would all work out. Next thing I knew, she left for Phoenix, where her grandparents lived. She cut off all contact with me. Nine months later, my grandfather sat me down with his lawyer. A woman brought a baby in and handed him to me. My grandfather said that they'd made a deal with Stacie—they would pay for all of her college tuition, any grad school, books, living expenses, everything, if she signed over all of her parental rights and never tried to contact Michael or I."

Emma bit her tongue. A thousand questions were trying to spill out of her mouth, but she knew she had to give Nate time to tell the story the way he wanted to tell it.

But holy shit.

"I tried to find her after that. Hired a PI and everything. He finally found her in California, I called, she said not to contact her again and hung up."

Emma pressed her lips together, but couldn't stop her foot from tapping against the floor. She couldn't interrupt.

"I tried to call her again; she'd changed her number. I mailed her a package; it came back to me unopened. I went out there and she'd moved."

Emma opened her mouth, then closed it without a word— something she was very proud of.

"My grandfather found out and he sat me down and told me that this was how it had to be. He couldn't have me distracted from my path to med school and the family business. Before I even saw Michael, Granddad made sure he had the best pediatrician, the best nanny, the best…car seat. Everything was taken care of. I didn't even pick out his name. I'd messed up by getting Stacie pregnant, but Granddad was fixing things and I needed to stop fighting it. Then he told me that *she* hadn't fought. She hadn't argued, hadn't tried to negotiate, had never asked for a visitation arrangement, hadn't even asked to talk to me. She'd given up. That's what got to me and made me stop trying to contact her."

Nate looked over at Emma. "My grandfather was a controlling, intimidating bastard. He essentially dictated everything in the family and I never saw anyone stand up to him. But, dammit, once I held Michael in my arms, I couldn't understand how Stacie couldn't have fought. There isn't anything I wouldn't do, anyone I wouldn't fight, to make sure he was okay."

He stopped talking and Emma wanted so badly to respond, but wasn't sure she should. The idiot woman had walked away from Nate too. She'd left when he tried everything to be *with* her.

Finally she couldn't take it anymore. "Maybe that was what she was doing."

Nate looked at her. "What do you mean?"

"Maybe she was making sure he was okay. Maybe giving him up, fighting with her own instincts to keep him and raise him, was the battle *she* had. Being with you, with your family's money and advantages, had to be better for him than a single mom who was starting college."

Nate stared at her. "Are you kidding me right now?" he finally demanded.

"What do you mean?"

"You're defending her to me? Seriously?"

"Nate, I watched Dena raise Shannon. I know how hard that is. If someone had come to Dena and said, 'Let me raise your kid in the lap of luxury, she'll never want for anything, she'll be safe and happy and healthy and *you* don't have to give up your plans or your dreams. We'll essentially give you anything you need to make those plans and dreams come true', she would've jumped at it."

He frowned. "What kind of motherly instinct is that?"

"He went to her before she'd even had the baby right? And she was a scared kid. She hadn't formed any attachment to Michael yet when the offer was made. He'd given her a get-out-of-baby-jail-free card. She signed it all away before she even thought about it."

Nate shook his head. "You are, hands down, the most difficult woman I know."

"Me? I didn't do anything to you."

"I tell you the heart-wrenching story about Michael's mom giving him up for money and you defend the girl to me. Figures."

He didn't sound mad though. Emma suspected that he knew what she said was true. Had even occurred to him before she'd said it.

"She was seventeen. Give her a break. And *not* keeping in touch had to be less *heart-wrenching* for her."

"I was seventeen too."

"But Grandpa didn't give you much choice, did he?"

"None at all."

"And you survived. Now it's your turn, truth or dare me."

"That's it? No sympathy? No, 'wow you did a great job, Nate. Michael's a great kid'? Nothing?"

"You know Michael's a great kid and you told me that he was raised by nannies, so why should I tell you great job?"

Nate shook his head. "There's really no impressing you, is there?"

She gave him a smile. "It's hard to impress me with single parenthood, Nate. I've seen it up close and personal and without money for private planes and private schools."

"As soon as I was done with med school, I was hands on with him. As much as I could be."

Emma regretted her quip. She'd seen Nate with Michael. He was a fantastic dad. Of course, the nannies and money helped, but there wasn't anything that could replace a dad who was involved and cared about his kid.

"But yes," he admitted before she could take it back. "Everything had to be easier for me than it was for Dena."

Emma shrugged. "Dena had *me*. So, you know, it was a cake walk."

He grinned and it did funny things to her stomach.

"You don't think Dena would have traded you in for a private plane given half a chance?"

Emma grinned too. "Only if I took Shannon with me when I went. There were days she would have traded both of us for a good margarita and a guy who could find her g-spot."

Nate's eyebrows shot up. "Is that right?"

Emma chuckled. "Most women would give a lot for a good margarita and a guy who can find her g-spot."

The air in the truck seemed to instantly heat a few degrees. Emma found herself breathing deep and fixating on Nate's mouth.

"I didn't realize we were so rare a species."

That pulled her gaze back to his and a surprised laugh escaped her, even as *her* g-spot said *oh, baby*. "Cocky much?"

"I would think *you* would appreciate that about me. Being damned cocky yourself."

"I appreciate a lot of things about you." She smiled. "Especially things having to do with cock."

She could tell from his smile that he'd been expecting the comment. "You don't let guys get away with that, do you, Emma?"

"Being cocky?"

"Not finding your g-spot. There's no excuse for that. You need to help point the way."

"Oh, I'm not at all shy about telling people what I want," she assured him. "Especially in the bedroom. I'm all for getting exactly what I want there." She liked the direction of this conversation. If he wanted to prove that he was a pro at the g-spot-finding thing, she'd be happy to let him.

He hesitated, his gaze on her face like he was studying her or looking for something. Then he sat back. "Exactly."

She blinked. "What?"

"We have a lot in common."

"We do?"

"I like things my way too. In fact, I insist on things being my way. I have a feeling we might clash a lot."

What the hell was he talking about? The conversation had been on a very nice course there for a minute. "Unless we want the same things."

He didn't say anything for a few seconds. When he did, he again surprised her. "Truth or dare?"

She studied his face as he had hers, but didn't have a clue what he was thinking. "Truth."

"How anxious are you to go to bed with Bruce?"

She felt her eyes widen. Her physical therapist? Was that bothering Nate because he worked with Bruce professionally? Or for another reason? She was tempted to tease Nate with a *very*, to see his reaction. But this was Truth or Dare. She had to stay true to the game. "Not anxious at all."

Something flickered in Nate's eyes but she couldn't identify it for sure. "Who are you anxious to go to bed with?"

She didn't have to answer. That was two questions on one truth, like he'd refused to do when she'd asked.

But, dammit, she wanted him to know the answer.

"You have no idea?" she asked.

He sat looking at her. His gaze went to her mouth, then came back up to hers. "That was a dumb question."

"Because you know the answer?" Her heart was already beating faster.

"Because it doesn't matter what the answer is."

Well, *that* wasn't true. "I think you should let me answer."

"No." He faced forward again. "Drop it."

Yep, he definitely knew the answer. "Nate, we could—"

"Drop. It."

His voice was low, but the command was so firm that she stopped without thinking. She blinked at him. Holy crap. "You use that tone of voice in the bedroom and I'll drop whatever you want—my panties, to my knees—"

His hand was against her mouth before she could blink. "Fuck, Emma." He looked pained as he stared at her.

She smiled behind his hand. Another reaction. A good one. He wasn't resistant. At all. She lifted a shoulder and waited for him to move his hand.

Finally, he sighed and dropped it. "Knock it off."

"What? It's called *Truth* or Dare."

"I'm calling Michael." Nate settled back in his seat and pulled his phone from his pocket.

"What? No." She reached out and grabbed the phone. "You need to relax."

"It's been forty-five minutes."

Forty-five minutes of her making him sweat. She loved it.

"And the cops haven't showed up, you haven't seen any naked people running around the yard, and no one's carried a keg in," she said.

"The keg could already be in there. Along with the naked people."

The keg was probably already in there, but at least they hadn't brought in another. "Nate…"

"Give me my phone, Emma."

He was using her name more. What did that mean? Anything? She was tempted to tuck the phone in her bra and tell him he had to retrieve it. Instead, she said, "Use that voice again."

His jaw tightened for a moment. "I don't know what you mean."

She smiled. "Yes you do. That sexy, I'm-in-charge voice. I bet you use that in surgery all the time."

"I am in charge in surgery."

"And with Michael, right? You use that tone with him?"

"I'm in charge with him too."

Yeah, clearly, she thought. But wisely didn't say it out loud.

"Do you use it in the bedroom?" she asked, dropping her own voice. "I mean, it doesn't matter. I'm going to *imagine* you using it in the bedroom anyway."

He frowned at her. "What do you mean you'll imagine it?"

She felt a surge of triumph. She was getting to him. "I mean, I'll think about you taking charge and saying things like 'take your clothes off' in that voice...later. You know."

He was still frowning. "Later?"

"Yes. Later. When I'm at home. In bed. With my vibrator."

He looked like she'd punched him in the stomach.

And now *he'd* be thinking about her with her vibrator thinking about him later. Mission accomplished.

"I'm going inside." He opened the door and started to get out.

Her feeling of achievement disappeared instantly and she reached out to grab his sleeve. "What? You can't go in there!"

He pivoted to look at her, one foot still on the running board. "Why not?"

"Because it's nuts!" She looked toward the party house. "And geez, they'll think you're the dean of the college or something."

He lifted an eyebrow. "Excuse me?"

"Seriously, Nate. You look like you could be a professor. Or someone's dad."

"I am someone's dad."

"Someone who is going to *hate* you for going in there and embarrassing him."

"What do you suggest?"

She looked at the house again. Then sighed. "I guess I could go in."

He pulled his foot back into the truck and shut the door. "You think you could pass for a college student?"

"Sure."

"Emma, you're twenty-eight."

"So, what? Watch this." She could get into that party. She could look the part enough that a few guys who'd already been at the beer and shots for a couple of hours would totally go for it. She dug into her purse and pulled out a ponytail holder and a travel pack of makeup remover towelettes.

She hated to mess up her hair and makeup, but this was for a good cause. Shannon deserved to have fun with her friends without her boyfriend's crazy father crashing the party.

Emma pulled her hair up into a ponytail, aware of Nate's eyes on her. As she lifted her arms, her breasts pressed against the soft material of her shirt and there was no way he could miss that her nipples were hard. But dammit, she was aroused and it was his fault.

He swallowed hard, but said nothing.

She ran a towelette over her face, removing her eye makeup in particular. Without eyeliner and mascara she lost a good three to five years.

Finally, she pulled off her looser top, leaving her in only a spaghetti strap tank and skirt.

Nate coughed and shifted on the seat.

That was worth some of it right there.

"Don't...do anything stupid, okay?" she asked as she reached for the door handle.

"You're going to go in, make sure they're in there and not... you know," Nate said.

"Gambling?" she asked.

"N—well, yes, that too," Nate said.

She rolled her eyes. He needed to lighten up. "Too?" she asked, messing with him. "You want me to be sure they're not watching an R-rated movie? Oh, but wait, they're eighteen so they can do that."

It wasn't exactly a subtle way to make a point, but Nate had already said that everyone was more subtle than she was. And with him, she was starting to think that direct and in-his-face was the best way to go.

Which completely worked for her.

"Make sure they're not…naked," Nate finally said.

"Okay, I'll confirm they're snorting the coke fully clothed." She pushed the door open, but felt Nate grab her arm before she could get out.

"Make sure they're okay," he said.

She looked him directly in the eye. "I already explained to you how much Shannon means to me." She pulled her arm from his grasp. "Don't piss me off by assuming that you care more about them being safe and happy than I do."

She got out and slammed the door behind her. But she immediately heard the sound of the electric window going down. She turned back. Nate leaned out the window. "If you're not out in fifteen minutes, I'm coming in."

"You're worried about me?"

"I'm worried you'll get into a drinking game or dirty dancing with someone and I won't get the status report on Michael."

What an ass.

But him being an ass was giving her a great excuse to go into the party and make sure Shannon really was okay. Shannon was a great kid and could be counted on to make good decisions. Most of the time. There were two girls who had graduated last year, Ashley and Carrie, that seemed to have a negative effect on Shannon's IQ—it dropped when they were around, and Shannon often ended up doing things that she later realized were really stupid. It was very possible Ashley and Carrie were at the party tonight.

All of that, however, was information that Nate did *not* need to have. She scratched her nose with her middle finger as she said, "Just for that, don't expect me out in less than twenty minutes."

She should limp as she walked up the sidewalk with Nate's eyes on her, she thought. But she didn't limp. The cane was a security blanket ninety percent of the time she used it. Her hip did get tired if she went for a long time. Like when she'd shopped all day with her sister, Isabelle, and then stood on it for an hour at a coffeehouse where three of Shannon's friends were doing a series of one-act plays. Other times, she took the cane along to remind herself not to go too far or fast.

And the difficulty she'd had the other night with yoga poses she'd done hundreds of times had pissed her off.

But mostly she was fine. Better every day.

She got to the front door and took a deep breath, pasted on a big smile and knocked hard on the door.

The music was loud and she wasn't sure anyone could hear her knock anyway. She reached for the doorknob and started to turn it, when the door swung in.

A big guy holding a plastic tumbler full of something greeted her. "Uh, hi."

Emma waited for his attention to return to her face. It took a minute.

"I was wondering if Heather's here?" she asked.

She'd met Shannon's friend who was throwing the party several times but she didn't want to see Heather. However, the party looked crowded enough that Emma could pretend to look for her and never actually find her.

"She's here somewhere," he said, stepping back. "Come on in. I'm Landon."

"Hi. I'm Emma," she said, scanning the front room for a sign of Shannon or Michael. If they saw her, they'd be confused and maybe mad at first. She could help them understand that she was helping them, but it would be easier if she could simply confirm that they were fine and then get out without them seeing her.

"If you need a drink, it's all in the kitchen. The poker game is in the back room and there's a mad game of Black Ops going on in the bedroom upstairs."

Awesome. Black Ops. Exactly her idea of a good time.

She ducked behind a big guy in the doorway to the living room and checked the room. No Michael or Shannon. She slipped around the colonnade that separated the living room from what would have been a dining room, but that held bedroom furniture instead as the housemates worked to get as many people living there—and sharing the rent—as possible.

People were sitting on the bed, standing near the dresser and leaning against the computer desk talking, laughing and drinking.

She wound through the dining room/bedroom and into the hallway that would lead back to the front foyer. She didn't see them anywhere. Dammit. They better not be naked upstairs. She didn't want to walk in on that. She rounded the corner, wondering if she could slip upstairs. There was a small closet to her left, the kitchen was across the hall, and the staircase was a few feet and around the corner to her right.

Emma quickly poked her head into the kitchen. There were three guys standing around a keg of beer.

Nate was right about that.

But no Michael and Shannon. They had to be here though. This was Heather's house and Michael's car was out front. The door leading into the kitchen from the backyard opened and four people came into the house.

"We need some more beer out there," one guy said.

"And Heather said there are marshmallows in here," a girl said, heading for the cupboards.

"Marshmallows?" the guy manning the keg asked.

"We're going to roast them over the fire pit," she said, slamming a cupboard and yanking another open.

"Here, I found Cheetos," another guy said.

"You can't roast Cheetos," the girl told him.

"Why would I want to roast Cheetos?"

"I thought we were going to roast marshmallows," the girl said with a frown.

"Go ahead," the guy said. "I've got Cheetos."

"You're an idiot," she told him.

He shrugged and grabbed a handful of Cheetos from the bag.

They grabbed cups of beer, the bag of marshmallows the girl finally located, the Cheetos and another bag of chips and went back outside.

There were people out back. Hopefully, Michael and Shannon were among them.

Emma stepped into the kitchen. "Hi, guys," she greeted the boys around the keg.

They all straightened when they saw her. Emma had been getting similar reactions from men for years, but it never grew old.

"Hi," one of them finally said.

They were at least five years younger than she was, but they weren't minors and they were cute. She grinned. "Hi."

One pushed forward in front of the others. "I'm Jake." He held out his hand.

When she took it, he pulled her close. "I'm Emma."

"Very nice to meet you, Emma. You a friend of Heather's?" He didn't let go of her hand.

"A friend of a friend."

"I'm a friend of Heather's," Jake said. "And I'd be happy to be a friend of a friend with you."

Cute and flirty. Just how she liked 'em.

Why an image of Nate flashed through her mind right then, she couldn't say. Nate was hot. Good-looking. Gorgeous even. He played football, so he was in great shape. And he had those hands. And those lips. And that ass... But he definitely wasn't *cute*. And there was no flirting. Sure, he said a few things that made her toes curl, but they weren't flirtatious. Hell, he'd been essentially telling her to shut up when she'd most recently had the urge to say "take me now".

"How about a beer?" she asked Jake, taking her hand from his. She inched toward the back door. She needed a peek into the yard. If Michael and Shannon were there, she was good to go.

If not... Hell, at this point she was tempted to go back to the truck and tell Nate that they were there even if she never put eyes on them.

Her phone chimed with a text and she glanced down.

What the hell are you doing?

Nate.

God, the man was infuriating. Couldn't he back off and give her some time? Geez.

She typed back, *Kicking ass at quarters.*

She wondered if Nate had ever played quarters. It was a popular drinking game from college, but when he'd been in college he'd had an infant son. She didn't see Nate as a quarters type of guy. She'd seen him drink with the guys at Trudy's after a game, but he never overdid it, never got the point of making an ass out of himself or being out of control.

That thought hit her—Nate was always in control. He'd said something in the truck...what was it? She wracked her brain. Something about liking things his way... *Insisting* on things being his way. That was it.

Nate liked to be in control.

In everything.

She accepted the glass of beer from Jake with a smile. She saluted him and took a big swig.

Nate Sullivan absolutely had a domineering, I'm-better-than-everyone-else attitude going on that drove her nuts a lot of the time. But she could come up with some scenarios where that take-charge tendency might not be a bad thing.

That could be hot as hell.

In fact, she was certain that it *would be* hot as hell.

CHAPTER
FOUR

NATE KNEW that Emma wasn't playing quarters. She wouldn't do that while she was supposed to be looking for Shannon.

Unless she had Shannon playing beside her.

No. He shook his head as he stomped up the sidewalk. That wasn't fair. Emma was just trying to annoy him.

With success.

As usual.

She was also being difficult when she told him she wouldn't be out for at least twenty minutes. He'd told her he was coming in after fifteen. It had been fourteen. He could be difficult too.

And didn't care what anyone thought. He knew—too well—how even something innocent and fun could get out of control and change a life forever. The night Stacie had climbed into his backseat had been her grandmother's seventy-ninth birthday. They'd been at her party. He'd brought her flowers. They'd had cake and ice cream with her. Then he'd gotten her granddaughter pregnant.

There hadn't been any alcohol or music involved, no convenient bed nearby, no one else around engaging in the same behavior, no short skirt like Shannon had been wearing tonight and he'd still knocked up his high school girlfriend.

He didn't care what anyone thought—worrying about Michael and Shannon tonight made sense to him. And his was the only opinion that he counted.

He lifted his fist and banged on the front door. He hadn't liked putting this all in someone else's hands anyway. Emma was lucky he'd stayed in the truck at all.

It took far too long for anyone to answer, so he let himself in.

There were people everywhere, but no one gave him more than a glance. And as long as they weren't Emma, Michael or Shannon, that was fine with him.

He was tempted to stand by the front door and bellow Emma's name. He didn't typically have to raise his voice to get things done. In the surgery suite, it was all about him. He did raise his voice on the football field but that was more because it was fun versus getting results. On the field, he did, however, expect everyone to do what they were supposed to do, to be where they were supposed to be, to give their whole focus to what was going on.

Like he'd been expecting Emma to do. She was supposed to go inside, locate Michael and Shannon and then come back out. Simple.

She, of course, was the one person who could make him want to yell.

"Emma!" he shouted.

There was music playing, but it was low enough to allow conversation. In other words, everyone in the vicinity heard him clearly. Heads swiveled in his direction. But none of them were Emma and no one offered information about where Emma was. He'd heard music coming from the backyard too and assumed more of the party was out there.

"For fuck's sake," he muttered, stomping toward the back of the house.

He rounded a corner and nearly plowed into someone.

A curvy blond. Who smelled wonderful and familiar.

He grabbed her hips as she gripped his arms to avoid landing on her butt.

"For God's sake, Nate," Emma said with a scowl.

"What the hell is taking so long?"

"I've been in here for *ten* minutes."

"Fifteen. And it's enough time to have a beer." He smelled it on her breath.

She nodded. "Enough time to blend in, act cool, check things out and *not* do anything stupid. Like yelling."

"The yelling did exactly what I wanted it to do."

"Call attention to the fact that you're here spying on your kid?"

"Get you front and center."

Her eyebrows went up. "You do like bossing me around, don't you?"

He did. Heaven help him, but he did. He loved that he'd called her name and she'd been on her way to him. It was not something that he should get used to, he knew, but he did like it. He nodded. "There's something about taming a wild spirit."

Her eyebrows went up even higher. "Is that right?"

It was right. Emma was exactly the kind of woman he should stay away from specifically because she wouldn't go for any taming. A guy couldn't be in charge with a woman like Emma. The best he could do was jump in and hang on for the ride.

That wasn't Nate's style.

But her tone did not sound offended or snotty. She almost sounded...intrigued.

"We all sometimes want what we can't have," he told her, setting her away from him.

She didn't move far. "You can have me, Nate." She shook her head as she looked up at him. "I shouldn't admit that. I mean, you're the last guy I ever thought I'd want to give any power to, but man, I'm not going to be able to stop thinking about that kiss. If you want to boss me around a little, I'm not going to complain. At all."

Heat surged through him and he almost reached for her. Almost. Hearing her say that she would give over some power. That was going to be hard for him to stop thinking about too.

"You're giving me power?" he asked.

"Yes. I don't usually let on so blatantly that a guy's getting to me. I like to keep 'em guessing. But I don't think you'll play that way. I think I need to be more up front with you to get what I want."

He gritted his teeth. Dammit, this woman tied him up in knots. She wanted him? No way. Not really. He was hard to get and Emma didn't like that. "I don't *play* at all, Emma. I don't like guessing and I don't like teasing."

"Like I said, up front. Nate, I want you. Take me to bed."

Her tone wasn't light and teasing like usual. She sounded entirely serious. Too serious.

His entire body tightened. Everything in him strained toward her and he wanted to push her up against the wall right now. Thank God she was so full of herself. That was the only thing holding him back. She was certain he would cave, that all it took to get to him was a few words. With Emma, he was going to need some action behind her words. Some proof positive that she could do things his way. And he was never going to get that.

"No."

She frowned and seemed to take a moment to process the word. "What?" she finally asked.

"I'm not taking you to bed, Emma."

She put a hand on her hip. "Why not?"

"Because it's more involved than you know."

"Fill me in."

"No."

It was so much easier to keep things to one syllable with her. The less he engaged in this conversation, the faster it would be over. Even talking about taking her to bed was making his body throb.

"Na—"

The backdoor in the kitchen, which was around the corner from where they stood in the hallway, banged open. "Hey, guys, need some more ice."

Emma and Nate looked at one another.

"Michael," she whispered.

He nodded. That was definitely his son's voice.

Emma looked around, then focused on something over Nate's shoulder. She reached past him and he heard a doorknob turn, then she pushed him into the closet.

She stepped in with him and pulled the door shut.

"What are you doing?" he asked as pitch blackness surrounded them. And her scent surrounded him. And the feel of her pressed up against him in the tiny space sunk in.

"He can't see us," she said. "He'll be furious."

She was right, of course. "No one seems to care that I'm a little furious myself," he said dryly.

She laughed lightly. In the darkness, the sound seemed to slip over him like a caress. "I don't think you can be a little furious. You're furious or you're not."

"All right. I'm furious."

"Oh, you are not. You're fine," she said.

She wiggled and he felt his hand drift to settle on her hip. Not that he moved it once it was there. He even curled his fingers slightly, testing the firmness of the muscle underneath and soaking in the heat from her body.

"I'm not sure I'm fine," he said after a moment. His voice was husky and he couldn't help it, or change it.

He couldn't see her, but somehow he could sense where her mouth was. It wasn't very far from his.

"What are we talking about again?" she asked. She sounded breathless.

He liked that more than he should.

"How to make me fine."

"Anything I can do to help?"

She moved closer. Or he did. In either case, their mouths ended up millimeters apart.

"Because I'm here for you, Nate," she said, her breath against his lips.

Her hands splayed on his ribs, causing him to suck in his breath. Then she slid her palms to his back and pressed against him.

"Whatever you need."

Damn. There was no way he was going to keep saying no to her. Not indefinitely. Not completely, at least. She thought she had him wrapped around her finger. She thought she was in control.

She was wrong.

"Kiss me," he commanded softly.

He felt her hesitation. Yep, he'd surprised her.

"Two simple words, Emma. What's the problem?"

"No problem at all." She rose onto her tiptoes and put her mouth against his.

It took two seconds for him to forget the point he was trying to make.

She tasted amazing—hot and sweet and oh so willing. That was what he wanted. What he needed. She could talk, flirt, lick her lips, wink, wiggle her hips...*act*...however she wanted when they were in the full light and she could gauge his responses and expressions and body language and adjust accordingly. But here, in the dark she had no idea what he was thinking or doing. And her reactions were one hundred percent honest.

He backed her up against the door, dropped his hands to her ass and deepened the kiss.

She arched against him, moaning.

Hell yeah, baby, and that's just a start.

Her fingers dug into his back muscles, pulling him closer. Nate complied. He ran his hand down her thigh, hooked behind her knee and drew her leg up, then leaned in, fitting his pelvis to hers. She gasped and he ran his hand to the curve of her ass, then down between her legs, his fingertips brushing the satiny material of what he could now tell was a thong.

Emma ripped her mouth from his. "*Nate.*"

He brushed over her clit, thin silk all that separated his fingers from the sweet flesh.

He felt the shiver go through her and had to hold back from grabbing hold of the thong and ripping it from her body.

"I'm feeling better," he told her huskily.

And he was. Oh, he was. He was hot, throbbing, *needing*, but he felt great. Emma wanted him. He could make her moan. She was on the verge of losing control. And it wasn't an act.

"I'm feeling damned good myself," she said. She ran her hands down to his ass and pulled him close again. "I can't wait to see how I feel when we have a horizontal surface."

The things he was going to make her feel...

Nate caught himself a breath away from kissing her again. He wanted to go there with her. He wanted to make her scream, make her beg, make her *his*.

And that wasn't ever going to work.

He wanted to conquer her, possess her, tame her.

He generally preferred his women already...tame. Sweet, unassuming and totally fine with him setting the pace and tone of their interactions.

For him, it was part ego and part convenience.

It made life easier because he wasn't waiting on someone else's decision and didn't have to deal with them making the wrong one. He'd experienced having someone else call the shots in his life—and call them badly. He wasn't doing that again.

That's why he and Rebecca, the woman he sometimes kind-of dated, worked so well. They'd met in medical school and had hooked up at a fundraising dinner a few years later. She came to town every couple of months to visit her parents for a week, and had no problem letting him make all the plans and decisions while she was here. She sat back and enjoyed what he came up with. Then she left.

Emma, on the other hand, was the type of woman to demand a man's attention—and to take it from other things. She was the opposite of unassuming. And she wasn't going anywhere. Not only did she live here, but she was one of his teammates' sisters. A teammate who was also a friend.

Getting involved with Emma was a bad idea. A really tempting, potentially world-rocking, disastrous bad idea.

"Let's go back to your house. Or my house. Or the nearest hotel," Emma said, running her hands up and down Nate's back. The guy was built. She'd known it, and admired it, before, but touching all those hot, hard muscles was so much better than she'd imagined. Now if she could get her tongue on them, things would be fantastic.

"We're not going anywhere, Emma. I'm here to make sure Michael's okay."

Damn, this guy had nerves—or hormones—of steel. She'd never had to work this hard before. This was not fun. She was going to have to go all out.

"Fine, vertical will have to do."

She wanted his hands on her. It was crazy. Nate made *her* crazy. She'd known she was attracted and would have gotten naked with him in a closet long ago given the chance, but now that she'd kissed him, now that he'd been up against her, his hand on her ass and his tongue against hers, she wasn't going to rest until she'd had him. All of him.

"Vertical will have to do for what?" he asked.

It was completely dark in the closet, but Emma could hear that he was amused from his tone. "Will do for getting naked and nasty."

"Nasty?" Nate repeated. "Not an appealing term, is it?"

Smug. And superior. And…sexy as hell. He seemed so uptight and that was exactly what pushed her buttons and made her want to show him how wonderful nasty could be. She'd love to see Nate get dirty. She wondered if he had it in him. He had the sexy, bossy thing going on, but maybe he acted so overbearing to cover up some nerves about what he could offer a girl.

That was kind of sweet. And she'd love to be the one to show him how to get down and dirty.

"I promise it will be appealing. It will be better than that. I'll talk you through the whole thing."

There was a heartbeat of silence and then he gave a low chuckle that seemed to cascade over her spine and send tantalizing waves of sensation out to her whole body.

"You're thinking that I'm not sure how to do nasty? Is that what you're saying?" he asked.

"Maybe our ideas about nasty are different."

His voice was rough as he said, "That's a good possibility."

"But I don't mind, Nate. I like things simple and straight up sometimes. And I promise that I won't say anything to any of the guys or whatever. I won't even tell my sisters. Let's go for it and have some fun. No worries."

"Emma."

"Yeah?"

"You have no idea what you're talking about."

Ooh, that sounded promising. And whether or not it was true, she wanted this guy naked and against her *now*.

"Show me. Let's go. Right here, right now. I'm taking my top off, Nate. Then my bra, then my skirt and thong. I will be naked, right here in front of you in T-minus twenty seconds."

"I am *not* taking you up against the door in a closet at a college beer party."

"Please." She said it quietly and let her sincerity seep into the words. Maybe he didn't think she was serious. And she was. Oh, she was.

"No." He cleared his throat. "Dammit, Emma."

"We're both grownups, we want each oth—"

"Stop it. I'm not doing this. And I'm certainly not doing it while my son is on the other side of the door, planning God-knows-what with his girlfriend tonight."

How could she want to screw his brains out and strangle him to death at the same time? Emma huffed out a breath. "You're killin' me here."

"I've got to think of Michael. As long as he's here, I'm here—with my pants *on*."

"Fine. But this conversation isn't over."

"Do conversations with you ever really end?" he asked, that soft amusement back in his voice.

"Not when I want something. You better remember that."

But she realized that pushing him wasn't going to work. Tempting him was kind of working, but Nate wasn't falling in line like guys usually did—big shocker. She was going to have to give her strategy some more thought.

"Okay, get out of here," she told him, a plan forming. "Go back to the truck. I'll handle this."

"How?"

"Don't worry about it. I'll get them out of here." She put her hand flat on his chest. "That's what you want, right? That's the objection to going at it like hot teenagers at a frat party—that your kid is outside?"

"Right."

"Then I'll get them out of here."

"Fine." He paused. "I'm still not taking you up against this door."

He'd said it that way before. He hadn't said, *I'm not doing you up against this door* or *I'm not going to fuck you up against this door.* It was *take you.* She wondered if the word choice meant anything. She also wondered why it made her panties so much wetter than the other ways of saying it.

"Fine. But there are a lot of doors in the world, Nate."

He sighed. It was a familiar sound. "How about we get outside of this one? I think that would help a lot of things."

Ha. He wasn't immune. But she'd play this his way. For now.

Emma cracked the door and looked around, then stepped through, straightened her top and skirt and headed for the kitchen. She trusted that Nate would get out of the house without causing any trouble.

Stepping into the kitchen she worked on looking sick and put a hand over her stomach. "Hey, can you help me?" The guys standing beside the keg talking, turned. "I need to talk to Shannon. I don't feel so good."

One of the guys looked alarmed. "Girl, don't you puke in here." He steered her toward the sink.

"I need to talk to Shannon."

The other guy in the kitchen yanked the back door open and yelled, "Shannon! Come here!"

"What do you want?" Emma heard Michael call back.

"She's got a friend in here who's about to hurl."

There was a pause, then Shannon said, "I do?"

Emma almost grinned at that. Shannon was going to be shocked to see her.

"Come on!" the guy insisted. "Get her out of here. She's had too much to drink or something."

Emma groaned. "I think so too. I shouldn't have done that last shot of tequila."

The guy next to her handed her a glass of water. "You shouldn't mix tequila and beer."

Yep, that was a good life lesson right there. That she could have taught him five years ago.

Shannon came into the kitchen from the backyard. She stared at her mom's best friend. "*Emma?*"

Emma gave her a barely-there shake of her head, then groaned again. "I don't feel so good."

Shannon was very bright and she and Emma were close. Shannon would trust her and play along without question. At least until she could get some answers about what was going on. "Yeah, you don't look so good."

Emma frowned at her when the guys weren't looking. Shannon gave her a grin. Emma looked great and she knew it.

Shannon put an arm around Emma's shoulders and steered her out of the kitchen. Michael had stepped into the house and of course, noticed Emma right away. But he didn't say anything. Shannon gave him a wink and he shrugged and went for the fridge, pulling out a soda and leaning back against the counter, seemingly to make chit chat with the other guys in the room. Emma knew it was to keep an eye on Shannon and to see what was up.

Shannon led Emma through the hallway, past the closet where she and Nate had been minutes before and Emma's whole body flushed just walking by the door. That guy had…something.

Something she wanted.

They finally stopped at a tiny bathroom and Shannon pushed her inside. "What are you doing here?" she asked as she shut the door.

Emma straightened from her my-stomach's-killing-me position and looked in the mirror over the sink. She messed with her hair and noted that her lipstick was completely gone. It was on Nate, as a matter of fact. She blushed and turned away from the mirror, concentrating on Shannon. "Nate's here and he's pissed."

"He's *here*? What do you mean?"

"He's outside."

Shannon frowned. "He's been calling all night."

Emma nodded. "And if Michael had picked up, even once, his dad wouldn't be outside casing the joint."

Shannon crossed her arms. "That's not normal, you know."

Emma had to agree. And yet, she got where Nate was coming from. "Listen, he's concerned and Michael's not handling it well."

"Isn't it normal to want to go out with your girlfriend?"

"Of course. But the secrecy and avoiding the conversation isn't helping Nate trust you guys."

Shannon sighed. "I guess. It…hurts that he won't give me a chance."

Emma knew, deep down, that it wasn't that Nate didn't want to give Shannon a chance, but she wanted to slug Nate for making Shannon feel that way.

"Sneaking around and avoiding him isn't going to do you any good."

"But if we do things Nate's way, I'll never see Michael."

Emma sighed. "We'll work on it. We'll figure something out. But you've had some fun tonight. Let's go home."

"You don't understand."

"What's not to understand? You and Michael are in love and your whole world is all about that right now. Nate doesn't want you to be in love because he wants Michael's world to involve other things. It's pretty easy to get, honey," Emma said.

"I thought you'd be on my side."

Emma frowned. "I always have your back. Why else do you think I would willingly spend the entire evening with a guy who makes me nuts?" Of course, now that she'd kissed him and made him laugh and seen the overreacting-protective-dad side of him, she wasn't quite as opposed to spending time with him.

"You've been with him all evening?"

"Yes, trying to slow him down and distract him. We were at the Washburn."

"Nate Sullivan went to the Washburn?" Shannon asked, clearly stunned.

"Yes. He wanted to know what Michael was sneaking around to do."

"And you went with him?" Shannon asked.

Shannon and Dena had heard plenty of Emma's complaining about Nate and the way he made sure to come to at least one of her rehab sessions a day and hassle her.

"I was making sure he didn't do anything stupid," Emma said. "Protecting *your* butt."

"Then you brought him *here*."

"I didn't have a choice. But I can keep him from coming in here, if you cooperate. Have Michael take you home."

"I haven't given it to him yet," Shannon said, her eyes filling instantly. "I haven't had a chance. It's almost like he's avoiding being alone with me."

She didn't have time for teenage drama, Emma thought. Normally she thrived on drama but Nate Sullivan was right outside. He was more than enough for her to handle in one night.

Shannon had planned to give Michael a special leather bracelet she'd had made for him. She had a matching one. The word *Forever* was stamped on the outside of the bracelet and their names were carved into the inside surface.

Forever seemed like a bold statement, but what did Emma know about it? She'd never wanted to give anyone anything that would mark them or demonstrate to the world that they were together. She didn't know how it felt to want everyone to know someone belonged to her.

Her thoughts skittered to Nate.

And she quickly tried to turn them in another direction.

But it didn't work.

Nate wasn't the type of guy to belong *to* someone. He was very much his own man. She couldn't imagine him tattooing a woman's name on his body or even allowing a woman to tell another woman to back off. And even if he was the type to wear a wedding ring or something, he wasn't about to wear *Emma's* ring.

Strangely, Nate's son was a romantic. He was a computer guru, but he also had an artistic side. He'd drawn things for Shannon that were amazing. He'd written her a poem. He'd written her love notes. Emma wouldn't have put a proposal and elopement out of the question. Which scared the hell out of her.

She liked Michael. She wanted Shannon to be happy. But they were *eighteen*.

Dena, on the other hand, thought it was not only romantic to think of them running off together, but she would probably pay for the gaudy pink Vegas wedding chapel and the Elvis-imper-sonator minister.

Emma sighed. Sometimes it was like having two teenage girls who needed her guidance.

"Maybe you should do it another time—" Emma started to suggest.

"No. It has to be now. His dad is pushing him to make all these big decisions about his future and I want him to know that I want to be there, no matter what."

Emma looked into those big brown eyes and caved. Shannon had gotten purple sparkly roller skates out of her at age six and had gotten her hair colored with pink streaks at age fourteen thanks to that same look in her eyes. "Fine. You guys get out of here. I'll try to stall him so you have some time once you get home, but you better get it done. It's almost pumpkin time, Cinderella."

Shannon grabbed her into a hug. "Thank you, Em. We'll leave right now."

Emma went with Shannon to retrieve Michael and explain that they needed to head home. He started to get belligerent, but Shannon whispered something in his ear and he calmed down.

Emma did *not* need to know what Shannon had said.

They decided to go out back again and then slip around the side of the house and get into the car. Emma was fairly certain Nate had gone back to the truck, but she couldn't guarantee it and Michael didn't want to run into Nate on the front steps or sidewalk.

When they were out the door, Emma made her way to the truck. She took her time, mostly sure that Nate wouldn't drive off and leave her here. She could buy the kids a few minutes that way. But she needed a bigger diversion for Nate.

The perfect idea came to her right away.

She almost rubbed her hands together. She knew exactly what she wanted to do.

And now she had the perfect excuse.

She stopped on the sidewalk beside the truck.

She rolled her head and shoulders, trying to loosen up. She needed to keep him busy, distracted, and from going after Michael and Shannon. She *should* be able to distract Nate. Dammit. That was what had always bugged her. She wasn't *sure* she could distract Nate.

But she'd never given it her all.

She started to reach for the truck door, but it swung open before she touched it.

"Get in here."

She wrinkled her nose. "Such a gentleman." She slid into the front seat next to him.

"They're on their way home?" he asked, putting the truck into drive.

He pulled away from the curb and Emma realized she was going to have to work fast. She wanted Nate to take the long way home. She wanted Nate to *want* to take the long way home.

"There is definitely some major sexual tension between us," she said, pivoting on the seat to face him.

He didn't look surprised at her words. He looked tired.

Awesome. That was a great reaction.

"Yes, there is."

"I think we should do something about it. Get it out of our systems. Because, frankly, it's a pain in the ass and annoying." Sleeping restlessly because of dirty dreams about Nate was definitely annoying.

"You don't have to act on every urge, Emma. Just because something would feel good doesn't make it a good idea."

"Why does it have to be a good or a bad idea? Why can't it be neutral? Why does it need that much thought?" she asked, crossing one leg over the other and letting her skirt pull higher on her thighs. "We do it, then it's over. It doesn't need analyzing, does it?"

He glanced over and frowned. "Stop it."

She couldn't help smiling. That was his you're-getting-to-me voice. At least in her mind that's what it was. "I love that voice."

He took a deep breath as he pulled up to a stop light and looked her straight in the eye. "You don't want someone bossing you around in bed, Emma."

Now they were getting somewhere. He was bossy in bed? That didn't surprise her. What did surprise her was the way her heart rate revved hearing it.

"I don't know." She'd never had a guy take charge in bed. She'd been with guys who knew what they wanted and weren't shy about telling her, but that was different than someone who actually took over. "I get tingles all over when you say that stuff."

"Emma." His voice was low with warning.

Definite tingles.

"Come on, Nate. Lighten up. One time. Like two hours."

"No."

"How about a whole night?"

"No."

"A weekend?" She could go for that.

His scowl intensified. "No."

"*What* is your problem?" She knew he wanted her. She was willing and ready. Why was he fighting it? "We're talking about a fling."

"You don't want to have a fling with me, Emma."

Oh, he was wrong on that one. "I don't? Give me one good reason."

"I like to be in charge. And you don't take instruction very well. You wouldn't like me bossing you around."

Yep, that sounded like it should make sense. But her body didn't think so judging by the increased temperature and the difficulty sitting still she was suddenly having. "You'd try to boss me around?"

"Definitely. I boss everyone around."

She watched him carefully. "What if I think that's hot?"

"You wouldn't. Not for long anyway."

"Maybe I would—"

"*Emma*," he said impatiently. "I'm a controlling asshole."

"*Nate*," she said, mimicking his tone. "I'm gonna do what I want, when I want. I'm not too worried about you being controlling."

"I call the shots—all the shots—in my relationships."

"And when I get tired of it, I'll leave. And what's with the *relationship* thing?"

"You don't want a relationship?" he asked.

"With a controlling asshole? No thank you." She grinned at the pained expression on his face.

Bold. She needed to be bold here. That was almost never a problem, but she had butterflies in her stomach at the moment. *Go big or go home.* She reached for the hem of her top and pulled it over her head. With the fitted tank she hadn't needed a bra. Her breasts were now bare, her nipples beaded, her arousal clear.

Even being half naked in front of Nate made her hot.

It was dark outside and the windows on the sides of his truck were tinted. The windshield, of course, was not. The streetlight shone in, illuminating her clearly.

He wasn't touching her. He wasn't saying anything. *He wasn't naked.* But she was already trembling slightly, breathless, and feeling like everything in her was drawing tighter and tighter, waiting for release.

And that was with him simply looking at her.

She might be in trouble.

Nate didn't speak. He didn't move. But he also didn't protest or act offended.

He sat watching her, his gaze slowly taking in every detail. Goose bumps sprung up all over her body.

She'd stripped for guys before. She'd been more bare than this. But she'd never felt this exposed.

Damn, the guy was good.

The light turned green and Nate accelerated normally, as if nothing unusual was going on in his truck at all. But he pulled into an empty parking lot and behind a building that was closed for the night.

Once the truck was in park, he turned to face her.

Without a word, she hooked her thumbs in the top of her skirt and began pushing it down as she lifted her butt off the seat.

"No."

Her gaze snapped to his. His posture was casual, the position he might assume in the middle of a business meeting or during a conference call. But there was an intensity in his gaze that should have intimidated her. Instead it made her feel like getting closer. A lot closer.

"You don't want me to stop," she chided softly, inching the soft material down.

He met her gaze. "Stop."

She did. She wasn't sure why, exactly, but something—the look in his eyes? The tone in his voice? Something else, something indefinable—made her obey. She put her butt back on the seat.

He studied her for several heartbeats. Finally he said, "Turn toward me."

She did.

"Lean back."

She rested her upper back against the door, her feet toward him.

"Spread your legs."

Now they were getting somewhere. She bent one knee,

putting her foot on the seat and letting the other foot slide to the floor, her legs apart.

"Pull it up."

She knew what he meant. She pulled the hem of the skirt up, bunching the material at her waist, revealing the white thong underneath.

She licked her lips. "Are you going to take anything off?"

"No."

Man, he said no to her a lot. "No?"

"No." A simple repetition of the word. No further explanation, no elaborating.

Emma narrowed her eyes. "You playing along or not?"

"You don't want to play with me, Emma."

"Oh, I do. But I want both of us in the game."

"No."

Damn him and that fricking word. "I'm more than half naked here," she said. "What's going on?"

"You started taking your clothes off."

"You didn't try to stop me."

"Why would I stop you?"

"So you *do* want to get naked with me?"

"No."

Emma pulled a deep breath in through her nose. "Nate," she said calmly, but firmly. "What the fuck are you doing here?"

"A gorgeous woman with the best breasts I've ever seen starts to undress in my truck? There's no way in hell I'm stopping that," he said simply.

She couldn't even concentrate on the compliment. "But you're not going to do anything with the best breasts you've ever seen?"

There was a flare of heat in his eyes even though he said, "No."

That little flicker was enough to keep her going. He wasn't blase about this. Not really.

"And you're not going to touch the best breasts you've ever

seen?" she asked, cupping her breasts and running her thumbs over her nipples.

They were so sensitive that she felt the pleasure streak straight to her clit. The way Nate watched, his eyes darkening, his lips tightening, urged her on. She didn't even wait for the inevitable *no.*

"And you're not going to suck on the nipples of the best breasts you've ever seen?" She rolled one nipple between her thumb and forefinger, her pelvic muscles tightening as she did it.

Nate's fist clenched on the seat next to him. He didn't say no. But he didn't say yes either.

Emma ran her hand down over her stomach to her mound. She rested her hand there, her fingertips skimming over the crotch of her thong. "If you like my breasts, you should see the rest of me."

"Enough."

But the huskiness in his voice took some of the sting out of the command.

She ran her middle finger up and down over the silk covering her clit. It felt damned good, but it wasn't even close to what she needed.

"Come on, Nate. It's sex. I know I give you a hard time and that I'm a smartass ninety-nine percent of the time when you're around, but I promise you, I won't criticize your technique or give you any pointers." He needed to lighten up. And unbutton. Figuratively and literally.

He gave her a half smile, but he didn't look exactly amused. "You think you know a lot, don't you? You think you've got me figured out."

She shrugged and ran her finger over her clit again while she circled her nipple. "You're a guy. No offense, but you're pretty straightforward."

"Is that right?"

Nate wasn't known as a player like some of the other guys, but she had no doubt that he had as much female company in—

and out—of bed as he wanted. And she was sure he wanted that on a regular basis.

"Emma."

There it was. Low and commanding, matched with that intense look in his eyes…she was a goner. And she couldn't wait. "Yeah?"

"If you don't have the finger vibrator in your purse, you're going to be in big trouble."

CHAPTER
FIVE

EMMA'S EYES WENT WIDE. "I do."

"Get it."

She reached so fast, she almost fell off the seat. The vibrator had been a gift with the purchase of her favorite flavored lube and massage oil, and she'd wanted to show her sisters so she'd thrown it in her purse. She was *really* glad she had.

She pulled the bumpy purple plastic device from her purse and handed it to Nate.

He shook his head.

"You want me to do it?" she asked.

"Yes."

Holy crap, a yes from him.

"When I tell you to," he added.

She stared at him, the tingles in her body gaining strength, her tummy swirling, her heart pounding. "Are you going to boss me around after all?" she asked.

"You want a taste of this?" he asked.

That was a loaded question. Her gaze dropped to his fly. His erection was apparent.

"Emma."

Her attention went back to his face.

"Answer me. Do you want to see what it might be like with me?"

She nodded quickly.

"I'm in charge."

"Okay." She so wanted to fire that vibrator up. He was making her hot and crazy.

"For the next seven days."

Her mouth dropped open. "You want seven days of sex with me?" She could so do that. She'd even cancel a couple of classes. The girls in those classes would understand.

"I want to be in charge for the next seven days," he repeated.

"In charge of…"

"You."

She sucked in a quick breath at his answer. But she didn't have to think about it. At all. "Okay."

It was clear she'd surprised him. He closed his eyes and shook his head. "This is a bad idea."

"Nate." She waited until he opened his eyes and looked at her. "Do it."

He seemed to make a decision. "I will insist on a few things."

"Such as?"

"Your undivided attention. No other men, no dates, no sex, no one-night stands. No time with your vibrator unless I'm there. Nothing coming up to interrupt what I want to do with you."

"Yes," she said quickly. She might end up regretting this, but she couldn't imagine saying anything other than yes to this.

Hell, she wasn't too proud to admit that she wanted to know what this was like. With Nate. Only with Nate. For some reason. He was right that she might not like it, or at least, might not like it for long. But she wanted to try it. With him.

She narrowed her eyes as his gaze again roamed over her body. That was probably why he'd chosen seven days. He could have had her, and bossed her around like crazy, for an hour or two. But he'd said seven days. Because he wanted to scare her off.

The jerk.

"Pull your thong to the side."

And just like that she forgot that she was annoyed with him. He really was good.

He thought he was going to discourage her by being domineering. He had no idea how stubborn she could be when she wanted something. She did as she was told.

As she moved the thong out of the way, Nate grew more stone-like. He seemed to freeze. Nothing clenched or twitched or blinked. His eyes were riveted on her.

She turned the vibrator on with a click.

"No." His eyes were back on hers. "Not until I say so."

Fine. She laid it on the seat next to her, still buzzing. That little reminder was going to be there for both of them.

"Touch yourself."

The lighting from the parking lot was low but it was certainly enough for him to see what he wanted.

She ran her finger over her clit and down to where she was wet and hot. She dipped her fingertip inside and then slid up again, circling her clit. If Nate thought she was going to shy away from this, he was crazy.

"I notice your hip range of motion seems to fine."

Her hip? She hadn't thought about her hip since he'd thrown her cane back into the truck.

She grinned at him and slid her finger further into her own heat. "Best rehab session yet, Doc."

He didn't reply, didn't smile, just watched her finger move.

This felt good. She wouldn't lie about that. She knew her body. But half the pleasure was watching Nate watch her. He was settled into the seat, his posture and body language the same as if he was watching a TV show. A fascinating TV show that he didn't want to miss a second of, but still, only a TV show.

But there was something—maybe it was her imagination or a feeling in the air—that made Emma certain he was as hot and wound up as she was.

Nate didn't do wound up. He yelled on the football field. He'd get up into a fellow player's face if something went wrong. She could imagine him chewing someone's ass in the operating room if needed. But "wound up" was not a term she'd associate with Nate. He was in control, even when he was pissed off.

"Faster." His voice was soft but still commanding. "You need more than that."

She was stroking in and out, up and over her clit, then inside again, but the pace was leisurely, a warm up, priming for things to come. Or so she thought.

"I thought that—"

"I'm positive that you know how to get yourself off," he said over the top of her. "Now do it." The last three words were delivered, softly and firmly. And caused her stomach to flutter.

Well, yes, she did as a matter of fact, know how to do that, thank you very much. And if he thought he was going to win this game of chicken, he was sadly mistaken.

She sped her rhythm slightly, slicking over her clit, shivering as the spot grew more sensitive. Her breathing sped up too. If she wasn't careful, she'd go right over the edge like this.

"Nate—"

"More."

He was in control. He'd warned her she wouldn't like it. She couldn't hesitate already.

She increased her pace, slid in further, pressed harder.

She had every bit of Nate's attention though and that was almost enough to give her an orgasm right there.

Is that what he wanted to see? That he could drive her all the way without even a touch?

Talk about cocky.

Well, she had plenty of her own cocky. She slid her finger all the way in, then added a second. She heard Nate pull in a breath through his nose. She gave him a slow smile and stroked deep in and out, again and again with both fingers, increasing the speed each time.

She was getting close. If she added stimulation to her clit she'd be coming in seconds. And her body was taking over. She was going to go all the way, whether she wanted to play with Nate or not, if she kept this up.

Her body was all for it.

Tipping her head back against the truck door, she let her eyes slide shut. She brought her unoccupied hand to her breast, playing with her nipple in the way that she'd used often enough when she was alone.

Nate's eyes were still on her. She could feel his gaze even with her eyes shut and the heat ratcheted up, her pelvis felt full and her muscles were beginning to tighten in that delicious pre-orgasm state.

"Get the vibrator."

His deep words worked on her nerve endings and she had to suck in a deep breath. Without opening her eyes, she felt around on the seat for the finger vibrator. She clasped it and started to withdraw her fingers.

"No."

She paused.

"Fingers deep. Eyes on me."

Holy orgasm, Batman. Emma's eyes locked on Nate's, boldly doing exactly as he said. It wasn't like she was suffering here. She pressed the vibrator to her clit, stroking her fingers deep, watching his nostrils flare and his jaw tighten. The sensations began to swirl out of control, her deep muscles clenching, her heart racing, the heat sweeping over her.

"Emma."

It was one gruff word. She wasn't even sure he meant to say it. But that was what pushed her over the precipice.

Her orgasm hit, stronger than any she'd produced on her own in the past. Her eyes slammed shut as everything in her coiled tight, then let go at once and she held her breath, letting the waves of pleasure crash over her and through her.

She stayed like that, fingers still but remaining deep, vibrator on, letting the tremors slowly quiet and fade.

When they were gone and all that was left were tingles in her scalp, pelvis and the bottom of her feet, she finally breathed, tossed the vibrator onto the seat and slumped back against the door.

There was no sound in the truck. No shifting on the other seat, no hard breathing, no begging her to move onto his lap and finish this right.

Reality hit and she drew her legs together, both feet on the seat.

She'd masturbated herself to an orgasm in front of Nate Sullivan.

Um, wow. There really wasn't any other term that fit.

Finally, she opened one eye.

He was still reclining comfortably, watching her.

Emma blew out a breath and sat up, shifting to pull her clothes back into place and slip her tank top back on.

Now what? His house? Her house? The silence was going to drive her crazy. "Well?" she asked.

"Very nice."

She blinked at him. Very nice? Very *nice*? "What the hell are you talking about?"

"You showed an impressive ability to follow my instructions," he said smoothly. "I'm pleased."

She peered at him closely. Was he at least fighting a smile? Was he messing around with her? She couldn't tell. "Oh, great," she said sarcastically. "So glad you're *pleased*."

He turned and put the truck into gear and pulled out of the parking lot without another word.

During the drive Emma replayed the entire thing, trying to figure out when exactly she'd decided that she didn't care if

Nate totally took over or not. Because he most definitely had taken over.

About the time he'd told her to pull her skirt up, she figured.

She'd been trying to overwhelm him with lust and he'd totally turned the tables on her.

Score one for Nate.

But this wasn't over.

And heck, she was walking away with a nice consolation orgasm even if he'd won that match.

The truck rolled to a stop and Emma became aware that they were outside of Dena's house. The big truck rode so smoothly she'd almost forgotten they were on the move.

"Be sure to keep your phone on."

She looked at him. He had to be joking. "That's it? What's happening?"

"I'm dropping you off. I saw Michael's car pull away from the house. I assume that means Shannon is safe and sound inside."

"But what about…us? The seven days?"

"I'm in charge," he reminded her.

"Yeah, yeah. I know you get off on that. But, Nate, I have some other ways that you can feel good." She braced a hand on the seat between them and leaned closer. "I promise that you'll feel like the king of the world once you're in my bed."

That got a half smile from him. "Keep your phone on."

He was going for a booty call. She sighed. It was a pain in the ass to think about going home and then getting called out again, but whatever. He needed to be ordering her around. Fine. She could put up with it if it meant she'd eventually get him naked too.

She grabbed the vibrator and started to put it into her purse.

"Give that to me."

She looked at him. "You want it?"

"You won't be needing it. No orgasms, no vibrators unless I'm there, remember?"

A shiver of desire went through her. "You don't think that little thing is the only toy I have do you?"

He held out his hand. "It doesn't matter. You won't be playing with any other toys until I tell you to."

She handed it to him. "Be sure you bring that with you the next time we see each other." She grabbed her purse and her cane, then opened the door. "You're kind of high maintenance, you know that?"

She was out of the truck and about to slam the door shut when he said, "You have no idea."

Nate kicked ass at football practice on Sunday.

"Nice hit, Sullivan." Cody Madsen slapped Nate on the back as he strode past.

Ryan Kaye was still getting up from the ground.

Nate appreciated being a football player every day he got to be one. He appreciated being a defensive back every time he laid out a receiver. And today, there were three very sore receivers on the field. Ryan Kaye being one of them.

"Damn, man," Ryan said, rubbing his ribs. "What I'd do to piss you off?"

"You caught the football."

"You're not putting extra muscle into this today?" Ryan asked. "'Cause I've been hit by you before and it didn't feel this bad."

"Keep talkin', Kaye," Nate told him. "And keep going for the ball. You haven't felt nothin' yet."

Ryan laughed and jogged up the field. Nate gritted his teeth as he headed back for the line of scrimmage. He wasn't exactly pissed off. He was on edge though and trying to work off some major pent-up emotion. He was frustrated, tense, mad at himself —yes, mostly that last one. Definitely.

And there was no getting away from the reason why.

Because her fucking brother was their fucking quarterback who was fucking calling out the plays. Nate couldn't avoid him. Or the fact that every time he heard someone yell Dixon's name Nate thought of Emma.

Of course, he'd been thinking about Emma nonstop since the night in his truck anyway.

How could he not?

He'd seen her naked. He'd watched her touch herself. He'd watched her orgasm. And most of all, she'd done it all because he'd told her to.

Damn, that was what really got him going…and had kept him up all night.

She'd hung in there, had met him challenge for challenge. He'd kept pushing, and instead of her backing off, he'd been treated to the hottest fucking thing he'd ever seen.

Then, in spite of him being crystal clear about the fact that *he* was in charge and would be the one to call her—something he'd decided he would definitely not do ever—she'd texted him. Saturday afternoon. And it wasn't *hi, how's it going?* No, she sent him questions like, *Where's the strangest place you've ever gotten a blow job?* and *If I was going to cover my body in flavored syrup, do you prefer strawberry or butterscotch?*

He'd gotten to the point that hearing the chime of his text message made him hard.

He should have known she wouldn't sit around and wait. He should have known she'd make this difficult.

And he should have known he'd love it.

Like he loved the text photo she sent him of her in a long, silky hot pink nightgown. And in a hot pink teddy. And in a hot pink bra and panty set. And then without the hot pink bra and panty set…or anything else.

He'd replayed the text message strip tease a dozen times.

But he'd still resisted texting her back. Or calling. Or going to her condo, throwing her on the nearest firm surface and doing all the dirty things he'd been dreaming about since Friday night.

"Run it again!" Coach bellowed from sideline.

Nate jerked out of his thoughts of Emma.

"Let's go!" Conner called. "Huddle up."

The defense lined up as the offense gathered to decide the play.

Nate took his place. It wouldn't matter what the play was. He was going to take someone's head off.

"Sullivan, you're on Kaye again. You're busting his ass today," Brian Axel, one of the linemen, said. "And that amuses me."

Ryan flipped Brian off.

Well, he was glad Brian was having a good time. "Got him," Nate said.

"It's a good day to be on our side of the ball, boys," Conner called as he took his position behind the center. Then he gave them all his best shit-eating grin.

And that led to the most pathetic thing Nate had ever thought in his life—Conner's smile reminded Nate of Emma's.

He gave a little growl.

Maybe taking Conner out of practice would help. Then Nate wouldn't have to see that fucking grin. Conner was a friend and a teammate. Typically they were on the same side and Nate didn't mind Conner razzing the guys on the other side. But today was a scrimmage and the defense was matched against the offense. Conner was the opponent today and his swagger made Nate grind his teeth.

Because it also reminded him of Emma. That woman had boldness to spare.

Which brought firmly to mind the way she'd shown it off Friday night.

The image of Emma laying back, thighs open, breasts bare, her fingers between her legs would be burned on his memory until the day he died.

He definitely wanted to take Conner out of practice. Nothing permanent. Conner was the best QB in the league, after all. But Nate wouldn't mind knocking the wind out of him.

He eyed Shane Kelley, the offensive lineman who would try to keep Nate away from Conner. Shane was a big guy, there was no denying that. He outweighed Nate by fifty pounds and had two inches on him.

Of course, Nate was faster. And there was the massive amount of pent-up sexual frustration he had going on. If he channeled that, he could get to Conner.

Nate watched Conner as the rest of the offense lined up. Even if Nate didn't get through to him, it would hurt like hell trying. He would at least be beat up, sore and tired after practice.

He'd had a hell of a long night the last couple of nights. He needed to sleep tonight. He had surgery in the morning and if he spent another night like last night, he'd be worthless.

With the offense set, Conner called the play and the sound of twenty-two grown men groaning and grunting, helmets smacking and feet pounding filled the air.

Nate was supposed to cover Ryan. Instead he put his head down and went straight ahead, Conner in his sights.

The next thing he felt was a brick wall hitting his chest right before his ass hit the ground. The next thing he heard was Shane Kelley saying, "I don't think so."

"Hell, yeah!" he heard Conner shout.

Nate turned to see the football fall perfectly into Ryan's outstretched arms.

"What the fuck?" Brian yelled, stomping toward Nate.

Nate rose slowly, stretching to his full height and faced Brian squarely. "Back off, Axel."

"You missed your cover."

"Yep."

"That's bullshit, Sullivan."

"Get over it." He shoved Brian.

That didn't go over well. As expected.

Brian shoved Nate back, Nate grabbed Brian's jersey and

they went at it for the ten seconds it took their teammates to jump in and pull them apart.

"Get your head out of your ass," Brian said as Cody shoved him the opposite direction from Nate.

That was exactly what he needed to do.

The offense huddled again and Nate took the opportunity to catch the eye of one of his defensive brothers. He tipped his head toward Shane. Travis, the lineman, nodded his understanding. Travis would take on Shane, giving Nate a chance to get through the line.

Theoretically.

They lined up, Conner called the play and they snapped the ball. Travis charged Shane, blocking the bigger man, allowing Nate to dart to the right and spin. Shane shouted, but Nate was already on Conner. He knocked their quarterback to the ground with a satisfying thud.

It was, of course, understood by everyone that the quarterback didn't get hit in practice.

Even if they didn't go at him full force, injuries could occur and they needed Conner to be in top shape.

Then again, they had several weeks of practice before league play started. He'd have time to heal.

Nate stood over Conner. "How do you feel?"

"Like you're a jackass," Conner told him. He pushed himself to his feet as Shane grabbed the collar of Nate's jersey and spun him around.

"What the fuck, Sullivan?" Shane asked.

"You missed your block," Nate told him calmly.

"The hell if I did. Your boy Travis missed *his* to come after me."

"And you don't think an opponent would quickly figure out that you're the guy to get rid of if they want to get to Dixon?" Nate asked.

"Take it easy, guys," Cody said, putting a hand on Shane's shoulder.

Cody was a running back and smaller than Shane, but he could at least slow the guy down.

"What the hell?" Ryan asked, pushing in to where his friends were gathered.

The rest of the team was likely wondering all the same what-the-fuck and is-Sullivan-crazy stuff, but they would let Shane, Ryan and Cody handle it. The five guys were a team within the team. They didn't just play together, they worked together too. All being in emergency services—a cop, a firefighter, a trauma surgeon and two paramedics—they had a lot of opportunity to spend time together working in sometimes tense situations where they had to depend on and trust each other. When the five of them were on a scene, everyone else knew that letting them take the lead together would guarantee the best outcome. They were a hell of a team, on and off the football field and they often chose to blow off steam together socially too.

"I was mixing things up, keeping everyone on their toes," Nate said.

"I'm talking about Conner's ankle," Ryan said.

Nate turned back to find Conner limping as he tried to step on his left ankle.

Okay, he could take Conner out of practice for that. He wasn't the team physician, but during practice, when Doc Porter wasn't there, Nate filled in.

"You should rest that," he said to Conner.

"Fuck that." Conner tried to step down again, winced and pulled his foot up. "Dammit, Sullivan."

"You're not going to make me actually test and treat you, are you?" Nate asked.

Dammit. He wanted Conner to sit out the rest of the day. That was it. Nate didn't want him hurt. And Nate didn't want to have to treat something he'd caused. Then he would feel like shit. All because of Emma. That girl really did cause a lot of trouble.

"No, you're not treating me," Conner said with a scowl. "I

don't know what your problem is but you're hitting like you're out for blood today. Stay the hell away from me."

Nate sighed. "Let me look at it."

"No. Hell no." Conner stepped down again, this time able to bear weight. "I tweaked it. It's fine."

"I'll hold him down for you, Doc," Shane said, giving Conner a grin. "It'd be my pleasure."

"All of you stay away from me." Conner limped a few steps away.

"What's with him and you now?" Cody asked. "I thought he was all for you and Isabelle living together?"

Shane laughed at that. "Conner's not all for anything having to do with his friends and his sisters. Iz and I are going to live together, period. Conner's telling himself he's fine with it because we're engaged. But now that it's real, he's hating it. And me a little bit."

Shane didn't look particularly fazed by that. Shane never had been particularly fazed by Conner's feeling regarding Shane being with Conner's sister. He'd fallen hard and fast for Isabelle and only humored Conner because it made things easier on everyone if Conner felt he still had some say in Isabelle's life.

Shane had joined the Hawks the year after Nate, Cody, Ryan and Conner had been added to the roster. He was a hell of a player and probably the best cop in the city. The guys had quickly learned to trust and respect him on scenes and on the football field. But Shane had set his sights on Isabelle almost from day one, so he and Conner's rapport had been…interesting from the very beginning.

"You need to look at his ankle," Ryan said to Nate. He was watching Conner limp away.

Nate sighed. "Fuck. Fine."

"I'll help you hold him down," Ryan said with a grin at Shane.

Ryan was also involved with one of Conner's sisters. He was a member of Conner's paramedic crew so they spent long shifts together even outside of the football team. Where there might not be an emergency scene that called the guys all together for weeks at a time, Ryan and Conner saw each other almost every day.

But Ryan didn't rub it in with Conner like Shane did.

Nate studied these men. Maybe he should take notes. If he was going to be involved with Emma… He shut that down right away. He was not going to be involved with Emma in any way that her brother needed to know—or worry—about. It wouldn't be long lasting, no matter what it turned into.

Cody started after Conner. "I'll get him. He's not pissed at me."

"You sure?"

Cody stopped and turned back to Shane. "Why do you ask? Why would he be mad at me?"

"You spend a lot of time with Olivia. His *baby* sister." Shane lifted a shoulder. "So, I'm asking."

Cody pinned him with a serious stare. "Olivia and I are *friends*. And she works for me. I can't be messing around with her."

Cody was the fire chief at Fire House Three and Olivia was his administrative assistant. The way Nate understood it, Cody and Conner had been friends since college. Cody had known the Dixons longer than anyone.

Ryan shook his head. "I don't know. There are all kinds of workplace romances that go on. Sex on desks, on copy machines, in coat closets…"

Cody shifted his weight from one foot to the other and cleared his throat. "None of that's happening."

Nate grew interested too. Cody looked really uncomfortable.

"You're right. Your workplace is a little different. You having sex with Olivia in a fire truck, Madsen?" Shane asked.

Cody looked over to where Conner was standing. "Shut the fuck up, Kelley."

"You *are*?" Ryan asked. "I knew it. Amanda said no way, but I knew there was something going on."

Cody stalked back over to where they were standing. "No," he said, his voice low. "Olivia and I are not having sex *anywhere*, but I don't even want my name, Olivia's and the word sex mentioned in the same sentence around Conner. You two are giving him enough headaches." He shoved Ryan back.

Ryan laughed. "All I know is that if I was spending that much time with Amanda and trying *not* to be attracted to her, it would make it even worse."

Cody shook his head. "We're friends," he repeated.

"No worries," Shane said, slapping Cody on the back. "She can't be interested anyway."

Cody scowled at him. "Why not?"

"Because you know the movie *P.S. I Love You* by heart, you've spent the night on her couch a dozen times and never made a move, and I know her dirty little secret," Ryan said.

Cody frowned, looking back and forth between Shane and Ryan. "What dirty little secret?"

"That *you're* the one who makes those fudge peanut butter brownies she's famous for at the fire house," Ryan said.

"*You* make those?" Nate asked. Those brownies rocked. He'd heard the firefighters gushing about them and he'd teased Olivia enough about not having any at the hospital that she'd finally brought some down.

Cody slugged Ryan in the arm. "So what? We bake together. Big deal. And how do you know I've spent the night and not made a move?"

"Olivia told Amanda," Ryan said. "And I guess she sounded disappointed when she said it."

Cody stared at him, clearly unsure what to say to that.

Nate grinned. The guy liked Olivia. It was clear. Of course, getting involved with one of Conner's sisters would be most complicated for Cody as Conner's long-time trusted friend.

Conner joined them. "What the fuck are you all talking about? Can we get back to practice?"

"We're talking about how you're not mad at Cody because he's not sleeping with any of your sisters," Ryan said, with a huge grin.

Conner frowned at them all suspiciously. "*That's* the topic of conversation?"

"Well, you won't listen to us because we're making Amanda and Isabelle happy," Shane said. "Apparently, you want your sisters unhappy and—"

"If you say horny or unfulfilled or anything else about sex, I will knock you on your ass, star offensive lineman or not," Conner warned Shane.

Shane laughed. "I was going to say cranky, but yeah, I guess that has to do with sex. Isabelle gets cranky when she's not getting any. Not that that happens much."

Ryan nodded. "Amanda too."

Nate bit his lip. Hard. Emma got cranky about not getting her way sexually too. But he was *not* supposed to know that.

"You're right. I'm mad at both of you," Conner said. He scowled at Cody.

Cody held up his hands. "Hey, don't look at me like that. I'm not sleeping with any of your sisters."

"But you won't take Emma off my hands."

Nate's spine went straight and stiff. What the hell?

Shane laughed. "What's that mean?"

Cody sighed. "Conner's been *joking* about me hooking up with Emma and trying to settle her down."

"Sit down, Dixon," Nate said firmly. Joke or not, he didn't want to think about any guys hooking up with or settling Emma down. He liked her...unsettled. "I want to look at the ankle. Or I'll have Coach bench you."

Conner gave him a dark look, but Nate's tone and threat were serious and Conner knew that. He dropped onto the grass and stretched his leg out.

Nate crouched by Conner's feet, pulled his shoe off, not necessarily gently, and peeled off his sock. Nate began prodding the tissues around the joint.

"You would be okay with Cody dating Emma?" Shane asked. "Seriously?"

"Emma needs to be tied to one guy," Conner said.

"It's okay for *Emma* to date one of your friends, but not Amanda or Isabelle or Olivia?" Nate asked, digging into the lateral ligaments that he was fairly certain Conner had strained.

"Ow! Fuck," Conner bitched. Then he shrugged. "One guy, even if it's a friend, would be preferable to her changing men as easily and often as she changes shoes."

Nate frowned. He didn't like that analogy at all. He looked at Cody. "Why haven't you taken him up on it?"

Cody shook his head. "Uh, no thank you. Emma's great but she exhausts me. She'd be a handful."

Well…yeah.

"Exactly why Emma's the one I need some help with," Conner said. "I've only got two hands and twenty-four hours in a day. I need some backup."

Nate rotated Conner's ankle in a way that would twinge those ligaments if they were inflamed.

"Ow! Dammit, Doc."

Yep, definitely a ligament strain.

"I'm not man enough for Emma," Cody decided.

Shane and Ryan laughed. Cody had plenty of women who thought he was more than man enough…for pretty much anything. He'd autographed his share of cleavage. Apparently, there was something women liked about firefighters.

And Cody was a nice guy.

Women also loved that.

They all did public appearances. It was in their Hawks contracts. It was promo to get people to come to games since asses in the seats were what paid the bills. They read to kids at elementary schools and signed autographs in nursing homes and visited fans in the hospital. None of them protested, but Cody loved that shit. He was enthusiastic and genuine and people could tell his heart was in it.

Michael found the fan blog sites about the team wildly amusing—especially the ones where women gushed about the players—and regularly emailed and texted the guys quotes. They were all aware that Ryan was known as a ladies' man, Shane as the party guy, Nate as the sophisticated, serious one and Conner as the dynamic leader. And Cody was the nice guy.

"Aw, Emma's not so scary," Ryan said.

"I suppose not," Shane said. "At least not once you've seen her naked, right?"

The image from the night in his truck hit Nate hard and fast and he coughed, struggling to breathe for a moment.

Ryan grinned. "Better than that thing where you're supposed to picture everyone in their underwear when you're doing a public speech."

Nate knew—*everyone* knew—that Ryan and Emma had purportedly had a fling awhile back, but in reality they'd only ended up skinny-dipping together. They'd let Conner believe it was more because it drove him nuts, but Amanda had cleared that all up once she and Ryan were together.

But remembering Emma touching herself in his truck made Nate beg to differ with Ryan and Shane. Emma was plenty scary. Seeing her naked had put him in danger of never getting a good night's sleep ever again.

"You're gonna live. But you need ice and rest for twenty-four hours. Practice is over for you," Nate told Conner. He signaled for one of the assistants. "Ice!" he called. The assistant gave him a thumbs up and jogged toward the locker room.

"Well, don't cry over being the one to cause the injury, Nate," Conner said dryly. "No, really. I hate when you get all emotional and shit."

Nate grinned, stretching to his feet. "I'll try to keep my guilt and regret under wraps."

"Sullivan!" Coach shouted. "Get over here!"

Ryan smiled. "You're in trouble," he sing-songed.

Yep.

Nate strode to the sidelines.

"He okay?" Coach asked.

"He's out for today, but he'll be okay by Thursday."

"What's wrong with *you*?"

"Bad day."

The older man frowned at him. "You threw a punch at Axel."

Nate glanced at the field. "I know." Nate hadn't been trying very hard to hit Brian and the linebacker had dodged the fist easily, but fighting among teammates wasn't tolerated by Coach Henry.

Nate wasn't exactly the punch-throwing type. He yelled when a guy did something stupid, he swore when a play didn't work, he swore louder when *he* screwed up. But he didn't push and shove and punch.

Emma Dixon was really messing with him.

"And you made a play on Dixon."

"Yeah."

"Hit the showers," Coach finally said. "And the next time I see you, you better be having a better day."

That worked to get him away from Conner and all the reminders and conversation about Emma. She was more on his mind now than she had been when he'd wanted to hit Conner.

Nate gave Coach a nod and jogged off to the locker room.

He had some space now from Conner. He now needed a way to get the other Dixon out of his head. Emma was affecting his sleep and football. He couldn't let her start affecting his work. He had to get her out of his system.

As he rounded the cement wall that led into the locker rooms he came up short.

Emma was walking up the slight incline to the field level.

The second she saw him, she scowled.

This was just fucking great. But he'd known it was going to

happen. He was going to run into her. There was no way around it. He was friends with her brother, two of her sisters were involved with two of his other friends and teammates. There was no way to avoid this woman who had been making him nuts even before he'd seen her naked.

He was in big trouble now.

"You're done with practice?" she asked as she got closer.

"Yes."

She heard shouting from the field and glanced in that direction. "Everyone done?"

"Nope, just me."

He propped his helmet on his hip and rested his arm on it as he studied her. She was dressed in a teal sundress that made her eyes look even brighter and greener than usual. Which was exactly the type of thing he *didn't* usually notice or care about.

Her long, tanned legs looked gorgeous in the short skirt and the thin straps over her shoulders reminded him of the tiny tank top she'd worn—and removed for him—Friday night.

"You got kicked out of practice?" she asked, stopping in front of him.

"Yep."

"Why?"

"Because I'm an asshole."

"I'm shocked."

She certainly didn't act like she felt awkward after the other night.

Dammit. He'd told her *he* was in charge of what was going to happen between them. She'd texted him anyway. And now she was here.

"You better be here to see your brother."

She propped her hands on her hips and a gust of wind whipped her hair back, making her look even haughtier than she already did. "Why would I be here to see my brother?"

"Why else would you be here?"

"To find you and see why you haven't called me."

Even that made him hot and hard. She wanted him to call her. She was impatient about it. There was no way he could not be affected by that.

He gave her a lazy smile. "It's only been thirty-six hours."

She raised both eyebrows. "Thirty-eight hours and forty-one minutes."

She was something. "No pride, Emma?"

"You said that there's something about taming a wild spirit," she said, moving closer. "I've *never* chased a guy in my life, Nate. I figured the fact that I'm here would be making you feel really good about yourself."

It did. God help him.

"But you're not supposed to be chasing me. You're supposed to be waiting by your phone for my call or text. Remember?"

"I did that."

"For less than twenty-four hours. The schedule is up to me."

She narrowed her eyes and he braced himself for her to tell him to go to hell. That was what he wanted. Sort of. This was all about pushing her away, rubbing her the wrong way, turning her off. But the idea that she wouldn't be waiting with her phone on for him to call rubbed *him* the wrong way.

"Fine."

She turned on her heel and walked back down the cement ramp.

Nate watched her go, wishing that he'd kissed her first. He appreciated the sexy sway of her hips, the way her heels clicked on the floor, and the fact that she was walking away. She hadn't fought him, hadn't told him to forget the whole thing.

Nate made himself stand still and not run after her. But he could call her back. She'd come. And it would irritate the hell out of her.

"Emma."

The concrete made the sound carry easily and she stopped immediately and turned back.

"Come here."

He could see her start to retort, probably with a *fuck you*.

He didn't typically get involved with women whose first instinct was to swear at him.

The women that he spent time with were strong, confident and sexy. But they didn't talk like sailors. They were polished and sophisticated. They were certainly not virgins, but had not been particularly sexually adventurous prior to meeting him. They were curious, willing, and always in positions where they had a lot of demands placed on them, made a lot of decisions and were responsible for a lot of people. He'd been involved with the CEO of a highly successful makeup company, the chair of a prestigious charitable organization, a high-powered attorney and now Rebecca, a nationally renowned cardiac surgeon.

It was as if they made so many important decisions and had so much stress in their everyday lives, that being with him and surrendering their sexual adventures to him was a relief, a needed vacation, a true break from real life. They were enthusiastic and definitely enjoyed every minute of it.

And the fact that it was always short-term worked for them. Though he and Rebecca had been involved for a while, it was only for a few days at a time and they went weeks without seeing one another in between her visits. It was damned near perfect. When Rebecca was here, she was just what he needed. Then she left.

Emma wasn't going anywhere.

Emma also wasn't a high-powered, sophisticated woman who had been somewhat repressed in her sex life before him. She owned her own business, she was confident and independent, and it wouldn't surprise Nate a bit if she could teach him a few things sexually. And polished didn't really fit the girl who could do more tequila shots than Shane Kelley, knew more raunchy jokes than any of the guys on the team, and had been thrown out of a Hawks game for yelling at the ref. Twice.

But dammit, there was something about taming a wild spirit like hers. He would bet good money she'd never let another guy be so demanding with her. He knew from her brother's complaints that Emma didn't let anyone tell her what to do, including her older brother, sisters or their mother.

She stopped in front of him and looked up. "What?"

"Kiss me."

Her eyes widened, then she gave him a mischievous smile and stepped close. "Say please."

He fought a smile. "No."

She sighed. "You and that word." But she ran her hand up his chest to the back of his neck and pulled him down to her mouth.

Heat and want exploded in his gut the moment their lips touched. She was soft and sweet like this—a direct contrast to how she came across when she was using her mouth to *talk*—and he loved knowing this side of her. As he cupped the back of her head with the hand not holding his helmet, a part of him wished that he was the only man to ever know this side of her.

Which further fueled the desire to have this week to dominate and possess her. Even if it wasn't forever, she would be all his for these few days and he could have her do things she'd never done. Maybe not in the actual sex act, but certainly in the foreplay…and obedience.

A niggle in the back of his mind tried to remind him that he'd intended to avoid her completely for these days he had her waiting on him, but with her mouth under his, he had to admit that idea was not going to work out.

Emma arched against him, and he fought to keep his opposite hand on his helmet when he wanted to pull her up against him firmly. He'd had an erection for her since she'd asked him about taking her clothes off in his office. He wanted to play with her, but he also wanted to hike up her dress and drive deep.

This was going to be a test for him too.

She opened her mouth under his and Nate gratefully sank into her, his tongue stroking along hers, drinking in her moan and memorizing the way she gripped the front of his practice jersey in one hand while her other hand gripped the back of his neck.

Finally she pulled back and stood, staring up at him, panting slightly.

After a moment she said, "At least say thank you."

He did smile at that, briefly. "No."

She let go of him and stepped back, taking a deep breath. "Swear to god, Nate, I'm going to hear some *yes, Emma*s out of you or die trying."

And that was the moment when he fully gave up the idea of *not* calling her. "Keep your phone on," he repeated from Friday night.

"Yeah, yeah, I got it."

She looked at him for another second, then turned and again walked away. He finally let his grin loose.

Nate headed for the locker rooms and showered, then figured enough time had passed. He pulled his phone from his bag and texted her.

Meet me in Memorial Park in an hour by the pedestrian bridge. No panties.

He tucked the phone away. It didn't matter what she responded with. He needed to see if she'd do what he said with no more explanation or direction than that.

CHAPTER
SIX

NATE PULLED into Memorial Park an hour and fifteen minutes after he'd texted Emma. He made himself walk casually, hands tucked into his pockets, but he felt his heart rate picking up as he neared the bridge. He hadn't been excited about seeing a woman in a long time. And he'd just seen her. This was crazy.

"You're late."

She was perched on the railing of the bridge, wearing the same dress she'd worn earlier. She looked like Emma always looked—hot, sexy, free. She hadn't given any apparent special attention to her appearance. Yet seeing her there according to his instructions fired his blood.

He didn't respond to her sassy greeting. Instead, he stepped close, forcing her to spread her knees, cupped the back of her head and kissed her.

He was never going to get enough of her taste. It was that simple.

Emma wrapped her arms around his neck, pressing close and returned his kiss with enthusiasm. Nate wasted no time running his hands up the sides of her thighs, under the skirt of her dress and up to her ass.

Only silky soft skin met his touch. Perfect. She'd followed all of his instructions.

He ripped his mouth from her. "Let's go."

"Where?" the question was breathless.

"Playground." He took his hands from her and stepped back.

She started to slide to the ground, but then paused. "Playground? As in here in the park?"

"Yes."

"I think what we're going to be doing is illegal in public. And highly unethical at a playground."

"Are you saying no?"

Disappointment hit him, but he kept his expression clear, not letting on how much her answer mattered.

She could say no. She *should* say no. It would be better for both of them to end this before it went any farther.

"I'm not saying no." She slid to the ground and looked up at him. "I'm going to trust that you know exactly what you're doing."

Relief hit him hard and he worked to keep his face impassive. "Excellent answer," he said, once he was sure he could speak without sounding hoarse.

He took her hand and they started for the playground about fifty yards away.

The play area was covered in sand and boasted an elaborate plastic and wood bridge-tunnel-slide system, a swing set and an area for digging and building in the sand. It was encircled by six plastic picnic tables. Another ten yards away was a sand volleyball court and beyond that was a paved square with two basketball hoops.

It was too late for children to be out but three women sat at a table on the opposite side of the play equipment from where Nate stopped, sipping from cardboard coffee cups and chatting. A game of sand volleyball was also going on with two guys and two girls on each side of the net and six guys ran around the basketball court.

Everyone else was involved in their own activities and barely spared them a glance. It was dusk, so they certainly weren't sitting in broad sunlight and the table was at least thirty feet back from the court, so they were hardly front and center.

Still, this was very public.

If Nate wanted to push Emma's boundaries and make her uncomfortable—maybe even uncomfortable enough to walk away—this was a great place.

Nate took a seat on the bench on the side of the table across from the volleyball game. "On my lap," he told Emma. In order to hold her, he had to face away from the game, but Emma would be able to see all the other people clearly.

She sat sideways on his thighs, looping an arm around his neck.

"You can't let on what's happening," he told her. "You have to control yourself or these people will notice. You have to act like we're sitting here and talking. Nothing else." Unable to help himself he ran his hand up and down her back. "No touching me. You don't do anything I don't tell you to do. Understand?"

There was a definite heat in her eyes. Along with a curiosity and an excitement that made him want to throw her down on the grass and to hell with everyone else.

Which was another reason doing this in public was a good idea. He couldn't sleep with her. He already felt a pull to Emma unlike any he'd felt before, even the two women who had turned his life inside out. That made her very dangerous.

But he also couldn't go one more minute without touching her.

"I understand," she said, huskily.

"It's up to you to be sure we're not seen and yet you have to do everything I say."

She nodded. "Okay."

He ran his hand up her thigh, again under her skirt. In his

truck things had been hot and amazing. But it was about to get a lot better. "Spread your legs."

Emma moved her knees apart. He ran his hand up the inside of her leg, high enough to make her squirm but not high enough to get too hot. Yet.

"To answer your questions, in the men's room at an airport and strawberry."

He could tell it was taking her a moment to figure out what he was talking about. Her mouth curved as she recalled the questions she'd texted him. "A movie theater and strawberry for me too," she said.

His hand stalled in its stroking. "You've gotten a blow job in a movie theater?" he kept his tone light but he knew she was talking about *giving* a blow job and he wanted to punch whoever she'd given it to.

He'd known Emma for a long time, had observed her, heard her talking with her sisters, heard her brother complaining about her and the guys she dated. Emma was the wild child of the Dixons. But all at once Nate was hit by a powerful wave of what could only be called jealousy.

"Given one," she corrected. "If the question is the strangest place I've *gotten* oral sex, then I'd have to say—"

"I love your nipples."

The interruption worked. She sucked in a quick breath. He didn't want to hear about other guys touching and tasting her. He wanted to be all she thought about, all she wanted.

"Pull your dress down on the right."

She licked her lips, her eyes glancing around the immediate area. She shifted slightly, her buttock grinding into his erection and he gritted his teeth. Her chest now closer to his and blocked from the other people in the vicinity, she reached up and slipped the strap off her right shoulder, then pulled the right side of her bodice down.

He drank in the sight, his fingers curling into her bare thigh. Emma's breasts had to be the best he'd ever seen. Firm, the perfect size, pink nipples hard with arousal. It was strange that breasts could be that different woman to woman, but they were. And Emma's were the best.

He ran a hand down to her butt and lifted slightly, bringing her breast closer to his mouth. His lips closed around her nipple and she gasped.

"Shh," he cautioned, smiling against her. He ran his tongue over the stiff tip and felt her struggle to breathe normally as her fingers gripped his neck. He thought about the teasing texts she'd sent, the hot pink silk slowly disappearing from her body, and he sucked hard, making her groan, then swear.

"Dammit, Nate," she whispered.

He swiped his tongue over her once more, then looked up. "Act natural."

"You bet. Natural." Her voice didn't sound natural at all.

Nate hid his smile as he ran his hand up her thigh, nearing the juncture of her legs.

"Touch me or I'll hurt you," she said, digging her fingers into his neck slightly.

"I'll touch you when I'm ready," he told her, squeezing her thigh.

"Nate—"

"You're used to getting your way, all the time, with everyone, aren't you, Emma?"

She blew out a breath. "Yes. I'm good at it and I love it."

"I'm going to be exception to a few of your rules." He wanted to stand out in her mind. A woman like Emma could have any guy she wanted. He wanted her to want *him*.

She pulled back to meet his gaze directly. "Maybe I want the same thing."

"For me to be an exception to what you're used to?"

"And to be an exception for you too."

He studied her in the fading light, his thumb tracing back and forth over the soft skin on her inner thigh. She'd told him how she'd hated being lumped with her sisters and mistaken for them at times. "You don't really worry about blending in with all of the other women, do you?" he asked. How could she think that? Even without her outrageous behavior, Emma had a glow about her that drew people—not only men—to her. She exuded fun and happiness and mischief.

"Of course."

She ran her hand over the back of his neck into his hair and back to his collar. But Nate wondered if she was even aware of the action.

"How can you think that?" Nate asked. He was surrounded by beautiful, intelligent, funny women all the time. He worked with doctors and nurses and social workers and therapists who were all smart and compassionate and outgoing. But when he thought about who stood out and stirred his desire, it was always Emma who came to mind.

"I have three amazing, gorgeous sisters," Emma said, her eyes on his chin instead of his eyes. "And of the four of us I'm not the strongest, I'm not the smartest, I'm not the most beautiful, I'm not the sweetest. I'm the…loudest. And the most unpredictable."

And she'd become the loudest and most unpredictable to make her mark. Nate's chest tightened. Emma was unlike any other woman he knew—including her sisters—and it wasn't about her being daring or loud.

Not that he'd given it a lot of analysis before, but thinking that she was on his mind only because she had a naughty streak was…wrong. But it was hard to put into words what made him take notice.

"All of your sisters and about fifty other women were out at Trudy's Thursday night," Nate finally said, running his fingers up the bumps of her spine. Thursday was game night, or practice night in the off-season, for the Hawks and Trudy's Tavern was the post-game hang-out. Emma and her sisters never missed a game. Or an after party. "You were wearing a black T-shirt with Hawks in gold rhinestones over your chest and jeans that made your ass look amazing and high heeled boots." He lifted his hand to her hair and ran his fingers through the heavy strands. "I prefer your hair down, but that night you wore this sexy, twisted ponytail thing." He met her wide-eyed stare. "I have no idea what any of the other women were wearing."

She looked amazed, then puzzled, then she frowned. "You notice me because you're attracted to me."

"I'm attracted to you because I notice you," he said, realizing the truth of it. "There were other beautiful women there, Emma. Women I'm physically attracted to if I think about it. But I pick you out in a crowd, every time, for some reason. Something draws me. And every time I watch you or listen to you, I want you more."

The amazed look was back. She shook her head slowly. "Holy shit, Sullivan. You're good."

He grinned. "You have no idea."

Her gaze dropped to his mouth. "I have *some* idea." She looked back into his eyes. "But I think it was the jeans that did it to you on Thursday. I look fantastic in those jeans."

He chuckled. He had to admit that her confidence made him crazy—and made him want to tie her to his bed for about a week.

"The jeans were awesome," he agreed, "but..." Did he dare admit this to her? Or to himself?

If she was fishing for compliment, or proof that he wasn't as in control of his reactions to her as he let on, she had him hook, line and sinker.

"But?" she asked.

"But it doesn't explain why I got hard when I looked over at you sitting in the booth with your sisters and all you were doing was listening to something Isabelle was saying. You were completely quiet, squeezed into the booth on the other side of Olivia—no spotlight, no line of guys waiting to dance with you, no line of shot glasses in front of you at the bar as you won another twenty bucks off some guy who thought he could outdrink you. It was only you and your sisters and you had this soft little smile on your lips and you were stirring a straw around in a glass of ginger ale."

The look on her face now was beyond amazed. It bordered on incredulous. "How—" She had to stop and clear her throat. "How do you know it was ginger ale?"

"I've been paying attention," he told her, now fine with her knowing that. "You always drink ginger ale after you do tequila shots." He ran his hand through her hair again, loving the feel of the soft strands shifting between his fingers. "Why is that?"

She tipped her head back slightly as his fingers caressed her skull. "The tequila upsets my stomach when I have a lot."

"Maybe you should stop drinking before it gets to that point."

She closed her eyes and moaned as he deepened the scalp massage. "I never back down from a challenge."

Right. That was her M.O. Nate frowned. Was that all this was between them? He was pushing her and she was pushing right back?

"Besides, I needed the twenty bucks to pay Olivia back."

He stopped rubbing and lifted her head back upright. She blinked her eyes open and he waited until she focused on him. "There's no money riding on our challenge here. The one where you let me take charge of you for a week. You sure you're motivated?"

"I'm very aware of which challenge you're referring to," she said, the sass back in her voice. "And there's something better than money at stake here."

"Oh?" The ability to add him to the notches in her bedpost? Nate was suddenly irritated. She didn't want to blend into the crowd? Neither did he.

"Do you remember the first time we met?" she asked.

He frowned. "The reception after your brother and I made the Hawks." Cody Madsen and Ryan Kaye had made the team that same season. They'd been the new guys on the team and had been friends ever since.

She nodded. "Conner introduced us."

He remembered. "I asked if I could buy you a drink and you told me that I should try hitting on a girl who didn't know that I was the one who missed the tackle that cost us the conference championship my senior year at Iowa."

She grinned now like she had then. "I figure the foreplay between us started then."

He narrowed his eyes, remembering that night—and all the sassy comments she'd thrown at him since. "That was three years ago." And even then he'd been captivated. Maybe even more by her knowledge of football than by her bright red curve-hugging dress and the red fuck-me heels that went with it.

"That's a lot of foreplay," she said, leaning close. "That's a lot of time for me to wish I could have your hands on me."

She kissed him, running her tongue over his bottom lip, but not moving inside. She lifted her head. "The chance to finally be in your bed is motivation enough to even put up with you playing dictator, Nate."

"Then you're not backing down? Going to prove you can keep up, huh?" he asked, running his hand higher on her thigh, his fingertips brushing the sensitive skin she kept bare and smooth.

She gasped. "Yes. Definitely."

Without warning, without working up to it, he ran his middle finger along her cleft and over her clit.

She was hot and wet and his cock grew harder behind his zipper.

"Yes." Her head fell forward, her hair swinging in front of her face. "More."

He lifted his free hand, pulling her hair back. He wanted to see every bit of her expression. "You don't get this I'm-in-charge thing do you?" he asked, circling her clit.

"I do," she panted. "I get it."

"No more bossing me, Emma," he said, his finger sliding up and down over her slick flesh.

"Right. Got it. No problem." She slipped her hand between them.

The first contact she made with his aching erection nearly shot him off the bench. And he almost dumped her on the ground.

"Dammit, Emma. No touching me," he said through gritted teeth.

"Come on, Nate. You don't want that." She tried to kiss him.

He avoided her lips and reached up to grasp her chin. "Emma."

She looked at him, blinking.

"No touching me."

"Fine." She didn't look like it was fine, but she removed her hand from his fly.

Thankfully. He was about to explode as it was. When he did finally get inside her—

Nate shut that train of thought down immediately. He wasn't going to get inside her. That was the bottom line. He was going to show her that she *didn't* want to be involved with him, which would lead to her ending things long before it ever got to the point of him being inside her.

Which meant he should make the most of what he had right now.

He stroked over her clit. "Very good," he praised, just to rub it in.

She opened her mouth to retort, but he slid his finger into the delicious heat that seemed to instantly pull him deeper.

Her eyes shut and she tipped her head back, pressing against his hand.

Fuck she felt good. He pressed deep and pulled out, pressing in again before she could take a breath, urging more sweet heat from her.

"Eyes open, Em," he said huskily. "Don't let on that I'm

about to make you come right here and now with all these people around."

She shivered and her inner muscles clenched around his finger. Her head came up and she forced her eyes open, but her lips were parted with her quick breaths and her hands clenched the skirt of her dress.

"Relax," he commanded softly. "I've got you. Give in."

She wiggled her butt on his lap. "I'm close, Nate," she whispered.

"I know." He pressed his lips to her shoulder, breathing her scent in deeply, and added a second finger, stretching her, gliding along her inner walls, coaxing the ripples that he knew were inevitable.

He thought about all the nights he'd watched her dance and laugh and flirt with other men. All the times he'd heard her yelling from the stands at their games. All the times he'd seen her hug her sisters or tease her brother. She was gorgeous and sexy and yes, the jeans and the tank tops and the short skirts made him want to touch. But it was her smile when she was talking with her sisters, her laugh when she was playing her brother in pool—the moments when she didn't have to work to be the center of attention, the times when she didn't know anyone was watching—when she was in the moment, versus creating the moment, that made him want to drive her right over the edge.

He wanted to taste her. He wanted that delicious wetness all over his cock. He wanted her spread out on his bed where he could watch every inch of him disappear into her over and over. He wanted her screaming with pleasure. Screaming *his* name.

Damn, he wasn't going to sleep well tonight either.

She lifted a hand to her breast and squeezed her eyes shut again.

This time he let it go because he felt the beginning tremors. And frankly he didn't care if everyone in that park—in the *city*—knew he'd brought her to climax right here on this bench.

He flicked the pad of his thumb over her clit while pressing his fingers deep and she bucked against his hand twice and then her orgasm took over. Her muscles clamped down, her whole body shuddered, and she made a soft squeaking sound while trying to be quiet that he found adorable.

And when had he ever thought a woman's orgasm was adorable?

He was screwed.

As she came down from the orgasm, she leaned into him, looped her arm around his neck and leaned in to kiss his cheek. "You are my favorite controlling asshole, you know that?"

And the fact that he wanted to be her favorite everything? Meant that he was *completely* and *totally* screwed.

"We'll have to go to your place," Emma said, pushing off of his lap and pulling her dress back into place. "Olivia's home tonight."

Emma had lived with her sister Isabelle up until the time Isabelle had moved in with Shane. Olivia had lived with their oldest sister Amanda until Amanda and Ryan had moved in together. Nate suspected that Ryan had already proposed to Amanda but that he wasn't telling her brother yet. Ryan loved to mess with Conner, and shacking up with one of his sisters was a sure fire way to increase Conner's blood pressure.

Nate also stretched to his feet. He wanted to take Emma home to his house and not resurface for several days. Forget his surgery schedule and his board meeting and spending time with his son.

And that was why he said, "No."

She faced him, looking perturbed, but not particularly surprised. "You have an unhealthy attachment to that word."

"I suspect it's a word you haven't heard a lot in your life."

She looked gorgeous. Mussed and turned on and happy—in spite of looking put-out right now. And he'd done that to her. He was tempted to stick his fingers in his mouth and suck all of her sweet taste from them, but he tucked his hands into his pockets and worked on looking unaffected.

If scaring her off by giving her an orgasm in public wasn't going to work, then maybe he could piss her off enough to get her to walk away.

Of course, they'd been pissing each other off for three years and she considered it foreplay.

Not that he could disagree.

"I haven't heard a lot of no's," she conceded. "Especially from guys who've had their hands where yours have been."

His fingers twitched in his pocket. "Then I'm making an impression."

She put her hands on her hips. "And now I'm supposed to walk back to my car and go home. Alone?"

"And not use your vibrator—or your own fingers—for any kind of satisfaction," he reminded her.

She bit her bottom lip, looking like she had something she wanted to say. In the end, she shrugged and dropped her hands. "At least walk me to my car. It's getting dark."

"Of course." He'd parked beside her for that very reason.

They walked without touching or talking. At her car, he watched her unlock it with her key fob, then reached to open the door. "Keep your phone close," he told her.

He wasn't done with her.

He should be. No question about it. Their game was getting dangerous. But he wasn't.

She started to step into the car, then pivoted to face him. "When are we going to sleep together?"

His entire body reacted—his heart flipped, his gut clenched, his erection swelled and his nerve endings tingled. Fuck.

Never. That was the right answer. The one he should give her. He couldn't get involved with Emma. She wasn't the type to take his controlling ways for long and the more time he spent with her, the more ways he got to know her and enjoyed her, the worse it would be when she got fed up.

He'd done the head-over-heels thing before. Twice. It sucked when it was over and he wasn't doing it again.

"When it's time, I'll give you the signal."

"The signal? What is this magical signal?"

He had no idea. He wasn't ever going to give her that signal. But if he did… "I promise you that you'll know it when I give it."

She gave him a you're-kind-of-full-of-shit look. No one ever gave him that look. And damned if he didn't like it from her.

"I'll be holding my breath," she told him.

He couldn't help it—he gave her a quick, hard kiss, then nudged her into the car. Before he pressed her up against it and gave her a big, unmistakable signal right there in the parking lot.

There was something to be said for the endorphin high after a great orgasm. It was more intense than she'd realized. Because when Emma came down off of it, she came off of it hard.

She was bitchy and crabby and had consumed more chocolate covered pretzels since Sunday night than she had in all of the previous year combined.

She bit into another one with no remorse.

Nate had played her.

And won.

Fuck. How had she not seen that coming? How had she not been suspicious from minute one? Oh, that's right—she'd been too caught up in how hot he made her and that sexy commanding thing.

But now, three days later, with no phone calls, texts or visits, she realized that their giant game of chicken had come to an end. And she was the big, gonna-be-fat-because-of-the-pretzels loser.

He'd teased and temped and gotten her exactly where he wanted her—craving him and admitting it. *Admitting it.* She'd said, more than once, that she wanted him badly.

Oh, and she couldn't forget falling for his crap about noticing her smile and that she drank ginger ale. Brother—how had he gotten into her pants with *that*?

She was usually much better with men than this.

"What if we move that bookcase and turn it more toward the window?" Amanda asked Olivia.

Even though it was Emma's bookcase in Emma's living room facing Emma's window.

"That would give a lot better light to the plants," Isabelle said.

"We'll have to move the sofa."

All three turned to look at Emma in unison.

She regarded her three beautiful, wonderful sisters. And frowned. Even now as they rearranged her living room, they were dressed in shorts and cute shirts, their hair and makeup were done and they were cheerful and dedicated to the job. She, on the other hand, sat on the couch in cut-off sweatpants, a T-shirt she was pretty sure she'd washed a few days ago and hair that she had definitely not washed in the past twenty-four hours, pouting and OD-ing on pretzels.

But her sisters were always more put together than she was—and not just in their appearances.

Amanda and Isabelle were both engaged to wonderful men. In fact, Isabelle had the king of the over-the-top-romantic-gesture wrapped around her little finger. Shane knew how to make a woman feel wanted and loved. He never shied away from showing Isabelle, and the whole world, how he felt about her. Emma could admit to some serious jealous moments when it came to Shane. Not because she wanted *him*, but his style of romance definitely appealed to her. And then there was Olivia. She wasn't serious with anyone at the moment, but she had never—not even once—had a quickie or a one-night stand.

They were all more polished professionally too. Emma wore T-shirts and yoga pants to work, she opened the studio when-ever she wanted to, and her day was consumed with decisions like which bottled water to stock for her clients next month and if she should make the couples' yoga class twenty-five or thirty percent off for the weekend.

And here she was, surprised and offended, that a guy like Nate was blowing her off. Right. She was so not his type. Nate would be calling *any* of her sisters back—even if they had given in as easily as she had in the park.

Emma studied her sisters. Any of them would have gone for the fun in the park. None of them were angels. It was just that they were more…*something* than she was.

She'd spent a lot of time and energy being different from them. She hadn't wanted to be lumped in with them. And she'd succeeded. She was different from them. Just in not so wonderful ways.

Suddenly she was incredibly irritated with these three perfect women who could easily date the man she was falling for if they wanted to. "*What?*" she demanded as they all continued to look at her expectantly.

"You're going to have to get up if we're going to move the couch," Isabelle said.

"If you can't move it with me on it, then you're not moving it," Emma said, grumpily. And bit into another pretzel.

Amanda sat next to her on the couch. "What is that, your fourth bag in three days?"

"Fifth," Olivia said.

Emma glared at her. "We're going to have to review the Roommate Alliance. What happens in this condo stays in this condo, little sister."

"You're moping. And eating your feelings," Amanda pointed out.

"No shit."

"What's going on? You never mope," Isabelle said, sitting down on the coffee table.

"And you only eat your feelings when it has to do with a

guy," Olivia added from where she was dusting Emma's bookshelf.

"Do you mind?"

"You're attached to this dust?" Olivia asked.

"We've been together a long time now."

Olivia kept dusting. Emma slumped back against the end of the couch.

"Who's the guy?"

"No one important."

"Hey, what were you doing out with Nate the other night?" Olivia asked.

Isabelle and Amanda both sat up straighter. "Nate?" Isabelle asked.

Emma threw a pretzel at Olivia. "How did you know about Nate?"

"Dena told me. She said he came over to yell at her and you jumped in and the next thing she knew you were leaving with him."

Dena. Dammit. Dena had asked Olivia to teach her to bake, so the two had been spending Saturday mornings together.

"Nate? Sullivan? As in the bane of your existence?" Amanda asked.

"Yes. Definitely. That's him," Emma said.

"You and Nate went out?" Isabelle asked.

"I went *along* with him when he went after Michael and Shannon. He's trying to break them up and keep them from eloping and getting pregnant and…" She sighed. "He's nuts, so I went along to be sure he didn't make it on the evening news."

"And now you're mad at him because of something that happened with Shannon?" Isabelle guessed.

"No, he mostly behaved where she was concerned."

"How about where *you're* concerned?" Isabelle asked. "Did he say or do something?"

Had he ever. The bastard. Emma reached for another pretzel. Only two left. That was so not going to be enough.

"What did he do?" Amanda asked, looking concerned.

Emma had no doubt that given half a reason, Amanda would go find Nate and chew his ass. She almost smiled at that image. "He was his typical asshole self," Emma said. "He said and did a lot of things."

Isabelle frowned. "I do not get why the two of you drive each other so crazy."

Emma would have said sexual tension a week ago. But apparently that was just her.

Fuck.

She dug for a pretzel and pulled the last one from the bag. Damn. She was going to need to go to the store.

"You must have had a big fight," Amanda said. "Ryan mentioned that Nate was acting weird in practice on Sunday."

Isabelle nodded. "Shane said the same thing."

"Weird how?" Emma asked.

"Distracted and pissed at the world was what Shane said."

Distracted and pissed off? What did he have to be pissed off about? He'd won.

The guy made her insane. Emma pushed up off the couch. "Do we have any ice cream?" she asked Olivia.

"Stop right there," Amanda said in her best big-sister voice.

Emma turned, an eyebrow up.

"What happened with Nate? You two have been making each other nuts for three years but you've never reacted like this. Tell me what he did."

Isabelle grabbed Amanda's arm. "I told you it's nothing. If she needed help with something, she'd tell us. Or Conner."

Emma's eyes went wide as she looked at her older sister. Amanda was the protector in the family. Yes, Conner was protective, but Amanda had long ago taken on the role of defender. She'd handled more than one guy for her sisters over the years.

Emma flashed to a not-so-long-ago memory at Trudy's where she'd teased a guy a little too much and he wasn't taking no for an answer. Amanda had physically removed the guy's hand from Emma. And she'd ended up with a bloody nose because of it.

Emma couldn't let her think that Nate had done something to truly hurt her. It was just part of this stupid game they seemed to be playing and she'd let herself take it too seriously.

"He kissed me," she said simply. "And now hasn't called me and my ego's bruised."

All three of her sisters stood staring at her, mouths open.

Then Isabelle's lips stretched into a huge grin and she gave a loud, "*Yes!*" She swung to face Amanda. "I told you. I told you it was something like that."

Amanda still looked concerned. A little shocked, but concerned. "You said they'd slept together."

"You thought we *slept together*?" Emma asked Isabelle. Though it was close.

Isabelle knew Emma. They'd lived together and were the closest of the sisters. Isabelle had been her sidekick since Emma was five and Isabelle was four. If Emma was going to get into trouble, Isabelle was going to be there beside her.

"I figured if you and Nate were together for more than twenty minutes alone that, yes, clothes would be coming off." Isabelle grinned unapologetically. "There is a heat between the two of you that everyone within a few feet feels."

Emma's stomach flipped at that. So it wasn't her imagination? It wasn't wishful thinking?

Then she frowned and turned to stomp to the freezer. "Well, Nate's not aware of that."

"Of what?" Olivia said, watching Emma grab the carton of Chunky Monkey and a spoon.

"That our clothes are supposed to be coming off."

She dug into the ice cream, then froze. Dammit. She'd admitted that…

"You wanted your clothes to come off and he didn't?" Isabelle demanded from the doorway.

Emma turned. All three sisters were now crowded into the doorway between the kitchen and the living room.

There was no escape.

She sighed. "Yes. I mean, the kiss was…amazing. Both of them." She waited for her sisters' reactions.

They all grinned.

"But he didn't want to go any further."

"And you told him you wanted to?" Isabelle asked.

Emma nodded, her cheeks heating.

"Oh, boy," Olivia muttered.

Emma nodded again. "I know."

"And you think he was messing with you," Isabelle concluded.

Emma dug her spoon into the ice cream. "Yep. We've been doing this dance for three years. And he finally…dipped me and ended it."

No one said anything for a moment. Emma took a huge bite of ice cream.

A phone rang in the living room. Olivia was closest. She disappeared around the corner. When she reappeared she was holding Emma's phone. "It's Nate."

Even that made her heart trip. Dammit. "So what?"

"He's calling," Amanda said. "Don't you want to hear what he has to say?"

Emma put a big bite of ice cream in her mouth. "*No.*"

"Maybe there's a good reason for him to not call the last few days."

"Don't care."

Amanda narrowed her eyes. "Yes, you do."

"Fine." Emma set the ice cream down. "I do. And that's dangerous, considering I'm into him more than he's into me. So…I don't want to talk to him."

Her phone rang again. Then her text notification chimed.

She crossed her arms and waited. Then she hit the button for her voicemail and put it on speaker.

"Dammit, Emma, I told you to keep your phone on and close. Call me immediately."

He hung up and Emma looked at her sisters.

"He and I would never work out."

Isabelle was the first to start laughing, then Olivia, then Amanda. Finally Emma grinned.

"He seriously talks to you like that? *Call me immediately*? And he thinks that will work?" Isabelle asked.

Emma had to swallow before she replied. "You wouldn't believe some of the stuff he said." She was still having a hard time believing some of it. But she sure kept replaying it in her head. That and the way she'd responded to it.

There were definitely things her sisters didn't need to know.

Her phone started ringing again.

"Oh, for fuck's sake," Emma muttered. She did *not* want to talk to him. He'd be able to wear her down and that pissed her off as much as her falling for his let-me-be-in-charge-of-you-for-a-week bullshit. "I'm going to the store."

She headed for her room for a change of clothes and some makeup. Yes, she was making a store run for junk food, but she had a sudden urge to wash her hair, put on some lip gloss—at least—and change into clothes she was *sure* were clean.

Forty-five minutes later, she grabbed her purse and slipped on her sandals. "Anyone need anything?" she asked her sisters.

They had rearranged the couch, the bookshelf, the armchair and were now working on the computer desk.

"Wine."

"Strawberry daiquiri mix."

"Kahlua."

She grinned. "Glad the unpacking is going so well." This was for Olivia's knick knacks. They hadn't sweated and gotten dirty and needed liquor after moving her furniture in. Of course, Conner, Shane, Ryan, Cody and Nate had helped with that.

Emma stubbornly ignored the memory of Nate in faded blue

jeans that clung lovingly to his ass and a dark red T-shirt that clung lovingly to his shoulders, chest and stomach.

Ten minutes later she was pushing a cart through the liquor section of Carl-Mart. Carl-Mart was a slightly smaller, slightly more expensive version of the big, nationwide chain of stores it rhymed with. Emma thought it was funny. The bigwigs at the nationwide chain of stores it rhymed with did not. But there wasn't anything they could do about it. Of course the press around their *attempts* to do something about it had resulted in a ton of free advertising for Carl-Mart and they were doing very well.

She set a jug of margarita mix in her cart next to the bottle of wine as her phone rang again.

She pulled it out, determined to hang up on Nate, but realized it was Shannon before she pushed the dismiss button. She accepted the call. "Hey."

"You have to come down here." Shannon sounded panicky.

"Where are you?"

"Carl-Mart."

Emma stopped in the middle of the aisle. "Seriously? Why?"

"We're doing the scavenger hunt for Jane and Matt's couples' shower. Michael and I decided to hit Carl-Mart."

Jane was a friend of Shannon's from high school. She was two years older than Shannon but they'd hit it off in choir and had stayed close. Jane was marrying her high school sweetheart in a month or so. Shannon was one of the bridesmaids and they were having a couples' shower that evening. The main event was a scavenger hunt where the guests broke up into couples and had to find the five things on the list in two hours and not spend more than fifty dollars. All items were to be gifts for the bride and groom and could be anything from sentimental to silly, as long as they fit the criteria on the list.

"I'm here. What's the problem?" Emma asked, quickly grabbing a bottle of Kahlua and starting toward the chocolate-covered pretzel section of the store. No matter what Shannon's emergency was, Emma had to have those pretzels.

"You're here?" Shannon immediately sounded relieved. "Thank God."

"What is going on?"

"Nate's here."

Emma stopped dead in the middle of the cookie aisle. "What?"

"Nate's here. Like the other night. Michael is skipping out on some dinner thing and Nate's pissed so he came down here to find him. We're hiding from him in the women's dressing room right now."

Emma rolled her eyes. "How did he know you were here?" She grabbed the pretzels and started for the dressing rooms. Then she circled back and grabbed another bag. *Then* headed for the dressing rooms.

"He found Michael's copy of the shower invitation. Michael had written *Carl-Mart* on the bottom."

Emma shook her head. She wound her cart through the racks of clothing. "Where is he now?"

"Sitting on a bench up front waiting for us to come up to pay for our stuff."

"For fuck's sake," Emma muttered, turning her cart toward the front of the store.

CHAPTER
SEVEN

"FINE. I'll go talk to him," Emma said. "But you guys can't avoid him and *hide* from him. That's not going to help him trust you."

"I know." Shannon sounded sheepish. "We saw him and ducked in here without thinking."

Emma started to lecture her further, but changed her mind. She could do that later. She had someone else to lecture about their behavior right now. "Have fun. Be good. See you soon," she told Shannon before hanging up.

Emma knew that Nate saw her from fifty yards away. He didn't look surprised to see her. She parked her cart in front of him and sat beside him on the bench across from the check-out lanes.

They didn't look at each other, choosing instead to study the people coming and going from the store.

"They don't sell what you need here," she said, crossing her legs and leaning back nonchalantly, her fingers clasped, hands resting on her stomach.

"A twenty-four hour bodyguard to keep watch over my son?"

"Antipsychotic medication."

He didn't respond to that. "You were supposed to keep your phone on," he said instead.

"My phone was on." She worked on acting blasé. Like the fact that he hadn't called her didn't sting and like she hadn't figured out that he was just messing with her.

She could tell he was frowning without even looking at him.

"You were supposed to answer it when I called," he said.

"You were supposed to call me for sex, not to track down Shannon and Michael."

"You really don't know how to let someone else be in charge, do you?"

"Shocking, I know." She wasn't about to let on that she *wanted* Nate ordering her around. That had never happened with another guy ever and it sucked that it was Nate frickin' Sullivan when it did finally happen.

But she'd get over it. And as far as he was concerned, she was *already* over it. Or even better, there had never been anything to be over in the first place.

They sat in silence for another few seconds.

"Why are you here?" she asked. "It's a big public place. It's unlikely they'll be having sex here. They don't even sell beds or mattresses."

"They sell air mattresses and sleeping bags."

She turned to look at him then. She couldn't avoid ever looking at him again anyway, though it would be easier on her if she did. "Tell me you're kidding. Right now, Nate, or I'm buying a funnel and I'm going to start dumping this liquor down your throat."

He eyed the cart. "No flavored vodka?"

Even that tiny mention flashed her back to that night. Dammit. "I'm done drinking flavored vodka. Left a bad taste in my mouth."

Something flickered in his eyes and she wondered if he understood her underlying message.

If he did, he didn't give any further indication.

"Your solution is to get me drunk?"

"If you're staking out Carl's because you're afraid that your son and his girlfriend might get worked up walking past the sleeping bags, then yeah. You need to get drunk."

"Michael hasn't been home in three days."

Emma sat up straighter. "What?"

Nate nodded. "He hasn't been home and isn't answering his phone. At least, when I call."

Emma pressed her lips together. She hadn't known that. Why didn't Shannon and Michael understand that this behavior wasn't helping? They were making things way worse.

"He hasn't been staying with Shannon and Dena." Or if he was, they'd been hiding it from Emma. Which made Emma frown. That wasn't cool. She hated the idea that Shannon—and *Dena*—would start having secrets from her now.

"I called Dena and she told me that," Nate confirmed. "But all Shannon would tell her was that he's staying with friends."

Dena hadn't told Emma that Nate had called her either. That made Emma scowl. She was going to have to have a talk with her friend. She and Dena had always been a team. Or so she thought.

"Then you found out they were here and decided to come talk to him," she concluded.

Nate nodded stiffly. "If it's come to the point where he's leaving home and not talking to me, then…I need to try to fix it."

She liked that. Nate was admitting he might have a part in this. This was progress.

"I can call Shannon," Emma offered. "She's answering her phone."

"Did you know that Shannon has a friend getting married?"

Emma blinked at the seemingly abrupt change of subject. "Yes."

"Her friend is young."

"Twenty. But they've been together for five years."

"Great. They went to prom together. If you can make it through that you can make it through anything."

Emma hid her smile at his bitter tone. "Look who's judging here. Weren't you the one ready to get married at age seventeen?"

"Exactly. So I know what I'm talking about. That's way too young."

Emma didn't disagree with him that it was young to commit to someone forever. Look at her. She was twenty-eight and not sure how that would work. "Why is it bugging you?"

"It's not exactly a good role model for young, impressionable, in-love Shannon, is it?" Nate asked.

Emma shook her head. "Jane's not Shannon's role model; she's her friend."

"Who's in love and planning a wedding and all aglow. Don't you think Shannon might catch some of this wedding fever?"

"Did you say she's all aglow?" Emma asked.

Nate scowled.

She laughed. "Jane is young. She's in love. Weddings are fun and, yes, Shannon is having a good time being a bridesmaid. But do I think that means Shannon is thinking of proposing to your son? No."

But there was niggle of doubt in the back of her mind. Shannon was head over heels and worried that Michael was going to leave her to go to college somewhere far away.

"She gave him a bracelet."

"I know."

Nate finally turned to fully face her. "None of this bothers you at all? None of this makes you think that they're moving too fast or getting in over their heads?"

Emma sighed. She wanted to tell him he was being ridiculous. She wanted to laugh it off. But the thing was—he had a point. And he looked worried. Not like he wasn't getting his way, but like he was truly concerned. And *that* bothered her.

Dammit.

Two weeks ago, she would have had a lot of fun rubbing this in and teasing him with it. But now—whether it was the kiss or the fact that he'd shared about his past as a single dad bullied by his grandfather or that she was truly looking at him and seeing more than the man who so easily infuriated her—she didn't know, but it was bugging her that he was so worried.

She looked longingly at the liquor and chocolate in her cart. It was going to have to wait.

Or did it? She glanced at the check-out lines and saw one where the customer was finishing up. "Stay here," she told Nate, grabbing a bag of pretzels and her purse.

She paid for the bag and ripped it open, shoving three in her mouth as she walked back to Nate.

It was clear Nate was blaming Michael's relationship with Shannon for his sudden disappearance. She had to reassure him without further alienating his son.

Piece of cake.

"Let's go."

"I'm not leaving this store without talking to Michael."

"I know." She held out her hand. "But at least you can quit *looking* like a stalker."

Nate looked from her face to her hand, then back to her face. Finally he got to his feet and took her hand without another word.

She counted that as a small victory.

The woman was shopping in Carl-Mart, for God's sake, and she looked fantastic.

In fact, Nate was wondering which aisle the sleeping bags were in.

And she was here. Here when he was about to lose his cool and overhead page his son to the front of the store. Here when he was here—without a clue about what else to do.

He knew he was acting like a lunatic. But when Michael hadn't come home Sunday night and hadn't answered Nate's phone calls, he'd panicked. Shane took pity on Nate and checked all the police logs and hospitals, reassuring Nate that Michael wasn't in jail or hospitalized. But that still left a lot of options. When he'd finally swallowed his pride and called Dena, and Shannon had confirmed that Michael was alive and well and staying with friends, Nate had nearly thrown his phone through a window. He was relieved, of course, but pissed. Michael would have known that Nate would have been worried sick. It was this rebellious, inconsiderate behavior that had Nate acting like an idiot. He was camping out in Carl-Mart just for a chance to talk to his son.

Yet somehow when he'd seen Emma coming down the main store aisle toward him, he'd felt better. Relieved. Like he could be a lunatic and she would roll her eyes at him, but she wouldn't leave. Like he could confess all the things he was worried about and she'd give him that you're-a-nut-job look but she'd stay and probably point out a bunch of stuff he hadn't thought of. She might even convince him not to worry.

Now that she was holding his hand too, he wondered how he'd managed to avoid calling her the last three days.

It had been tough.

He'd had a crazy schedule at the hospital and clinic. He'd put in an extra workout. He'd hung out with the guys. But with the guys there was always talk about the girls. Ryan would mention Amanda, Shane would say something about Isabelle, Cody would tell a story he heard from Olivia, and Nate inevitably thought of Emma every time.

And then there was nighttime. When he was alone. Nothing to distract him, no way to avoid the thoughts of her and how badly he wanted her in the bed beside him.

Emma let go of his hand to reach into her bag of pretzels. And he missed her touch.

This was not good.

"There they are," she said, grabbing his arm to pull him into an aisle in the electronics section.

Nate couldn't help his smile. "Stalking isn't okay, but spying is?"

"No, none of this is okay," Emma said. "But this is better than sitting up front and scowling at everyone like they've all kicked your dog and pissed in your beer."

He looked at her with the combination of exasperation and amusement that was becoming very familiar. "I don't have a dog."

"That's one more thing that's wrong with you."

He shook his head. Why did he feel comforted having her with him again? He couldn't explain it, but the fact that it was hard to impress her drew him somehow and her matter-of-fact way of dealing with him—whether he was being an ass or bossing her around or telling her about Michael's mom—made him feel comfortable in a way he only felt with his buddies from the Hawks.

Emma leaned around the display of earplugs on the end of the aisle they were hiding in. "I want you to see what they're doing here. It's nothing to worry about but I know you won't take my word for it."

"Do *you* really know what they're doing here?"

"It's a scavenger hunt that's part of the couples shower." She dug into her purse as he peeked around the corner too.

Michael was holding two books behind his back and Shannon chose one side. He pulled it out to show her what she'd picked and she gave him a huge smile, grabbing the book from him. She looked at the cover of the book, then up into Michael's face.

And Nate stared, dumbfounded.

That girl thought his son walked on water.

There was something in her expression, the way she smiled, the way she tipped her head—something. He couldn't dislike or totally distrust someone who thought Michael was amazing.

He ducked back into the aisle with Emma.

"Here." She handed him what looked like an invitation.

It was, indeed, for a couples shower that day. He'd seen it. That was how he'd known to come to Carl-Mart today to find his son.

The invitation said everyone was encouraged to bring their significant other. The scavenger hunt started at three, with dinner to follow at a popular Italian restaurant at five.

"Why a scavenger hunt?" he asked, handing it back to her.

Emma removed the invitation and Nate realized there was a second card underneath it. "For fun, Nate. You've heard of fun, right?"

He read the back of the invitation.

Gather one item in each category as a gift for Jane and Matt. It can be fun, practical, silly, sexy...anything goes! Keep the total of all items under $50 (excluding tax). You've got until five o'clock sharp!

The list of items included *something to use in bed, something to make him hot, something to make her scream, something to play with* and *something sweet and sticky.*

He raised wide eyes to Emma's. "What the hell is this?"

She took the list back from him. "You're such a prude."

He hesitated, then stepped close to her and dropped his voice. "Really? Watching you make yourself come in my truck? Making you come in the middle of a park? Prudish behavior, Emma?"

He saw her swallow hard and her cheeks get a little pink. Then she shoved him back. "Knock that off, Sullivan. I'm not the sucker you think I am."

He frowned at that. "Sucker?"

She pointed her finger at his nose. "The *only* reason I'm here right now is because Shannon called me. This isn't about the truck or the park or your stupid ego thing, so keep your distance."

"Ego thing? Emma—"

"Seriously, shut up, Nate."

She looked almost…desperate. Like she *needed* him to stop talking about it. That was odd. So unlike Emma. She liked to talk about everything.

He decided to pursue it later. "Fine, tell me about this then." He held up the scavenger hunt list.

"They're getting those things here. In Carl-Mart," she said. "Just because your dirty mind instantly goes to nipple suckers and cock rings when you hear 'something to use in bed' doesn't mean those are the only options."

Hearing her say cock rings instantly made him hot. *Fuck.*

Rather than grabbing her, he said, "I thought I was a prude."

She shook her head like she didn't know what she was going to do with him. He had a few ideas. And using a nipple sucker on her was only the beginning.

"Look, see what they're getting. No cocks involved."

It should probably bother him that she was using the term *cocks* so freely in regard to his son's activities, but…it didn't. Again, her matter-of-factness made it less serious and less awkward somehow.

Michael was eighteen, after all. Sex was a part of his life whether Nate liked it or not.

Emma leaned around the corner of the earplug display again and Nate leaned with her, breathing in the scent of her hair.

"What is it?" he asked, not clear what was in the box Michael held. Though he didn't think Carl's sold cock rings, and definitely not in the electronics section.

Emma leaned back and smiled up at him smugly. "A book light."

A book light.

Something to use in bed.

"Very clever," he said.

"Exactly. So relax. They're fine."

"Item number two is something to make him hot," Nate pointed out.

She sighed. "You want to stick around and see what they come up with?"

He shrugged. Part of him did. But more of him wanted a reason to spend more time with Emma. Safe time. Time away from any temptation to show her that he didn't need any nipple suckers or cock rings to have a good time.

Not that he'd throw them out if she brought them along.

"They do sell condoms here," he pointed out.

"But you *want* them to use condoms, remember? No grand-kids yet?"

"You're right. That makes me feel so much better."

She laughed. "Come on. But they can't see us. Because this is ridiculous."

Maybe. But maybe it was great.

She started down the aisle in the opposite direction. Her sandals were flat today—which was unusual, and it made him roll his eyes that he knew that—but they still clicked on the tile floor and he said, without thinking, "I'm glad you're here."

She stopped instantly and turned. "*What*?"

"You're keeping me from being an absolute asshole. Thank you."

She blinked at him as if she was trying to decide if she had heard him right. He braced himself for her to say something nice or sweet. If she did that, he might not be able to keep from kissing her.

"Nate, it is my absolute pleasure to help decrease your level of asshole-ishness anytime I can. Honestly, if that level goes any higher, you're going to explode and there will be casualties."

Nope, not nice or sweet.

He grinned. That didn't keep him from wanting to kiss her though.

He strode forward, took her upper arm, pulled her up on tiptoe and covered her mouth with his.

She gripped his shoulders and pressed closer.

Since they were in Carl-Mart, Nate held back from putting his hands anywhere else. Barely.

When they separated, she looked up at him and sighed. "And not a sleeping bag in sight."

"Just wait 'til we get to aisle sixteen."

She shook her head. "I need you to stop kissing me."

"Not gonna happen."

"You don't get to not call for three days and then kiss me whenever you want."

"I warned you this was how it was going to go."

"And you said that I wasn't going to like it."

"Yes, I did." He didn't like where this was going.

"You were right."

Dammit. He'd known that would happen. He'd initially hoped it would happen.

But now…he was willing to hang out in Carl-Mart to be with her. This was absolutely not going according to plan. "I'm sorry to hear that," he told her honestly.

Emma stood looking at him, looking a bit conflicted if he wasn't mistaken.

"I get it," she finally said. "But I'm going to fix this right now."

She spun away from him and started down the aisle.

He definitely felt hesitant about following her, but his curiosity was stronger.

A woman was standing at the end of the aisle they were in, looking at the blenders.

"Hi," Emma said.

The woman looked at her in surprise. "Hello."

"I'm sorry for this."

"For what?" the woman asked.

Emma glanced at Nate. "I need to confess to a stranger in

public that I want to sleep with this guy."

The woman looked appropriately confused and uncomfortable. "I'm sorry?"

"Me too," Emma said, sounding very sincere.

Nate crossed his arms and waited. This was...interesting. Strange, but interesting.

Emma took a deep breath. "Okay, you're the witness," she told the woman. "He needs to know, officially, that he's won," she said, gesturing toward Nate. "I have to admit that he got to me so he'll stop turning it on and trying to make me all stupid."

Nate felt his eyebrows climb. This was definitely not what he'd been expecting.

"So here goes," Emma went on. "I want this guy. Bad. Really bad. He did it. He made me cave first." She spread her arms wide. "There." She turned to Nate. "Satisfied?"

Satisfied? Not by a long shot. But this was not where he wanted to have that conversation.

"Not the most appropriate word," Nate told her. "But if saying yes will get you to stop this, then yes."

"Great." She dropped her hands to her sides. "Sorry again," she said to the woman who was clutching a blender against her stomach like it was a shield.

The woman nodded, then glanced at Nate.

He had no idea what to say or do so he simply waited until she spun on her heel and hightailed it out of the aisle.

"What the hell—" he started.

But Emma slapped a hand against his chest. "Shh!" She walked quietly and slowly the ten feet to the end of the aisle and peeked around the corner.

She turned back and pointed, mouthing, "It's them."

Michael and Shannon, he assumed.

Unexpectedly, he was irritated at them being nearby. And wasn't that perfect? He'd come to keep an eye on them and now that they were close he wished they weren't.

But he needed to talk to Emma.

She hurried back to his side and motioned for him to follow her. They exited the aisle on the other end and managed to get behind a large stack of plastic storage bins as Shannon rounded the corner.

"Toys are over here," she called to Michael.

Emma and Nate both glanced behind them to find the toy section. Damn.

Emma motioned to him and they crept around the edge of the bins as the kids started toward the toys. Then Emma pointed at the aisle Michael had come from. Nate felt ridiculous as he slipped into the aisle stacked with alarm clocks and coffee pots, but safely out of sight while Emma stayed crouched behind the storage bins.

She peeked at him, then made a strange hand signal. He frowned and shook his head. She frowned and repeated the hand signal.

He rolled his eyes. They were using hand signals?

Emma finally sighed and straightened, walking toward him casually. "You'll never make it as a spy."

Speaking of people who were getting to other people.

"We need to talk," he told her.

"No." She grinned up at him. "You're right—that is a fun word to say."

"Emma—"

"Come on. We're here on a mission."

She started for the toy section, approaching it from the aisle along the far wall rather than the center lane.

Nate wanted to pick her up and throw her over his shoulder. He didn't care about the kids and the scavenger hunt right now. He wanted to know what was going on with Emma.

"Now be quiet," she whispered as they moved past the Play-Doh.

"Emma—"

She gave him a frown. "No, Nate."

How many kids had been told no in that same firm voice in that aisle by their mothers, Nate wondered.

When they got to the end, Emma crept around the edge of the display of action figures. What they were doing with the Play-Doh, Nate had no idea.

They heard a shriek from two aisles up followed by male laughter. They moved closer.

"I'd say that will work for something to make her scream," Michael said.

Shannon giggled. "For sure. That's creepy."

"Okay, next is something to play with."

"Play-Doh," Shannon said. "That would be perfect."

Emma and Nate glanced at each other and in unspoken agreement, slipped down the Lego aisle as Shannon and Michael came around the corner heading for the Play-Doh.

"Why is Play-Doh perfect?" Michael asked.

"It's so fun and so simple," Shannon said. "You can do a million things with it."

"I guess they could make it into obscene shapes," Michael said.

There was a pause and Nate risked a glance around the corner. He had to look then duck back but he saw Shannon was facing Michael. Michael's back was to Nate. Shannon stood with one hand on her hip and an expression that was part amused and part what-am-I-going-to-do-with-you.

Nate had *felt* that expression many times. Mostly with the woman who was now next to him. If Shannon was feeling what Nate so often felt, it meant she knew Michael was going to be a handful at times, but also knew being with him was going to be a hell of a lot of fun.

"Name ten obscene shapes they could make," Shannon said. "I can only think of two that you could do without a lot of artistic talent."

"There's at least four. This. And this. And there's the obvious one," Michael said.

"Hey," Shannon said, dropping her voice, "be good. There are kids around."

"I'm pointing, not saying anything."

Nate could hear the laughter in Michael's voice.

And, even though they were obviously talking about making a penis out of Play-Doh—among other things—he couldn't help but smile. His son sounded happy and, maybe even more importantly, comfortable. He was himself with Shannon. That was big, in any relationship.

Nate turned to Emma. "Let's go—"

"You know what they do sell here?" she interrupted. Her voice was a whisper but her irritation came through loud and clear. "Duct tape. And I'm not afraid to use it on you. One big piece over your mouth. *That* would be nice."

"Here give me the pink Play-Doh," Michael said from the next aisle.

"No way," Shannon told him. "You can't open that in the store and you are *not* making something dirty here in the middle of Carl's."

"I'll pay for it," Michael promised.

Nate could tell he was still smiling.

"Michael," Shannon said. "Put the Play-Doh down."

"Sweetheart, you're gonna have to come over here and take it away from me."

It was strange listening to his son flirt, but Nate felt more satisfaction than discomfort. Shannon clearly made him happy. Nate couldn't help but be pleased about that.

"I think I know how to get it away from you," she said.

Nate shifted. He wasn't going to be able to listen to all of their verbal foreplay. If they started talking more provocatively he was going to have to interrupt—he glanced at Emma—or leave.

Would he really leave his son behind with the girl who was capable of changing everything about his future, to spend time with Emma instead?

"Pay attention to *them*," Emma said, nudging him with her elbow. "This is why we're here, right?"

Allegedly, yes. But his focus was definitely fluctuating.

"You think you're gonna get physical with me?" Michael asked Shannon.

Nate shifted again. He whispered to Emma, "Maybe we should—"

"There are no sleeping bags over here either," she whispered back. "Relax."

"I think I'm going to get you to do whatever I want," Shannon said, her voice teasingly ominous.

Nate heard a plastic clicking sound.

Michael chuckled. "A Nerf gun?"

"Put the Play-Doh down."

"No way."

The next noise was a *thwump*.

"I can't believe you shot me!" Michael exclaimed.

Shannon laughed. "Direct hit."

"This isn't over."

"No way," Shannon said. "You wouldn't shoot me."

"Honey, you know you're number one when compared to most things," Michael said. "But this is Play-Doh."

Another click then a *thwump*. Shannon squealed, Michael laughed, and then Nate heard the sound of running feet. Emma pulled Nate back as the two teens went pounding past, Shannon chasing Michael, both laughing. They ran down the center aisle, then Shannon ducked behind the same plastic storage bins Emma and Nate had used to hide a few minutes ago. Michael took position behind a large rack of rubber balls. He'd lean out and fire a few shots, then duck back as Shannon fired on him.

"Oh my gosh."

Nate looked down at Emma. She was staring at him "What?"

"You're *smiling*."

He frowned. "So?"

"So, you do think they're adorable. I knew you would if you gave them half a chance."

"Happy? Yes. Clearly in love? Definitely. Adorable might be pushing it."

"Come here." Emma grabbed his sleeve and pulled him around the corner and into the Play-Doh aisle again.

"What are we doing?"

"Checking out their cart before they get back. Then you'll see there are no condoms and no sleeping bags."

All of a sudden, Nate didn't need to look in the cart. Shannon and Michael were…fine.

He wasn't thrilled the way the relationship was derailing Nate's plans for his son, but there were good colleges here. He didn't have to go to Boston to get a good education.

And there was a part of Nate that liked the idea of having Michael closer and around on weekends or even over for dinner during the week—theoretically, anyway.

He hadn't let himself think too much about how his life would change if Michael was hundreds of miles away at college. But it definitely would. Having him closer wouldn't be so bad.

He did, however, need to keep Michael from following in his father's footsteps in another important way. "I'm thinking you're right and we should throw some condoms in there for them in case they forget to pick them up."

Emma gave him a surprised look. "How mature and enlightened of you." She stopped by the cart and reached for something, handing it to him.

A jar of salsa.

"Get it?" Emma asked with a grin.

"Something to make him hot."

She nodded. "Innocent and fun. But useful," she added as she took the jar back and handed him a pack of bubble gum. "Sweet and sticky."

He got it. He reached past her, his hand brushing her arm. He withdrew the big rubber spider. "Something to make her scream."

"It worked on Shannon."

He tossed the thing back into the cart. "You've made your point."

"I'm glad."

They heard the kids' laughter coming closer again and Nate couldn't resist leaning around the end of the aisle. He looked in time to see his son grab Shannon around the waist with one arm and pull her in close. Then he kissed her.

Nate had to swallow hard.

That was romantic. And sweet.

Michael was in love.

Everything in Nate urged him to break it up, to protect his son. It felt like watching his son run into traffic after his ball and doing nothing to stop it.

Love made people dumb. Love hurt people. Sometimes irrevocably.

But…he wasn't convinced. No, it had never worked out for Nate. However, he'd seen his friends, Ryan and Shane, both fall hard, but well. They were happy, they were making their girlfriends happy, no one was folding at the first sign of adversity or lying or manipulating each other.

He had to let this happen for Michael.

On the off chance that it would work.

If it didn't—there were important life lessons learned from heartbreak too, he supposed.

The kids started back toward them and this time Nate grabbed Emma's hand and pulled her in the opposite direction.

They slipped around the corner as Shannon and Michael came into the aisle.

"We leaving?" Emma asked as they put more distance between themselves and the kids.

They could. But that would mean each of them getting in their own cars and going their own way.

"I'm not leaving until they leave," he said. It wasn't a complete lie. It was his reason that had shifted.

"Then what do you suggest?"

"This way." He led her toward the lawn and garden department and a minute later settled her into one of the outdoor chairs that was part of the patio set display.

"We're hanging out?"

"For now." He sat across from her, facing the toy section where Shannon and Michael were still messing around. He doubted they would have a reason to come back in this direction, but he'd see them before they saw him.

Emma crossed her long, gorgeous legs and regarded him. "You're going to want to talk about our feelings now aren't you?"

"I want to know why you think that I think you're a sucker."

"I'm not giving anything else up easy, Nate."

"When has anything between us been easy?"

"When you told me to pull my skirt up and I did it."

He instantly went hot and hard. He shifted in his seat. He cleared his throat. Yeah, that had been surprisingly easy.

"I think I like easy with you," Nate said.

She gave him a half smile and shook her head. "I don't think you do, actually. I think you like when I give you a hard time." She tipped her head. "It helps you trust me."

She was looking at him with far too much perception. And she was close to being completely right. He'd been there. The women who fell too easily, who were too interested, too accommodating, too willing, were hard to believe. When Emma said yes, he knew she meant it because she never hesitated to say no or tell him when he was being a jerk or that she thought one of his ideas was dumb.

"Never mind. Let's not talk," he decided.

"What are we going to do instead?"

"I could go grab a board game from the shelf."

"Oh, sure, you and I should totally sit here and play Life."

"Tell me about the sucker comment." But he was starting to suspect why she'd said it. She thought he was faking it all.

"First, you tell me about the girl who broke your heart."

He coughed. Dammit. "I told you about Michael's mom."

"I know. But I think there had to be another one. You're too smart a guy to think that one woman's betrayal means they will all hurt you. But you're also too smart to fall for three women who would hurt you."

Up until about a week ago, she was right on. Now he was beginning to wonder. Emma would be the third. If he let himself fall.

If he had a choice in the matter, anyway.

"There was another one," he admitted.

Emma glanced around.

"What?" he asked. He was about to open up and she was already distracted?

"Where did I leave my chocolate-covered pretzels?"

"Seriously?"

"This story is going to be good," she said, looking at him again. "A snack would be perfect."

"This isn't for your entertainment."

"Oh, I don't know. Some insight into you and your behavior? Definitely enjoyable."

He leaned in, watching her carefully. "Why so interested in getting insight into me and my behavior?"

She shrugged. "You're different than most guys. Not as easy to figure out."

"Thank you."

"You would think that was a compliment."

"I do. Men are very predictable where you're concerned, I would imagine," he said. He didn't have to imagine. He knew it was true. He'd watched enough men interact with Emma to know their pattern.

"Predictable how?"

"They take one look at you and decide they have to have you.

Then you say something or laugh or dance with them and they realize they'll do anything for you. Any guy, any time."

Her eyes were wide, her eyebrows nearly to her hairline.

He gave her a little smirk. He loved shocking her with what he knew about her. "I like being different than those guys."

She visibly relaxed, her expression smoothing. "Because, in spite of everything, you haven't decided you'll do anything to have me?"

Was that a bit hurt he detected in her voice? This was nothing to be hurt about. He was nearing the point of doing anything and the problem was that he had the stubborn streak, the money and the resources to be really over-the-top about it.

"I want to know if *you'll* do anything to have me have you," he told her.

She narrowed her eyes. "What does that mean?"

"With the other guys you don't even give it any thought. There's no real analysis on your part if you *want* a guy to be into you. He simply is. They all are. So you never have to give it any thought or effort. I want to know how much you want me to want you."

She seemed to be processing that for a moment. "How did we get back to talking about me? I want to know about the chick that broke your heart."

He'd gotten too close to a truth she didn't want him to know. Interesting. Fine, he'd tell her about Trish. He'd give her a chance to see that no matter how much he wanted her, he wasn't going to give up the control he needed to have. Emma needed to understand that.

"She was my fiancée."

CHAPTER
EIGHT

💋

EMMA SAT UP STRAIGHT. "You were *engaged*?"

How had she not known that? And why did it give her such a sick feeling in her stomach?

She knew the answer immediately as she looked at Nate lounging in the display patio chair. Because she liked thinking he was difficult and emotionless in general. But if he'd fallen for someone hard enough to *propose* that meant he was capable of deep, intense feelings. Just not for Emma.

"Yes. Michael was seven when I met Trisha."

Trisha. Yuck. She sounded like a stuck up bitch.

Emma made herself sit back in her chair and look cool. "Go on."

"Our grandfathers were friends. We were introduced at a charity event. She was the CEO of the charitable foundation— beautiful, sophisticated, the whole package."

And Emma was buying a cartful of liquor at Carl-Mart when he saw her. Real sophisticated.

Emma hated Trisha.

"Sounds like a match made in heaven," she commented.

"Yep. She was perfect for me. She even loved Michael."

She loved Michael, Emma thought. Michael was a great guy. He made her laugh, he'd fixed her laptop more than once, and they texted jokes and websites back and forth regularly.

"That's a good thing if you're wanting to *marry* a woman, I'd say," Emma replied.

"It is," Nate agreed. "Especially if that woman can't have children of her own."

Oh. Now she felt a twinge of sympathy for Trisha. "She wanted kids?"

"That's what she told me," Nate said calmly. "She told me the fact that she could be a mom after all meant the world to her."

Damn. Maybe even perfect women didn't always get their way.

"What happened?"

"Three months before our wedding I found out she was suffering from some medical complications."

His voice remained calm and even, but there was something in his eyes now that made Emma lean in. "Complications?"

Oh, crap. Had Trisha died of cancer or something? Emma was going to feel bad about the bitchy thoughts if that was the case.

"She was bleeding a lot, in pain, anemic," he said. "They decided they needed to do a hysterectomy."

Not cancer then. Or was it? There was such a thing as uterine cancer. "How old was she?"

"Thirty."

"Yikes. How long were you together?"

"Almost two years. And I'd already come to terms with not having more biological children. It was the only thing to do for her health, but I was, of course, concerned about what was causing the bleeding and pain."

"Was it cancer?" Emma blurted out. She didn't want Nate to be brokenhearted over a dead fiancée.

He shook his head. "Not cancer. It was scar tissue. From the two abortions she'd had."

Emma flinched, partly from the impact of the words and partly from the rage she could hear in Nate's tone underlying the words.

"How did that happen? She couldn't get pregnant," Emma said.

"She'd lied. She didn't *want* to get pregnant. She didn't want to deal with morning sickness and stretch marks. She also didn't want to change dirty diapers or get up in the middle of the night. She'd been specifically looking for a man who didn't want kids or who already had older kids and where there was no birth mom in the picture."

Emma felt her mouth drop open. She was quite comfortable with her bitchy thoughts and dislike for Trisha now.

"And, in case you're wondering, yes, both pregnancies she terminated were mine."

There was a definite pain in Nate's eyes that made Emma want to climb into his lap and hug it away.

And how idiotic was *that*? She and Nate might have a weird sort-of friendship, but it wasn't a hugging relationship. For sure.

"So you broke up with her," she summarized.

"Right in the hospital room before her surgery. I'm sure the entire hospital staff thought I was a huge asshole, but I didn't care."

Emma crossed her arms to keep from reaching for his hand. "So you had one girl who got pregnant and did nothing to fight for you or the baby and then you had another one who lied to be with you."

Nate gave her a funny look. "Thanks for the synopsis."

"It's no wonder you have a hard time trusting relationships. On top of how your grandfather manipulated everything in your life, it's amazing you aren't an asshole twenty-four-seven."

"I'm not?" he looked surprised at that.

She smiled. He wasn't. Not really. "Only because *we're* not together twenty-four-seven," she said. She did seem to have a way of bringing it out of him. "My brother and the guys on the team like you. My sisters all like you. Michael likes you—even if he doesn't listen to you."

Nate gave her a half smile. "You like me too, Emma."

There was a flip in her stomach at his words. But she still shook her head. "I like things *about* you," she admitted.

"You like that I'm making you work at this a little bit," he said.

And the cocky was back. That smug look, that arrogant tone. All the things that made her want to smack him.

All the things that made her want to make him crack, make him lose some of the superiority in the face of other emotions— passion, pleasure, joy. The dominance that made her want to get him to the point where he couldn't even remember to boss her around. Of course, Nate would always think he was better than everyone else. But she wanted him to...let *her* tell him that.

Dammit.

"Maybe it's like how much you like me sassing you. It's out of the ordinary."

"Maybe," Nate agreed.

No denial on him liking her sass? That was monumental.

"But I don't like you sassing me just because it's different," he said.

"But you do like it?"

His expression lost some of its teasing. "It's you. It's real. You were right—it helps me trust you."

Why did they have to be sitting in Carl-Mart right now? Emma so wanted to grab him and throw him back on the patio table and show him exactly how real she could be.

"This isn't a game," he went on while she was trying to decide if the table that was part of the set for one ninety-nine would hold them up.

Her eyes went to his. "What?"

"You told the lady with the blender that I won. That I made you cave first."

Her heart sped up and she had to breathe deep. "You haven't called in three days. What was that?"

"I wanted to see if it would bother you."

"You're a—"

"But not—" he went on over the top of her, "—because I'm playing a game and trying to get to say 'I told you so' first."

"Then why?" Her heart was hammering and she bounced her leg up and down. It was a tell. He would know that she was anxious about his answer. But she couldn't stop.

"I wanted to see if you'd let me get away with it."

She thought about that. She was confused. "And did you want me to let you get away with it? Or not?"

He sat studying her.

"Well?" she pressed.

"My first instinct is to say yes, I wanted you to sit and wait for me."

She started to respond but he went on again.

"But I wanted you to be bothered by it."

"I was," she said quickly and firmly. "I was plotting ways to get revenge. And most of them involved the genitals that I have yet to see."

He gave her a hot, though still cocky, smile. "And *that's* bothered you too."

"Yes. See? You win."

He sighed and shook his head. "I don't think I have."

"What do you mean?"

"Turns out I wanted you to show up on my doorstep, pound on my door and demand to know why I wasn't on *your* doorstep."

She wanted to talk. *Very* much. She had things to say. But he was on a roll and she liked what he was saying.

"But you didn't," he said. "So I was thrilled to hear that you want me. Bad. Because ditto."

Her leg bounced harder and her sandal slipped off her heel.

He leaned a forearm on the table. "*You* win, Emma," he said. "You've got me tied up in knots and willing to break my own rules."

She liked that. Too much. Was he playing with her now? If he was, he was good. She was falling for it. And hey, she liked hearing that she'd won. Even if she hadn't been aware there was a game.

"What does that mean?" she finally asked.

"I think I want to be more like my son."

This guy and his ability to surprise her were stressing her out.

"You weren't wrong when you said that I took everything on that scavenger hunt list sexually," Nate said. "Nipple suckers are almost exactly where my mind went."

Emma's nipples tingled at that.

"It's been a long time since I enjoyed being with a woman like Michael is enjoying Shannon. Having fun and laughing, letting myself be surprised and impulsive, being myself."

More of her tingled at that. "You're the one who's so convinced they're doing more than having fun and laughing."

Nate nodded. "But at least they're *also* having fun and laughing."

"You don't have that with the women you date?" She didn't know much about Nate's romantic life. She assumed he had one. She knew lots of women found him attractive. His football fans alone would keep him warm pretty much every night of the year. And there were lots of nurses and techs and so on at the hospital. Emma had always been sure that Nate had whatever he needed in the female department. The idea that he might not have made her…want to give it to him.

Dammit.

"I don't date much," he said. "There's one woman. Rebecca. I spend time with her when she comes to town. I see her on a monthly basis."

"But she's just a hook up?" Emma hated her too. The list of women she wanted to slap was growing.

Nate nodded. "More or less. She accompanies me to any dinners or fundraisers that I have to attend when she's in town."

"The fundraisers you're always taking my sisters to?"

Nate had always asked Amanda to his high-class parties before she fell in love with Ryan. Since then, Nate had started asking Olivia. Having Nate take either of her sisters out drove Emma crazy. He'd never asked *her*.

"Yes. But it's not…" His gaze flickered to something over her shoulder.

She turned to look. Michael and Shannon were finally making their way to the front of the store. They were holding hands and laughing.

"It's not like it is with Michael and Shannon," he said, focusing on Emma again. "It's not romantic or fun for the sake of having fun."

"You're going to start dating," she summarized. Great. The idea of him having sex with another woman made her stomach feel tight and sick. The idea of him acting the way Michael did with Shannon over another woman made her heart feel tight and sick.

"Yes. I'm going to try it."

She tied him up in sexual knots but now he wanted more. Fantastic. This store didn't have enough chocolate-covered pretzels to help her through watching Nate romance someone. "Good for you."

He smiled, clearly satisfied. "I think it will be good for me."

Michael and Shannon were on their way out of the store. That meant Nate was not at risk of ruining things between them today and that meant Emma could leave. She scooted her chair back. "Have a great time."

She'd taken one step away from the table when he said, in that deep, commanding voice, "Emma."

She pulled in a breath and turned. "What?"

"I would like to take you to the hospital's annual dinner dance on Friday night."

She hadn't been expecting that. "You want to date *me*?"

He rose. "Yes."

He was dressed in blue jeans and a faded green T-shirt. He hadn't shaved today. He was standing in Carl-Mart.

But she wanted him. Bad. Just like she'd told the woman with the blender.

There was no way she could date him, though.

She could sleep with him. She could give him a blow job he'd never forget right here in good old Carl's. But she could not see him in a tuxedo, dance with him, drink champagne with him.

She couldn't even play with Nerf guns and Play-Doh with him. Except…she glanced around…she already kind of had. They'd had a good time today. It was silly and spontaneous and —worst of all—had made her like him more.

She was acting like an idiot around Nate Sullivan. *Nate Sullivan*. She had become a desperate woman where he was concerned and she was shocked at herself. She had never, ever, begged a guy to have sex with her. She'd never, ever let a guy call all the shots.

But she was enjoying it.

And the biggest problem was that she thought she knew why she was enjoying it.

He said it was all about him, that he liked calling the shots, but she couldn't help it—he made it feel like it was about *her*.

She was difficult, she took a lot of time and energy. She knew that. More than one guy had told her she was too much work and that keeping up with her exhausted them.

Nate knew her. He knew she was a lot of work. But he said he wanted to date her anyway. Sure, he was bossing her around. That shouldn't seem like a sweet gesture, but it took time and energy to keep her on her toes too, and she loved that he was doing it.

And all that stuff about noticing what she wore and that she drank ginger ale at Trudy's? And now saying that he wanted to be more like Michael and have fun and enjoy things? The guy had to have panties dropping all around him and part of her loved that he'd decided hers were the ones he was interested in. For now, anyway.

And that was where she got hung up whenever she thought about all of this.

It wasn't only desire she saw when their eyes met. There was an exasperated affection there as well. He said that her sass made him know she was real and that he could trust her.

But it would get old. Eventually, the exasperation would outweigh the affection.

She'd been there before.

Romancing Emma was like mountain climbing. The training was challenging, the climb was exciting, but once you got the peak, there was nowhere else to go.

Usually she didn't care. As far as she was concerned, she climbed for those few moments of pleasure at the top and there was always another mountain waiting.

Until now. She had a feeling the view at the top with Nate was like nothing she'd ever seen.

And it was going to hurt like hell when she fell from that height.

"Uh, no."

Nate folded his arms. He didn't exactly look surprised. "Why not?"

She couldn't tell him the real reason why—that she was afraid of falling for him if they went to some dumb charity dinner. Definitely not. "Because you're not putting out."

"Maybe you need a guy to *not* have sex with you."

"*Why* would I need that?" She was definitely not getting dressed up if there was not going to be any sex

"Because all the other guys have sex with you."

That was flattering. "Hey."

"I mean, the other ones you date."

"You bossing me around and a couple of orgasms doesn't mean we're dating. And I had to do one myself, if I remember correctly."

His eyes darkened, clearly remembering it too. "I helped. Admit it."

He'd been a huge part of it. But she'd never admit that. "Quit messing with me."

"I'm not messing with you. Come to this with me."

"No."

"Michael is bringing Shannon."

"Good. Be a grown-up and show her you think she's okay and you're happy for her and your son."

He didn't try to stop her as she started for the front again. Which was good. Or so she told herself over and over. By the time she got to the car, she almost believed it.

"What about this one?"

Emma could not believe that she was helping her sister pick out a dress to wear when she went on a date with Nate.

Technically, it wasn't a date. Emma knew that. Olivia and Nate were friends and she'd gone with him to fundraisers and parties in the past. But Emma still hated it.

It sucked that Nate was taking another woman to the party, and it sucked that it was her sister, because she couldn't hope that Olivia would get sick from the shrimp cocktail or would turn her ankle in her heels.

Emma was curled on Olivia's bed, a pillow hugged against her stomach, her head propped on her hand. "That one's great," Emma told her.

"You sure?" Olivia smoothed her hands down the front of the royal blue cocktail dress. It had spaghetti straps and was fitted through the bodice with a flared skirt. With Olivia's creamy skin, pale blond hair and big green eyes, she looked amazing.

But Olivia was the perfect choice to go as Nate's date to the hospital fundraiser for other reasons as well. She was sweet and friendly and great at small talk and had never played naked Twister with any of the male physical therapists or flashed her boobs at any of the male nurses on a dare. Yes, Olivia would be the perfect person for Nate to have on his arm at the fundraiser. Emma not so much.

Emma was tempted to suggest the white strapless dress that was fitted from breast to mid-thigh but Olivia didn't quite have the breasts or hips to really make it work. She was stunning in the blue.

With anyone else, Emma would have loaned her some gaudy earrings or thickened her eye makeup so she was slightly less than perfect. But, of course, she'd never do that to her little sister.

"You're stunning," Emma admitted.

"What about the shoes?" Olivia asked, lifting her right foot.

"Wonderful."

Olivia faced her fully. "What about my eye makeup?"

"Impeccable."

Olivia put a hand on her hip. "Earrings?"

"Love them."

One of Olivia's eyebrows arched. "My hair?"

"It's exactly right."

"Emma Elizabeth Dixon," Olivia said, firmly. "What is wrong with you?"

Emma sat up slowly. "Nothing."

"Bullshit."

Emma's eyes went wide. "What's wrong with *you*?"

"You've had a dozen chances to ruin this, but you're not doing it."

"Why would I ruin it?"

"Because you don't want this to work out for Nate and another woman."

"You're not another woman. You're my sister and you're a *friend* of Nate's." Emma narrowed her eyes. "Right?"

"There," Olivia said. "Now at least you're acting jealous."

"I'm not jealous. Besides," Emma lowered herself back onto her side on the bed. "He asked me first and I said no."

"Yes, you've mentioned that. Four times."

"Well, I really don't want to go."

"That's bullshit too."

Emma thought maybe she was being a bad influence on Olivia. They'd only been living together for a couple of months, but Olivia was getting spunkier.

"You're scared of Nate Sullivan."

Emma sat up so fast she almost slid off the bed. "What?"

"You're scared of him. You're not going to this party because you're afraid of ending up in bed with him and then ending up in love with him."

Emma swallowed hard. "That's not it."

Olivia didn't say anything.

Emma bit her bottom lip and tried to keep quiet. Olivia was the sweet one of the Dixon girls. It couldn't be that hard to stubbornly outwait her.

But only twenty seconds passed before Emma said, "Fine, I…"

Olivia tipped her head. "Yes?"

"He knows I want to end up in bed with him. I've offered it more than once. I'm absolutely not scared about ending up in bed with him. I'd *run* to his bed at this point."

Olivia gave a triumphant smile and sat on the bed beside Emma. "Which means you're scared of falling in love with him since you're not scared of sleeping with him."

Emma sighed. Olivia was also the romantic of the group.

"I'm not going to fall in love with him, Liv." She was possibly going to end up with a serious unrequited crush, but it wouldn't be love.

Olivia looked at her for another long moment. Then she nodded. "Fine." She stood up. "I mean, if you're not afraid of sleeping with him or falling in love with him, the only thing keeping you from that party is that you actually don't want to go." Olivia crossed to the closet and pulled the white dress from the hanger. "Which is a relief," she said, turning back to Emma. "Because I wanted to wear this one instead." She reached up and unclipped her hair, letting the long tresses fall sexily to her shoulders. Then she kicked off the two-inch heels she was wearing. "And I can borrow your silver heels, right?"

Emma stared at her sister. "Those are four-inch heels."

Olivia nodded. "I know. They'll look great, don't you think?"

They would look…sexy.

"No. You should definitely not wear the silver heels."

Olivia looked surprised. "You sure? I think they'll go perfectly."

"And you're not wearing that dress."

Olivia couldn't show up in that white dress. It was hot. Even without the breasts and hips, Olivia would turn heads in that dress. And while Emma was a big enough person to make sure her sister looked *nice* when going out with Nate, there was no *way* she was going to let Olivia look *sexy* when going out with Nate.

Olivia put a hand on her hip. "Emma, if I'm going to that party, I'm wearing the white dress and the silver shoes."

Unless *Emma* wore the white dress and silver shoes.

She eyed the heels. It would be tempting to use her cane with those things on. But she didn't really need the cane anymore. Nate could take credit for a lot of that—with him she felt confident and daring and…safe. Which sounded strange. Nate couldn't have kept her bones from breaking in the car accident. But he had been the one to put her back together. There was something about that—about him—that made her feel like no matter what bad thing might happen, Nate would make it better.

And if she wobbled on those heels at the party, Nate would be there to hold her up.

It was a silly analogy maybe, but it made her get to her feet.

"Well, you're *not* going to that party."

Olivia gave her a smile. "That's more like it."

💋

"Dr. Sullivan?"

Nate turned to face one of the security guards, Frank. "Yes?"

"There's a woman outside. She doesn't have an invitation but she insists she's your date."

Nate pulled in a deep breath.

Emma. It had to be. Olivia wouldn't forget her invitation. She knew how this worked.

He shook his head. Emma had specifically turned him down for this and now she showed up?

She was so sure that he'd let her in? It was an invitation-only party. Two hundred dollars a plate. She wasn't getting past those doormen without him going down to claim her.

He should leave her there. Better yet, he should go down there and then say he didn't know her.

But there was no way he was going to do that. He liked her. Even though it meant she was running the show, if she'd decided she wanted to be here with him tonight, there was no way he would say no to that.

Plus, he couldn't wait to see her.

"Fine. I'm on my way."

He took his time though. He wasn't going to jump every time she decided to grace him with her presence.

At least, he wasn't going to let her know he was jumping.

Ten minutes later, he finally made it to the front doors.

Where he found Emma talking to the doormen as if they'd been best friends since grade school.

"Miss Dixon?" he asked.

She looked over her shoulder and her face lit up when she saw him. Nate groaned. It was so hard to be annoyed with her when she did that.

"Hi, Nate." She grinned. "Sorry I forgot my invitation. But I was busy with other things and didn't think of it. I hope you think it's worth it." She rose from the chair that someone had no doubt retrieved just for her. She executed a nice slow turn that showed off...everything.

The white strapless dress molded to her curves and showed off her gorgeous legs, the color emphasizing her golden skin.

And then there were the silver shoes. They made her legs look longer, her ankles dainty and they put her at the perfect height to push her up against the wall and kiss her.

Dammit.

Both doormen looked at him as if to say, *Totally worth it.*

She knew exactly what she was doing. And he was wrapped around her little finger.

The question remained as to whether he was going to let her in on that little secret or not.

"Come here." He stalked to one side, not waiting for her.

She followed.

When they were several feet from the hotel entrance he turned to face her. He had to work not to stare. The dress supported and cupped her breasts lovingly, exactly like he'd like to do with his hands. He lowered his voice. "You don't have an invitation and you turned my invitation down."

"I changed my mind."

"Why?"

"Because you said that I prevent you from being an absolute asshole. And here you are in public. I thought I could potentially be helpful."

It had nothing to do with her wanting to be here with him, huh? "Maybe I don't want help with that."

She grinned. "You're happy being an asshole at a charity fundraising event?"

"I should make you go home. I should embarrass you and not let you in." He knew if he ran his hands over her hips he'd feel firm muscles and warm skin. He wondered if he'd feel panties or the string of a thong.

"You could do those things," she agreed. "But I don't think you will."

He crossed his arms, itching to touch her. "Why not?"

"Because I don't think you'd hurt me like that. And because you do want to spend time with me tonight."

She was right.

She was also full of herself. More so than any other woman he'd ever been with.

And it was hot.

Fuck.

"Fine. But you're on your best behavior, and whatever I say goes."

"Aye aye, Captain."

"Stop it." He helped her step over the velvet ropes. "I'm glad you decided to leave the cane at home, by the way," he commented.

"I was afraid it might detract from my cleavage."

Nothing could detract from her cleavage. But Nate kept the thought to himself.

"Best behavior," he reminded her.

"Oh, I'll be the best you've ever had, Nate," she replied as people stepped forward to greet him, preventing him from a retort.

He did, however, manage to pinch her ass before shaking hands with the head of neurosurgery for St. Anthony's.

For the next two hours he kept Emma by his side. Not that it was difficult. She didn't seem inclined to leave him. Which he loved. Trisha had always been schmoozing. As the head of a charitable foundation, her entire career was about making nice with people who could make donations. Rebecca, too, often spent most of the evening carrying on her own networking conversations. Emma, on the other hand, seemed focused on him.

She had excused herself briefly to go chat with Michael and Shannon at one point, but she'd been back next to Nate after only ten minutes. Nate hadn't felt the need to stick close to his son and his date. There were other young adults their age at the party—children of the hospital administrators, community bigwigs and physicians—and Nate knew he needed to show Michael that he wouldn't hover, but would trust that his son would conduct himself with decorum.

Emma was also demonstrating a surprising level of propriety. He'd expected her to flirt with the males in the room and talk shoes with the women. Instead, she sipped champagne, she laughed and chatted with his colleagues, she gave the head of plastic surgery the recipe for a cleansing tea she swore by, and she gave the wife of the number one cardiothoracic surgeon the name of her favorite acupuncturist.

Emma seemed happy to stay with Nate and was mostly acting properly. Recommending acupuncture to a renowned surgeon's wife was borderline, but the woman had seemed thrilled. At one point, Emma had told a joke and Nate had held his breath for the punch line. Emma and Shane often had competitions for who could tell the raunchiest jokes and Emma often won. But the joke had been tasteful, funny and had drawn laughs from the group.

She hadn't even tried to touch him inappropriately. She hadn't looked up and licked her lips. She hadn't sucked the chocolate off any of the chocolate-dipped strawberries while he watched. She hadn't brushed up against him more often than necessary. Nothing.

He wasn't as pleased with all of that.

During dinner, they sat next to one another at a round table with two other couples. Both Nate and Emma knew Dr. Ben Torres and his wife, Jessica. Jessica was the older sister of Sam Bradford—one of the paramedics at St. A's that Conner and Ryan worked with regularly—and Sara Bradford, the woman Conner Dixon thought hung the moon. Even though she was happily married to a very protective, very *big* guy who also worked on Sam's paramedic crew.

The other couple was Dr. Matt Thompson, one of the best orthopedic surgeons in the city, and his date, Samantha.

Matt, Ben and Jessica were hardly the type of people that Emma needed to watch her manners and her mouth around. They were fun and laid-back. Moreover, Nate knew that Matt and Emma had talked—and flirted and danced—in the past. He certainly hoped it hadn't been more than that, but they were both regulars at Trudy's Tavern and both were known for short-term meaningless flings.

However, conversation was polite and pleasant. It wasn't exactly exciting, but it also wasn't tense. Matt was attentive to his date, who was quiet but seemed nice. They all talked football and about the hospital. Ben and Jessica were a great couple and had the rest of them laughing with stories about their kids and their twin nieces.

And not once did Emma put her hand on Nate's leg under the table or whisper something naughty in his ear.

Nate was getting more and more irritated by that.

She was perfectly pleasant and polite. Not at all like the Emma he knew and wanted to the point that he had barely tasted the rib-eye steak with Portobello relish or the flourless chocolate cake with raspberry coulis. Which also irritated him. He loved chocolate cake.

Though even as he ate it and tried to concentrate, all he could think was how much he'd like to smear it all over Emma before eating it. And he had some specific ideas about that raspberry coulis.

"Olivia sick tonight?" Matt asked.

Nate focused on the other man, finding that his date had excused herself from the table. Matt was regarding Emma over the top of his beer bottle.

Emma looked up from spreading the raspberry sauce around on her plate with her spoon. "No."

"But you got to come to the fancy party instead?" Matt asked. "I've never seen you so dressed up."

Nate bit into his cake firmly. Matt was also known for being mouthy and irreverent. His insinuation that he knew Emma well enough to know how she typically dressed made Nate want to stab him with his dessert fork.

"This dress is overkill at Trudy's and since that's the only place we've ever hung out, the fact that you haven't seen me more dressed up makes sense, doesn't it?"

Nate took a long drink of water to hide his smile. Her clarification had been polite but clear.

Matt grinned. "That dress is overkill anywhere," he said. "My heart about stopped when I saw you."

Nate frowned at the other man. Emma was obviously here with Nate, and Matt had a date, but he was hitting on her anyway? The guy had balls.

Nate waited for Emma to say something—something to put Matt in his place or something sassy and flirtatious or something more than...

"Thank you, Matt. That's sweet."

Sweet? Matt basically telling her she looked hot as hell was sweet?

Matt grinned again. "I'm guessing you borrowed it from Olivia though, right?"

Emma took a bite of her cake and chewed as she looked at Matt. When she'd swallowed she said, "Why is that?"

"It's about a size small for you, isn't it? Not that I'm complaining. That dress lets every guy in here know what he's missing or brings back a great memory, you know?"

Nate straightened quickly and stared hard at Matt. Had the asshole really just said that? "Thompson," Nate said, his tone low with warning. "You'd better—"

He felt Emma's hand on his thigh and he glanced at her.

She didn't look at him but she squeezed his leg, then lifted her napkin to her mouth and dabbed. "Do you know what I remember?" she asked Matt.

Okay, he could let her handle it. In fact, Nate couldn't wait to hear her put Thompson in his place.

"What's that, sweetheart?" Matt asked.

"That you're a great dancer. Will you dance with me now?"

What the hell? Nate watched with amazement as Matt agreed and came around the table to pull Emma's chair back and help her up. They walked to the dance floor hand in hand. Nate felt his blood pressure rising as Matt took Emma in his arms.

"I think that's a great idea," Ben said, standing and taking his wife's hand. "Let's dance, babe."

Nate realized he was gripping his fork in a position more conducive for inflicting puncture wounds than for eating cake and made his hand relax. He gave the Torreses a smile. "Enjoy."

As Ben and Jessica made their way to the floor, Nate's eyes were immediately back on Emma and Matt. He was about ten seconds from cutting in, but he needed to get his temper under control before he did it or Matt Thompson would end up on his ass in the middle of the Britton Hotel's ballroom.

Matt's ear was close to Emma's lips and she was whispering something. Nate sat up straight. He didn't like that one bit. She was fucking here with *him*. And she was supposed to be having a hard time keeping her hands off of *him*. And she was supposed to be suggesting dirty things she wanted done to her by *him*.

Nate stood and started for the dance floor as Emma ran her hand from Matt's shoulder, down his chest to his fly. Nate's blood pressure climbed to dangerous levels as he stalked toward them, but when he was about to grab Matt's arm, he saw Emma clench her hand.

She had Matt Thompson by the balls. Literally. And was squeezing.

Nate saw Matt's eyes widen and heard the squeaking sound he made.

"This is a nice place, full of nice people, and if you can't act *nicely* then you need to get the hell out of here. Got it, Thompson?" Emma asked him.

She flexed her hand and Matt nodded quickly.

"The next time you think you want me up close to your cock, keep this in mind," she said with one final squeeze. She let go of him, pushed him back and smoothed her hands over her dress. "Now I have a date to get back to."

She turned and nearly ran smack into Nate.

He took hold of her upper arms and stared at her. God, she was something.

She looked sheepish. "Sorry about that."

"About putting Thompson in his place? Don't be."

"I've been working hard to not embarrass you tonight. That's why I took him out here away from Ben and Jessica. But I had to shut him up."

"I know." It was crazy but he loved that she'd been thinking of him and not embarrassing him even while he hated that she'd changed her personality to fit in here with him tonight. He loved that she was unpredictable and spoke her mind and did whatever she wanted to do. He'd appreciated the more demure Emma tonight, but he hadn't *enjoyed* her the way he did the usual Emma.

"Do you want to dance?" she asked, giving him a sweet smile.

"No."

She instantly frowned. "Dammit, Nate. There are other words in the world."

"How about these?" he asked. "Do you remember how I told you I'd give you a signal when it was time?"

Her eyes went wide with understanding and she nodded.

"This is the signal."

"What is?"

"Me telling you that this is the signal."

Her mouth curved up and her eyes sparkled. "That's not a very good signal."

"It's communicating clearly, isn't it?"

"That you're ready to finally get naked with me? Yeah, it's communicating clearly."

"Then it's a perfect signal."

She was still smiling as she pulled her lower lip between her teeth.

"I should warn you, my physician says I have to wait six more weeks before I have sex."

He grinned. He should have known that would come back to bite him. "Your physician sounds like an asshole."

"A controlling one," she said, nodding.

"So…screw him."

She snorted and Nate's grin grew.

"This is a hotel," he pointed out.

"Yes. A very nice one."

"Hotels have beds. And showers."

"And walls and dressers and chairs," she added.

He moved in close and dropped his voice, running his hand down her bare arm. "You want me to take you up against the wall or on the dresser or bent over a chair?"

"Yes," she said breathlessly.

Heat and desire hit him low in the gut and coursed to his cock.

He was a fool if he'd thought for even two seconds that this would never happen. And the fact that he preferred the Emma who didn't hesitate to take a conceited surgeon by the balls when he got mouthy over the Emma who made polite small talk with the chief of surgery, was one more indication that fighting his feelings for her was impossible.

He didn't say anything more, simply took her hand and led her out of the ballroom and across the lobby to the front desk.

"I need to book a suite for tonight," he told the receptionist.

"Of course."

As they took his credit card and plugged information into the computer, Nate felt Emma shifting from foot to foot beside him.

"Nervous?" he asked her calmly, not looking at her because

he couldn't trust himself not to start something he couldn't finish here in the lobby.

"God no," she said with a laugh. "Eager."

That pulled his eyes to hers. It definitely wasn't nerves. As she looked up at him, Nate saw a combination of things that made him dizzy—excitement, desire, trust. And the thing that hit him hardest—happiness. He made her happy.

"We're also going to need room service to bring up some of the chocolate cake with the raspberry coulis," Nate said, turning back to the front desk attendant. "Two pieces. Big ones."

CHAPTER
NINE

HE HEARD Emma giggle and his palms itched with the getting-more-familiar-all-the-time tingles.

"Of course, Dr. Sullivan," the woman behind the desk said.

They got on the elevator and rode to the sixteenth floor without talking or touching. They walked to the door to the suite. He inserted the key card, surprised but pleased that his hands were completely steady. He pushed the door open and Emma stepped past him. He moved in behind her and let the door swing shut.

Emma turned to face him in the alcove. She spread her arms. "I'm all yours."

Those three words hit him directly in the chest. There were so many things good about those words.

He'd had fantasies about having Emma to himself in a hotel suite. He had lots of things he wanted to do to and with her. But he was also having an urge he hadn't had in a long time—almost too long to remember.

"Emma," he said in that low voice he knew she liked.

"Yes, Nate?" she asked, kicking one of her shoes off.

"You know how much I like being in charge."

"Yes, I do." She gave him a sexy smile that said she was fully on board and kicked her other shoe off.

The fact that she was here and ready to do whatever he told her to do made his heart thump. But at the moment there was something else he needed more.

He hadn't trusted a woman since Trisha, and it had taken him a long time to get there with her. They'd been together for more than two years before he trusted the idea of making it permanent. Her trial period had been *two years*. And it had still blown up in his face.

After that, trusting another woman with his heart, with his life, had seemed impossible.

But Emma Dixon made him believe he could do it. She made him want to do it. After only a week.

Yes, he'd known her for much longer but it had only been since the night in his truck that he'd let himself think about having anything with her beyond their teasing and arguing and sexual tension. He'd tried to resist it, but the idea had been there in the back of his mind, digging in and taking root.

He trusted her and that meant he could let go, let things happen...let Emma loose.

"That means that you're expecting me to tell you what to do," he said.

Emma reached behind her to the zipper on her dress. "Yes, I am."

"I want you to do whatever you want."

She froze and stared at him. "Excuse me?"

He grinned, tucked his hands into his pockets and leaned back against the door. He wanted to see Emma unleashed. On him. "That's what I want. I want you to do whatever you want."

Her hands dropped away from her zipper.

"Are you serious?"

"Very."

"I'm totally in charge?"

"Oh, I intend to cover you in chocolate cake later," he promised. "And then I'm going to bend you over that chair to lick it off."

She sucked in a quick breath and blew it out through pursed lips.

"But, right now, it's all you."

Slowly a smile curled one side of her mouth and she stepped close. "That's really nice of you."

"That's exactly why I'm doing it—to be nice."

She licked her lips, perusing him from head to toe. "Okay, let's go." She gestured with her thumb toward the bedroom.

Nate pushed off the door and sauntered into the bedroom, holding back from sprinting.

He started to sit on the bed but Emma stopped him with a simple, "No."

He turned to face her. "You're getting awfully comfortable with that word yourself."

She pushed him back from the bottom of the bed and took a seat herself. "Take your jacket off."

He did.

"And the tie." She leaned back, bracing her hands on the mattress behind her and crossing her legs.

He undid his bow tie and tossed it to the side, imagining his tongue running up the inside of those gorgeous thighs—finally.

He went ahead and toed off his shoes and unbuttoned his shirt, but when he tried to shrug it off she said, "No."

Nate cocked an eyebrow, but let the shirt hang open.

"Now the pants."

This was getting good.

He unbuckled his belt and slid it free, tossing it in the direction he'd thrown his tie. He unzipped and pushed the tuxedo pants to the floor and kicked them to the side. He'd worn black silk boxers and he stood watching her look at him, his blood heating and his cock swelling for her.

He hooked his thumbs in the waistband of the boxers but

paused. She hadn't said to remove them yet and he knew all about how important it was to follow directions.

Emma took her time looking him over. "This is going to be so good."

"What's next, Em?"

Her gaze flew to his. He was as aware as she was that he'd never called her Em before. It was what her sisters and her close friends called her. It felt intimate.

He intended to call her Em a lot from here on out.

"Lose the boxers."

The leg that was crossed over the other started bouncing, the telltale sign of her adrenaline levels climbing.

He pushed the black silk down, his eyes glued on her expression.

She didn't disappoint him. Her eyes drank him in and she pulled her lower lip between her teeth. Her leg bounced even faster.

She looked at him for so long that he finally cleared his throat.

She smiled without looking away from his cock. "Patience, Nate. Patience."

"You're the one who said we've been involved in foreplay for three years. I'm thinking we could jump ahead here a bit."

Slowly her eyes traced his body back up to his eyes. "I shared that sentiment a few nights ago in your truck. And in the park."

"And now here we are."

"And *I'm* in charge."

The look in her eyes made him groan. "And this is payback."

Her smile widened. "Something like that."

He stepped closer. She was looking very interested. Surely she wouldn't...

"Back it up, Nate." She didn't lean away, she didn't put her hand up, but she knew her words would stop him.

It was such a damned turn-on when she let him boss her

around that he decided to give her some of the same in-charge thrill.

He took a step back and stood in front of her naked but for his unbuttoned shirt, fully aroused and at her mercy.

She nodded with approval. "Touch yourself."

The same words he'd said to her in the truck. And damn it was hot.

Her lips fell open as he encircled his cock with his fist.

"Like this?"

"Very nice."

He grinned. Also words he'd used with her.

He stroked up and down the length of his cock. The way she watched him made him even harder. Her eyes were wide, her lips parted, her breathing fast.

"Faster. You need more than that." Her voice was husky.

Had she memorized everything he said to her in the truck? How many times had she replayed it in her mind? Had she'd used her hand again as she'd remembered? Or the finger vibrator? Or a bigger vibrator?

"I told you not to play with yourself," he said.

Her eyes flew to his. "What?"

"How many times have you gotten off thinking about that night in the truck?"

Emma opened her mouth, then snapped it shut, shaking her head.

Nate continued to stroke himself. "Twice for me."

She frowned. "Only twice?"

He chuckled. "I told *you* not to do it at all."

"It wasn't hot enough for you? Remembering all of that isn't enough to get you going?" she asked.

He stroked up and down, squeezing more firmly. "Does it look like I'm not going?"

She licked her lips slowly. "You're going *now*. Because you're pretty sure this dress is coming off at some point."

"That dress *is* coming off at some point," he said firmly. "But trust me, honey, that night was enough to keep me going for a long time."

"You sure?"

"Absolutely. The sight of you laid back, your skirt hiked up, your fingers busy on your clit… I think about that every time I even hear your name. And after that night in the park I can replay the sound of you coming and the feel of you clamping down around my fingers." He stroked faster, reliving the feel of her sweetness on his fingers.

Emma sat up straighter on the end of the bed. "I'm positive that you know how to get yourself off," she said, again repeating his words.

"I sure do, honey. Especially when I've got you fueling things."

"You think you're going to do that right here, right now, like this?"

"If that's what you want."

"I kind of do."

He'd prefer to be inside her but if this was what she wanted he had no hesitations about it. "I'd love to mark you like this, Emma," he said gruffly, his cock swelling as he worked it.

She sucked in a quick breath, her gaze riveted on his hand.

A few more minutes and he'd be done. But then he'd be able to start on her. His hand worked faster. The way she was looking at him was enough to produce some major dirty dreams. Her cheeks were flushed, her breathing fast, her lips pressed together.

Then she pulled in a long deep breath and looked up at him.

She gave him a slow wicked smile. "No."

"No?" No what? She was playing with him. He stopped moving, but did not unhand anything. "What do you want?"

"I want you to drop your hands."

He did.

She stood and reached behind her, unzipping her dress and letting it fall from her body.

She was completely naked underneath.

"No wonder I didn't feel a panty line."

She smiled as she stepped out of her dress, then sat back on the bed. She leaned back, her beautiful breasts bouncing slightly, spread her legs and stroked her finger up and down over her clit.

"Holy—"

He started to step forward, but she shook her head.

Fine. He put his hand back on his cock. They could do this together. No complaints from him.

"No, Nate." She lifted her hand to her breast, playing with the nipple. "No hands."

He groaned. "Come on, Emma."

"No." She circled her clit and dipped inside, thrusting her finger deep, then pulling back out to circle again.

"Em," he said, low, using that voice that always got a response.

"I'm planning on giving you something that will make you unable to keep from jerking off seven nights a week."

He couldn't help his grin. That bothered her. Did she honestly think that he wasn't affected by the memory of her? It wouldn't leave him. She'd been driving him crazy for a week. Longer really.

And it wasn't only her gorgeous body or her candidness about sex, it was how funny she was and how smart she was, and how she didn't let him get away with anything and how she was impressed by the right things—not money and fancy parties, but things like people being loyal to one another and the joy of seeing her sisters happy and Shannon and Michael laughing together—and that she was able to have as much fun in the middle of Carl-Mart as she did at Trudy's or even here in the hotel ballroom.

"I'm ready, babe," he told her.

"Now *you're* in charge."

He hesitated, his chest tightening. "What?"

"That's what I want you to do," she said. "Take control. I've been fantasizing about this for a long time, even before I knew that being in charge is what makes *you* hot. And it makes *me* really hot." She dropped her voice to a sexy almost-whisper. "Please, Nate. Boss me around in bed."

He wasn't going to have her ask twice. "Look in the right hand pocket of my pants."

She didn't question, she didn't hesitate. She leaned over and grabbed his pants from the floor by the bed and withdrew several condom packets. And the finger vibrator he'd taken from her the night in the truck.

Her eyes were wide, as was her smile, when she looked at him again.

"Lie back," he commanded.

She did, parting her thighs.

For a moment, Nate couldn't look away from all the delicious pinkness. He couldn't wait to lick and suck and plunge... He pulled in a breath. One thing at a time. She was all his, as was this room, for the night. They had lots of time.

Emma's hand hovered over her clit with the vibrator but Nate stepped closer, his knees bumping the bed, her legs spread on either side. "Put the vibrator on my finger," he told her.

She licked her lips as he stretched his hand toward her and she slipped the plastic ring over his index finger.

"Now turn it on."

Once it was humming Emma squirmed on the bed and Nate smiled.

"Now put my finger wherever you want it."

She took his hand but instead of pressing against her clit, she moved the vibrator to her left nipple. She ran the soft plastic head back and forth over the hardened tip, humming in pleasure along with the toy.

Nate almost forgot to breathe.

Then she moved it to the other side. He leaned in, letting her direct the motions of that hand, and braced his other hand on the mattress beside her. Then he took the extended tip she'd just pleasured into his mouth. He licked gently, then sucked, then licked again before biting gently.

She groaned and arched closer. So he did it again.

As he sucked, he felt her move his hand lower, the tip of the vibrator trailing over her ribcage, her stomach, her mound and finally to that sweet spot he'd been waiting for. He needed to see this. He moved back, putting one knee on the mattress between her legs, watching as she brushed his hand and the vibrator over her clit. At first she moved in small, gentle circles, but she quickly picked up the rhythm, pressing harder and harder.

She was in charge of his single finger, but that left three others and a thumb free. He relaxed his hand, his second and third fingers resting against the hot wet entrance that he couldn't wait to thrust into. His teasing touch made her moan again.

She was breathing hard, her unoccupied hand clenching the comforter beside her hip, but her eyes were wide open and locked on his face. Watching her eyes, he pressed his middle finger into the hot sheath of her pussy. Her muscles clenched around him and he withdrew and stroked in again deeper. She widened her legs and pressed harder with the vibrator on her clit.

"I don't want you to come," he told her.

"Then you need to stop looking at me like you want me to come," she said breathlessly.

Smartass. Even as he had her legs spread wide, a finger deep inside her, a vibrator on her, she still sassed him.

He added a second finger. "I mean it, Em. No coming until I'm filling you up and thrusting hard and deep."

She sucked in a long, shaking breath. "Then let's get after it."

"I want to see if you'll listen to me in *this* at least."

She shook her head, the comforter tousling her hair, making her look disheveled and sexy. "The chances are not good. I think you know that."

"Try." He said it firmly—the way he knew made her hot.

"Nate," she gasped, arching her hips closer to his hand.

"Hold on," he ordered her, thrusting his fingers deep and fast a few times, feeling the beginning ripples. Her breasts bounced, her bottom lip pulled between her teeth and her eyes slid shut.

She was almost there.

And he wasn't going to miss feeling this for anything. He tossed the vibrator toward the pillows, slid on a condom, put a hand around each thigh and pulled her to the end of the bed. He paused for a second to absorb the moment, the final moment before Emma Dixon was completely his.

Then he thrust forward, sliding into her slick heat. Her eyes opened and locked on his and his name spilled from her lips.

She was the perfect fit.

Her body sucked him in, bringing him as deep as he could possibly go. He was buried, hugged on all sides, her muscles massaging his length as her orgasm started to build from ripples to waves. He moved only slightly and she clamped down, her body resisting any attempt on his part to leave.

There wasn't a thing in the world that could have taken him away from this. He withdrew in spite of her body tightening around him, then thrust forward, hard and deep.

"Nate!" She cried out this time.

He pulled back and thrust again and again, her climax building quickly, gaining strength as he moved. But he definitely kept moving. He pumped into her, taking in every detail from how her earrings swung to how she arched her neck to how hard her nipples got to the way her inner thighs trembled.

And then she went over the edge, her orgasm grabbing them both, tightening everything, even making her toes curl, milking his cock like the firmest, sweetest fist he'd ever felt.

He gave in to his need then, thrusting hard again, this time letting go, his orgasm taking over, shaking his entire body. Shaking *him*.

He held his position, his eyes shut, basking in the sensations that seemed to have taken over his whole body, for nearly a minute. Then he braced both hands on the bed and leaned in, touching his forehead to hers.

"Good thing you took over," she said, running her hands up and down his back. "I would have never thought of all that."

He chuckled. "You've been thinking of nothing *but* that."

She tightened her inner muscles around him and he groaned. "Promise you're going to jack off to *that* memory."

"That memory and a whole bunch more we haven't even made yet."

There was a knock at the door. "Room service."

"Lea—" He had to clear his throat. "Leave it outside the door," Nate called.

Emma tightened her pelvic muscles and her arms around him. "Don't go."

"It's chocolate cake. I have to go." He kissed her forehead, then shifted back, pulling out of her and instantly missing the contact.

"Come right back."

Looking at her lying on the bed, rumpled and flushed and spent because of him, Nate wondered if there would ever be a time he *didn't* want to come back to her. It was hard to imagine.

The realization hit him hard in the chest and he had to cough and turn away from her.

Dammit. How had that happened?

He took care of the condom and grabbed a towel from the bathroom as he went past, wrapping it around his waist. He retrieved the dessert tray from the hallway and dropped the towel on his way back to the bed, carrying one plate in his hand.

Emma propped up on her elbows. "You have a weakness for chocolate cake?"

"Something like that." He broke off a piece of the cake, dipped it in the raspberry sauce that was in a little bowl on the side. "Ever since they set this down in front of me at dinner I've been imagining it spread all over you."

"You want me to get wet every time I look at a piece of chocolate cake from now on?"

He pinned her with a serious look. "Yes. And think of me."

She didn't say anything, but she licked her bottom lip in that way that drove him crazy.

That easily he was ready for her again.

He spread the cake from her inner knee to her inner thigh. Watching her face, he knelt at the end of the bed and put his tongue against the chocolate on her skin, licking up the frosting and the cake that was so moist it clung to her silky skin near her knee.

Emma met his gaze, putting her finger on her clit again and circling.

"You don't need me, huh?" he asked. He moved higher on her thigh, licking, then sucking some of the chocolate and raspberry combination from her.

"I've been doing this every night since your truck," she said. "I'm good."

He sucked harder, then bit gently. "I told you not to do that."

"Yeah, I know."

He reached for more cake and moved higher, wiping cake across her lower stomach, down to her upper thigh and over to her mound. "You're a handful."

"Yeah, I know."

He'd seen her, he'd felt her, but he hadn't tasted her yet. He took a dollop of frosting and knocked her hand out of the way, swiping the frosting over her clit. Then he leaned in and licked it off.

Her hips came up off the bed. "Nate!"

That was better. She couldn't do *that* to herself.

He proceeded to lick all of the chocolate off of her skin, her gasping growing louder and her wiggling getting more and more forceful.

He ended with his lips on her clit again. He licked and sucked and licked and sucked. She tasted even better without the chocolate. Then he slid two fingers into her sweet heat, stroking deep.

Her head was thrashing on the mattress, her fingers were on her nipples.

"*Nate*! Dammit!"

She put her feet on his shoulders and pushed him back.

"I'm not done with you yet," he said firmly. Would he ever be done with her? The question niggled, but he shoved it to the back of his mind.

"You better not be," she said, sliding to the end of the bed and then standing. "But there was a promise about bending me over that chair."

Everything in his body pulsed with heat and a resounding *yes*. He'd known sex with Emma would be amazing. He hadn't known it would make him an addict in the space of forty-five minutes, but he probably should have known that too.

"How can I say no to that?"

"I hope you can't. I've never met anyone who can say no as easily and often as you do."

He stepped forward and tipped her chin up. "When it comes to taking you and making you scream, there's nothing I wouldn't do."

Then he kissed her hot and hard, the rich chocolate and raspberry blending with the sweet, intoxicating taste of her and the feel of her arching to get closer, her hands on his back, her breasts pressing into his chest, his heavy cock pressing into her belly.

He pulled back and quickly spun her around, needing her again as if he'd never had her. The armchair was the perfect height for Emma's fantastic request. He yanked the chair around so the back was to them and then pressed her against it.

"Bend over," he said huskily in her ear.

She obeyed immediately, bracing her hands on the chair seat, her gorgeous ass offered up.

He knocked her feet apart and reached for more chocolate.

He spread the cake and icing up the back of her thighs and over the lower curves of her ass, then he knelt behind her and licked it all clean, making her wiggle and beg.

Finally when he'd tasted everything but her pussy again, he put his tongue against her, taking a long swipe from her clit along her sweet, wet cleft. He did it three times before thrusting his tongue inside her and circling her clit with his finger until he felt the beginnings of another orgasm.

She was amazing. He was going to have her over and over.

He swiftly stood, replacing his tongue with a finger and grabbing another condom. He somehow wrestled it on and then took her hips in his hands and thrust into her in one swift move.

She cried out, her neck and back arching and he reveled in the submissive position while acknowledging that she had him completely at her mercy.

He wanted her more than he'd ever wanted anyone and he'd already had her. Was in the process of having her. Yet he felt a hunger, a need to possess her.

That was it. It had to be. Emma was so strong, so sure, so free. He would never totally *have* her...and he'd always be drawn to the need to try to claim her.

He thrust deep, taking her, completely in control, at least at the moment. She couldn't use her hands, he couldn't see her face, she wasn't directing any of this, this was his show.

And yet he felt his orgasm building before hers. Oh, no. He wasn't going first.

As amazing as it still was to him, he knew that Emma liked him taking control, bossing her around, playing the dominate. He didn't believe for a moment that any of that would spill over outside of the bedroom, but in here, she was under his influence. And he wanted her to come hard.

He reached out and gathered her hair into his hand, pulling gently but firmly, arching her neck.

She groaned and he felt her pelvic muscles tighten.

"I want you to suck my cock after this," he told her. "I want you on your knees, taking me deep."

"Oh, *yes*," she panted, her muscles tightening again, harder this time.

And she liked dirty talk.

She was officially perfect.

"And later you're going to ride me. I want you on top of me, taking my cock inch by inch until I'm so deep you see stars. I want your gorgeous breasts bouncing and I want you looking right into my eyes as you come."

Her orgasm came on fast. She gasped, "Nate" once and then she clamped down on him. Goose bumps breaking out all over her body as she sucked him deep and milked him hard.

He drove into her, unrestrained, over and over, until his body went crashing over the edge with long, deep, satisfying pulses.

He stood and breathed for several long moments after she slumped forward on the chair. He ran his hand up and down her back, his other hand still gripping her hip, keeping himself imbedded in her. He never wanted to move.

He was in big trouble.

She was in big trouble.

Big. Trouble.

She'd been in trouble before. She thought she'd been in big trouble before. But it was nothing compared to where she was now.

All because of Nate Sullivan.

She should have known something like this would happen.

Still, she was walking down the long hallway of the professional building toward his office.

He'd texted her thirty minutes ago. All it had said was *My office at noon, short skirt, no panties.* She'd followed it to the letter.

Now as she approached his office door, the adrenaline was

coursing. She hadn't seen him in two days and she was more than happy to show up for a noon quickie. Okay, it wasn't classy or romantic. But classy and romantic were going to take some practice. For now, this was just fine with her.

"Hi, I'm—"

"Miss Dixon, right this way."

The receptionist at the desk rose and started own the hallway that led to Nate's actual office versus the exam rooms that Emma knew from personal experience were the other direction.

The woman stopped at the door and gave a quick knock.

"Send her in, Shelby." Nate's voice came from the other side of the door.

"Have a great day." Shelby gestured at the door, then started back toward her desk.

But Emma could have sworn she saw a smirk before Shelby turned away.

So she knew why Emma was here. Emma grinned and turned the knob. She didn't care if the whole world knew.

"Doc Sullivan, I'm feeling a little hot," she said as she stepped into the room. "I'm wondering if you have anything you could give me for it." She swung the door closed behind her.

Nate pushed his chair back and stood, stepping around his desk. The look on his face made her shiver with anticipation.

"I have exactly what you need."

Exactly what she'd been hoping he'd say.

He was across the room and had her pressed against the door before she had her next smart-ass comment fully formed in her mind.

He cupped the back of her head, bringing her in for a deep, wet kiss as his other ran up the outside of her thigh, gathering her skirt as he moved. This skirt wasn't tight like the one she'd worn the night in his truck. This skirt fell in soft pleats that flared about mid-thigh. Unlike the one from the other night, this one didn't stay up when bunched at her waist.

His palm ran over her left cheek, then his fingers grazed the soft, wet cleft between her legs.

"I'm hungry," he uttered against her lips.

She didn't have time to respond with anything more than a sharp gasp as he went to his knees before her.

He ran his hands up and down the outside of her thighs. "Hold it up, Em."

She was having a hard time breathing as she slowly lifted her skirt for him.

She'd never felt so slutty—or hot or wanted. It was awesome.

With the flared bottom of the skirt, she couldn't see him, but she felt his hot breath as he leaned in. She started to move her feet apart, but he caught her left calf in his hand and lifted her leg to drape it over his shoulder.

The first swipe of his tongue was up the inside of her thigh. He followed it with small kisses along the same wet path. At the top he paused and sucked and Emma knew she'd have a mark. Her heart raced at the idea.

Her head fell back against the door as Nate's fingers spread her open and he put his mouth on her clit. He licked and she gasped, then he sucked and she cried out.

He continued, her noises getting louder. Her entire body responded, sensations racing from her toes to her earlobes, then centering on him—his mouth, the two fingers he slipped into her, the delicious words he muttered against her, like "sweet", "hot", "more" and "come".

And only a few hot moments later, she did.

He, thankfully, held her up as he stretched back to his feet, then covered her mouth with his. She tasted herself on him and the lingering pulses from her orgasm throbbed through her.

She needed more. A lot more. Like all of him. Now.

She wrapped her arms around his neck and arched against him, pressing against his erection. Nate kissed her thoroughly.

Then he let her go, smoothed her skirt down and stepped

back. He licked his lips, straightened his tie and gave her a little smile.

She knew that smile. He really did love being in control.

"That's it?" she asked. "I gave up chicken quesadillas for this?"

Nate chuckled and headed back toward his desk. "Honey, I dare you to find chicken quesadillas that can make you feel like *that*."

She sighed and straightened her clothes. "Well, no, not without *a lot* of guacamole."

There was a knock at the door.

He gave Emma a wink and called, "Yes?"

"Your next patient is in room three, Dr. Sullivan."

He shrugged into his long white coat and Emma couldn't help but feel a little flip in her stomach. He looked so good as the in-charge doctor.

"You called me down here and started all of this, knowing that you had a patient waiting?"

"It's Mrs. Murse. She's always early."

He'd slipped her into his day. Emma decided to feel good that he couldn't go any longer without seeing her rather than offended that he'd penciled her in for fifteen minutes between patients.

She turned the doorknob. "Just so you know, I'm going to have quesadillas with guacamole now."

He laughed. "Enjoy."

She pushed the door open partway. "And I'm going to eat them naked."

That made him pause. "Oh."

"And if you were there, I'd show you just how much I like guacamole. On *everything*."

He coughed. "Emma—"

She gave him one of his own sly smiles. "Too bad you have patients waiting." Then stepped through the door and started down the hall.

But not before she heard him groan.

Maybe that would teach him not to call her down here in the middle of the day for a not-quite-a-quickie.

Though she kind of hoped it wouldn't.

Emma stomped up the steps to Dena's front door and let herself into the duplex she considered her second home. She needed to talk to Dena—the least judgmental person Emma knew. "Dena! I need some cookies!"

She knew that Olivia had been teaching Dena to bake. Olivia wasn't home tonight—she was helping her buddy Cody shop for new ties or something—which meant Dena better know how to make Olivia's Double Chocolate Chewy Whatever cookies. Emma didn't know the official name. She just knew that they were the best damned thing she'd ever tasted.

And that included the chocolate cake with raspberry sauce from the other night.

Her whole body shivered with the memory of that cake. The only thing even close to being as delicious as Nate's cock with that cake smeared on it was the Whatever cookies.

She needed some of them. Now.

Because she couldn't afford any more of that chocolate cake, Nate's cock was with him in Chicago at the moment, and she needed to stay far away from his cock anyway.

"Dena!" she hollered.

Her friend came down the stairs, her phone pressed to her ear. "That's fine, honey. I'll see you in the morning." She disconnected her call. "What's got your panties in a twist?"

Nate.

No question about it.

She missed him. How had *that* happened? The out-of-this-world sex thing was, of course, part of it. She was thinking she might miss that for the rest of her life. But she also missed him beyond that. She missed him making her roll her eyes, missed him bossing her and then sighing resignedly when it didn't work, missed him making her laugh, missed making him laugh.

The I-need-more sex she could handle. The rest was making her crazy.

The noon-time hook-up in his office had been enough to make her addicted.

Then there was the late night phone call the next night where he'd talked her through another do-it-herself kind of orgasm and him showing up at her yoga studio after hours two nights later and making her go through a whole yoga routine while he sat and watched. Even the watching had made her hot. Amazingly, her hip hadn't hurt at all as she moved through the more advanced poses. Then they'd had sex right on her favorite yoga mat. The one she used for teaching all of her classes. She could barely get any work done now she was so distracted.

Then he'd left for Chicago for some medical blah, blah, blah conference for a week and she hadn't seen him since.

"I need you to make me cookies and then you and Shannon and I are going to watch movies all night." She was going to ignore her phone. Because she was equally distracted whether he called or not.

"I'm all for cookies and movies," Dena said. "But Shannon's out tonight."

"How late?" Emma asked, tossing her purse on the couch and kicking her shoes off.

"All night." Dena gave her a smile. "Since Michael's dad's out of town, they decided to go camping with Ashley and Carrie and their boyfriends and some other people."

Emma frowned. "Some other people? Who?"

Dena shrugged. "I don't know. Some kids Ashley and Carrie know."

"From college?"

"Probably."

Emma stared at her friend, amazed that Dena didn't seem the

least bit concerned. "They're camping. With a bunch of older friends. Most of whom you don't know. *Because* Nate's out of town?"

"That way he won't bother them."

But when he "bothered" them, he kept them safe.

The thought came out of the blue and hit her hard.

After running interference over the past couple of weeks, Emma was acutely aware that, while he acted crazy a lot of the time, Nate was coming from a very sincere and understandable place. He loved Michael. He wanted to protect his son. He'd never really had to worry or come down on Michael before Shannon showed up. He'd parented Michael but it hadn't been complicated or difficult like it was now.

So he was overreacting most of the time. Was it better to be too protective rather than too trusting?

When the kids were barely eighteen—and having sex and drinking and staying out late with older kids known to be bad influences—yes.

Maybe it was because he was out of town that she was so aware of the way he would have reacted to this. Maybe it was that she thought he was a damned good father and she wished Shannon had had a little more of Nate's brand of parenting. Maybe it was that Emma *had* been given a taste of Nate's brand of parenting. Her brother and her older sister Amanda would have both followed her into a party and pulled her out if needed. Dena herself had pulled Emma out of a couple of sticky spots. She'd been far more relaxed in her approach to Shannon and her escapades for some reason. And Emma had tried to stay out of it as much as she could. Shannon wasn't her kid.

But everyone deserved to have at least one person in their life who was willing to go over the top for them.

And while it might piss her off, Shannon needed to know that she had someone that was committed to keeping her safe no matter what.

Maybe Nate was rubbing off on her, but Emma felt confident

that it was a good thing. She'd rather be like Nate and have the kids frustrated but alive and well, than have the kids think she was cool…and get hurt.

Emma had always been aware that Shannon and her friends did stupid things sometimes. All teenagers did. But she hadn't realized how nice it was to have someone concerned about it— and willing to jump in.

Emma put a hand on her hip. "And you're cool with this?" Of course Dena was cool with this.

"Sure. They're going to do a bonfire and some skinny dipping." Dena smiled. "Kid stuff. They're having fun."

"Dena…" Emma trailed off. She'd never questioned Dena's parenting before. Well, not out loud. She'd simply always been there to pick up pieces and clean up. "I don't think it's a good idea."

Dena looked surprised. "It's nothing you haven't done before."

Emma couldn't argue with that. That, however, did not make it a good idea. "So, I know what I'm talking about. And so do you. Bonfire? Camping? You know they're going to be drinking. Do you honestly think drinking and fire and swimming all go together?" Geez, she sounded like Nate. But she couldn't stop.

Dena frowned. "It's kid stuff," she repeated. "Shannon's a smart girl."

"Who's in love and having the best summer of her life and is no way going to say something to ruin either of those things." Michael was a good kid too. Beyond intelligent. But Emma knew too well how easy it was to go along with bad ideas when she was in a big group, having fun and the adrenaline was flowing. Not to mention the alcohol.

And Nate wasn't there to step in or curb it. He wasn't there to go storming out there and break the party up. That meant someone else would have to do it.

"You didn't care about the party at Heather's," Dena pointed out. "Why do you care about this one?"

Emma opened her mouth, then shut it. That was a good question. The party the other night had seemed like a harmless, normal teenage thing to do. Tonight didn't.

But the party the other night had occurred before she spent so much time with Nate.

He'd shown her a really attractive side to being protective and bossy. Being bossy with his son was different, of course, but being on the receiving end of Nate's attention was an intense, and strangely comforting, place to be. She knew Michael felt it— deep down if he really thought about it. And she wanted Shannon to also feel the security that came with someone caring about her every move.

There were a dozen bad things that could have happened the other night at the party Shannon and Michael had been at. There were at least that many things that could go wrong tonight.

And two weeks ago she would have laughed her ass off if anyone had told her she would ever be seeing things from Nate's perspective.

"So I should tell her no," Dena said, clearly not a huge fan of that idea.

"Yes," Emma said. "But I'm not sure that will do a lot of good." Shannon was, as she'd pointed out to Nate numerous times, eighteen.

Dammit.

"What do I do?" Dena asked.

That was a great question. But there was no way Emma was going to be able to enjoy her cookies and sit back and watch a movie while she was worrying that Shannon would have a couple of wine coolers and jump in too deep and drown.

She sighed. "Do you know where they're camping?"

Dena nodded. "I know how to get there, roughly."

"Where is it?"

"It's someone's uncle's place or something."

"It's private land?"

"Yeah."

That could make things better or worse. Better if the owners knew they were there and even if they were in attendance. If it was an organized party and the hosts knew the waters, it would be safer. But if it was a teenage hey-I-know-a-place-we-can-go type party, then it could be worse. If the land owners didn't know about the party and found out, they could call the cops and turn the kids in for trespassing.

In which case having Shannon and Michael be eighteen—and no longer minors—would mean a bigger penalty.

Emma grabbed her phone. "Did the owners invite the kids over?"

Dena shrugged. "I have no idea."

Emma dialed Shannon's number, but it went to voice mail. Of course.

"Come on," she told Dena. "Looks like we're going camping too."

Forty-five minutes later, they bumped down a winding dirt road leading out to what appeared to be nothing more than a cow pasture. They were well outside the city limits and it was getting dark. Emma hoped this was right.

Dena braced her hands on the dashboard as they hit yet another huge pothole. "At least give me credit for finding out where they were going to be," she said.

Emma rolled her eyes but said, "Yes, at least you did that."

They came over a small rise and saw the flames of a huge bonfire in the distance. Emma killed the headlights, grateful there was still enough sun to see the general direction they were headed in. Not that being on the road was doing them a lot of good. The pasture itself couldn't have been more rough and bumpy.

"There they are." She slowed down and rolled up slowly, then pulled off the path when they could see the kids and cars, but were far enough back to not be noticed themselves.

"What are we going to do?"

"Get up closer and see what's going on."

"And hang out? Jump in to save them if someone starts to drown?" Dena asked.

"Yes. And you're going in first," Emma told her.

"You were a lifeguard too," Dena said.

"But I'm not the one that thought this party was an okay idea," Emma retorted. "And I do heavily chlorinated water, *not* river water."

They got out and walked up on the campsite, careful to stay in the shadows. Several cars and pickups were parked around the perimeter of the fire pit and they were able to use those as cover.

"Do you see them?" Emma whispered to Dena.

"There." Dena pointed.

Shannon and Michael were on the side of the fire closest to where Emma and Dena were. They were dancing to the music that was booming from one of the truck radios. Shannon wore flip-flops, denim shorts and a green bikini top, her hair fell past her shoulder blades, loose and wavy as if it had been wet and had dried in the summer air. She looked happy and young and uninhibited.

Michael was gazing down at her. The sunset behind her lit his face and for a moment Emma felt her eyes tear up. He looked like a guy in love.

He also looked a lot like his father.

Her stomach tightened and she had to take a deep breath. She wanted to see that look on Nate's face when he looked at her.

And that was the stupidest thing ever.

"You're out already?" A tall guy approached Shannon and Michael and offered two plastic cups of something. "Drink up, drink up. We made lots."

"No thanks, man," Michael said. "Gotta take care of my girl."

Emma liked that kid. At least one of them was being responsible. Nate needed to give the guy more credit.

"Come on," Emma whispered to Dena. They moved closer, staying behind cars, but keeping Shannon in sight.

"This is so good." Shannon giggled. "I think I'm getting loopy."

Michael leaned in and kissed her. "You are. Good thing I'm here to keep an eye on you."

"I love when your eyes are on me."

Emma sighed. They were sweet. But Shannon was getting drunk and there was a huge-ass fire four feet away from them and she doubted there was a fire extinguisher anywhere in the vicinity. They were surrounded by other teenagers who were also drinking, several miles from the city—which meant driving home under the influence for those not camping for the night— and only a few yards from a drop off to the river. Emma didn't know how high they were, but from the sounds of the water below, it wasn't an easy jump. All someone had to do was tip back a couple of drinks and stagger too close to the edge and there could easily be a broken bone. Or a broken neck.

"Target practice time!" one of the boys called from over near some of the pick-ups.

Emma straightened. Oh, no way.

She was pleased to see that Michael also pulled back slightly from Shannon and gave attention to the new development.

"What's going on?" he called out.

"You're going to *shoot* stuff?" someone yelled.

"They're airsoft guns. Plastic. They sting but they won't hurt anybody," the first guy said. "We're just gonna shoot bottles and cans."

Uh-huh. No. Drunk teenagers with guns? Of any kind? No way.

Emma grabbed Dena's arm. "You have a choice to make here," she hissed, making her decision quickly and easily. "You can go over there and make your daughter come home or let her get charged as a minor in possession, because I'm calling the cops in two minutes."

She didn't miss the irony of party girl Emma Dixon calling in a tip to the cops about an underage bash.

It might be an overreaction. She might be taking this Nate-isn't-always-wrong thing too far. But one thing she could say for Nate and his crazy-overprotective tendencies—when he went overboard he committed to it and went all the way.

Dena looked from Shannon to Emma and back again. "Why can't you go over there and make her come home?"

She could. Absolutely. She'd only feel slightly ridiculous, in fact.

But Emma had to at least give Dena the chance to be the one to show Shannon that she had someone who would do anything for her. If anyone was going to be over the top in protecting Shannon, it should be Dena.

"Because *you're* her mother, Dena."

Emma cared about Dena. They had some fun memories and Dena had been there for Emma through the worst time of her life after her dad died. As a teenager and college student having an older friend with a couch she could crash on, a car she could borrow, and some real-world experience had been cool and Emma had also loved being around as Shannon grew up.

It was only over the past few years that Emma had started to feel like she was growing up and maturing—in spite of what her older sister and brother thought—and leaving Dena behind. Emma found herself relating to her older siblings more and more often as Dena frustrated and disappointed her.

She was hoping to help Dena grow up too. But if she kept mothering Dena's daughter for her, that was never going to happen. And Dena and Shannon's relationship would suffer. Emma knew that. Shannon needed to respect her mom and that was a lot to ask a lot of the time.

"I can't do that to her," Dena finally said with a shake of her head.

Emma huffed out a frustrated breath. She understood. She'd

felt the same way the other night when Nate had insisted on following the kids. But Emma wasn't Shannon's parent.

"Come on then." They headed back for Emma's car. Once they were shut inside, Emma made the call to the police reporting a party with a fire, underage drinking and possible guns.

That combination worked nicely to get several squad cars there within fifteen minutes.

In the commotion that followed, Emma and Dena were able to drive away unseen. But Emma headed directly for the police station. They were going to have to pick Shannon and Michael up.

And she was definitely making Dena pay Shannon's fine.

They were still sitting in the station an hour later when Emma's phone rang. It was Nate.

Crap.

She took a deep breath and answered. "Hi, Nate."

"Michael called me from the police station," he said without preamble.

"He did?" She was genuinely surprised. Michael knew she and Dena were there. They planned on taking him home as soon as all the paperwork was complete. She'd figured he'd keep it from Nate at least until his father got home. If not forever. "Are you freaking out?"

"No."

That also surprised her.

"He said that they're not fining him because he was sober and has no previous offenses on his record."

She already knew that. "That's great. Shannon has to come up with five hundred bucks because she was drinking, but she has no priors either."

"Hopefully that will make her think twice next time."

Hopefully. Nate sounded calm. She frowned. "You sound fine."

"I am fine. Shane said you were already there."

"Oh. Yes. We came down to pick Shannon up."

"He said you were there when they got there."

"Um, right."

"Emma."

His voice was low and firm and had the usual effect of causing tingles to dance up and down her spine.

"I can't do the phone sex thing right now," she told him quietly, sneaking a look at Dena, who was busy texting on her phone.

He chuckled. Actually *chuckled*. His kid was in jail and he was chuckling.

"Did you know about the party?" he asked.

She cleared her throat and shifted on the bench. But what was she going to say? "Yes, I knew about it."

"And did you know about them getting busted?"

"Yeah."

"Were you there staking out the party?" he asked. He sounded amused.

She felt her mouth curl. "Only for a little bit."

"Thank you."

His words were completely unexpected. "You're thanking me for calling the cops on your kid?"

There was a long pause on Nate's end. Then he said, "*You* called the cops?"

Oops. "Uh…yeah. But they were all being stupid. I mean they had a bonfire and someone could have fallen off the edge of the cliff—"

"They were on the edge of a *cliff*?" Nate demanded.

She definitely wasn't going to tell him about the guns—airsoft or not. "It wasn't a *cliff*," she amended. "A tall…bank. There was a short drop to the river—"

"They were drinking at the *river*?"

She was going to shut up now.

There was another long pause while Nate, presumably, took some deep, calming breaths because when he spoke again he said, "Yes, thank you. Thank you very much for calling the cops."

He sounded sincere. And cooler.

"Maybe I should have pulled Shannon and Michael out before the cops got there," she said.

"No," Nate answered. "This was a good lesson. Even though he's not in trouble—at least not with the cops—I'm glad Michael saw this side of things."

"Okay. Good."

"It was the right thing to do, Emma," Nate said.

That made her smile grow and she felt warm in her chest. Which was ridiculous. She was letting him boss her around *and* she was reveling in his praise? Pathetic.

"I was hoping that you'd let him crash on your couch tonight," Nate said.

"Michael? Of course."

"I can't let him stay over at Shannon's—that would send the wrong message," he went on. "But he doesn't want to be alone at home."

She smiled at that. "Isn't it nice when they still act like kids from time to time?"

"It really is."

She could hear the smile in his voice too.

"Besides," he added. "It'll be a good excuse for me to see you when I come pick him up in the morning."

She closed her eyes. Nate Sullivan had evoked so many emotions in her in the time she'd known him that she felt like she had a kaleidoscope inside when he was around. This sweeter side was as affecting as the hot side.

"You don't need an excuse to come over," she said softly.

There was another pause, then he said, "I'm making note of that. Just so you know."

"Good." She bit her lip on saying anything further. Like *I miss you* or *hurry home.*

"I'll be home tomorrow then," he finally said.

"You know where to find me."

"I definitely do."

As she disconnected, the only way to describe how she was feeling was warm and fuzzy. But she kept it to herself, because if she said it out loud to anyone who knew her, they would assume she'd had a personality transplant.

CHAPTER
TEN

EMMA HEARD the knock on the front door at five a.m. Blurry-eyed she shuffled down the dark hall. What the hell? If Shannon had snuck out and come over to be with Michael or something, Emma was going to yell. She'd only yelled at Shannon once ever, and it was because Shannon had reached for a hot pot of water on the stove and it had scared Emma to death. And that had been fourteen years ago.

She wouldn't have heard the knock if she'd been in her bed. But Michael would have from the couch. Little did Shannon know, Emma had insisted Michael take the bed. He was too tall to fit on the couch comfortably. She, on the other hand, curled nicely into the cushions and had been sleeping peacefully.

Emma unlocked the three locks on her door. There had been one when they'd moved in, but when Shane, the cop, had seen it, he'd promptly installed two more. When she finally yanked the door open, she was fully expecting to see the eighteen-year-old girl she loved like a sister.

Instead she saw the man she was very afraid she was beginning to love. And nothing at all like a sister. Or a brother.

"Nate?"

Before her hand could touch the handle on the screen door, he had it pulled open and was up against her, pushing her back with his body, one hand at the back of her head, fingers tunneled into her hair, his eyes locked on hers. When they'd cleared the door, he pushed it shut, quietly in spite of the intensity she felt in him.

"When you said tomorrow I didn't think you meant in a few hours," she told him, softly, letting him move her, letting him press her up against the wall in the hallway.

Nate didn't reply. Instead, he covered her mouth with his and kissed her deep and hot and wet, making her moan. He ran his hand up under the leg of her short shorts, his fingers finding the bare skin of her butt and making her gasp. Then he pulled the front of her tank top up, exposing her breasts and dipped his knees to take her nipple in his mouth making her moan his name louder and grip the back of his head.

Her nipples were so sensitive and he seemed to know exactly how to make the hot sparks of need race straight through to her core.

He sucked as he stroked his fingers over her butt, moving closer to where she needed him most.

"You have to be quiet," he told her, lifting his head only slightly. "Can't wake everyone else."

"Kitchen," she panted. "Please." Her bedroom was the farthest from the living room, with Olivia's room, a bathroom and a closet between it and the kitchen.

He straightened, then scooped her up with both hands under her ass. She wrapped her legs around his waist and her arms around his neck, kissing him deeply as he strode down the hallway to the kitchen.

He stepped through the swinging door and deposited her on the edge of the kitchen table. "Take 'em off," he said gruffly, undoing his belt and unzipping.

As she wiggled out of her shorts, she watched him sheath

himself with a condom. She itched to touch him, but ached more to have him inside of her. She dropped her shorts to the floor and Nate stepped between her knees, stroking one finger up and down through the wet heat between her legs.

"Yes, Nate. God."

He didn't need any more encouragement than that. He cupped her butt and moved her forward as he arched his hips, sliding home.

It didn't matter how many orgasms he'd coaxed from her, her body welcomed him as if she'd never known anything like the sensations he evoked. She took him deep, pressing every inch of her she could against him. She wrapped her legs around his waist again and her arms around his neck as he started to move.

The stupidest part was that she felt...right. Not just good. Not hot or hungry or any of those feelings he so easily brought out in her. But right. Like she was where she was supposed to be.

And when she let that thought sink in, she felt something else —really damned scared.

Emma pulled his head down, putting them forehead to forehead. He couldn't see into her eyes like this and at the moment she wasn't sure she could hide these feelings from him.

Nate's thrusts were deep and slow and Emma felt them along every nerve ending and inch of skin.

"You feel amazing. I've been thinking about you nonstop."

Her body responded to his husky voice like it did to his touch, growing softer and warmer and wetter, wanting more and more of him.

"I can't get enough of you," he told her, stroking in and out, steady and deep, filling her.

The words made her inner muscles grip him harder.

"The feel of you, the way you sound, the way you taste..." he continued.

She arched, wiggled, shifted, not able to get any closer but not feeling close enough.

Nate caught his breath and she felt an incredible surge of power.

"I missed you, Em," he said hoarsely.

That was the spark she needed to send her careening into an intense orgasm. She tightened her legs around him and muffled her cry against his shoulder. He put a hand against the back of her head, holding her to him and came right on the heels of her climax, his fingers tightening in her hair as he rode it out.

They stayed entwined for a few minutes afterward, their breathing and heart rates slowing.

Emma clung to him the whole time, not wanting to let go and not wanting him to see her face. She was sure every single stupid emotion was going to show.

Finally, it was Nate that pulled back. Of course it was. Emma couldn't do it. She never clung to guys—figuratively or literally —but she couldn't let Nate go.

"I didn't mean to do any more than kiss you," he told her smoothing her hair back from her face.

His hand on her cheek made her bite her bottom lip to keep from saying something revealing. Something like "if you wanted to touch me like that forever, that would be okay with me."

"I meant to kiss you and ask you to dinner Saturday night."

This was Saturday night. Technically Sunday morning. "You want to take me to dinner in a week?" she asked.

He stepped back and tucked himself back in, straightening his clothes before he bent to retrieve her shorts. "Yes." He let the shorts dangle from his fingertip. "I would love to take you on a date."

Her heart tripped. Dammit. "A date?" That was maybe not the best idea if she wanted to keep from falling all the way in love with him.

He smiled. "Yes. A date. Dinner. Maybe a movie or something."

She grabbed her shorts and slid from the table, shimmying them on. "Are you going to at least call me for 'lunch' at your office before then?" It was out of place with his nice invitation. But it was a defensive move. He was not acting like the Nate she thought she knew, that she'd always known. The one who had no qualms about telling her she was too loud or too crude or too flirty or too...lots of things. The one who bickered with her. The one who bossed her and made her hot.

She could handle all of those guys.

"I'll think about it every day," he said, his eyes darkening slightly at the reminder about their last lunch. "But it's a crazy week. Since I've been gone, we've packed my schedule this week. Lots of surgeries, longer office hours. And I need to spend some time with Michael."

"He's fine, Nate," she felt compelled to say. "He was the one with the level head at the party. He was looking out for Shannon."

"I know." Nate ran a hand over his hair. "But we need to reconnect. I've been gone from him too."

She understood all of that. What she didn't understand was why she wanted so much to be one of the priorities that he wanted to reconnect with this week. How stupid. She wasn't even a girlfriend. She was a...fuck buddy. That he was going to take on a date.

"Say you'll go out with me next weekend."

"If I can spend the night." She had to keep this on a level she could understand and deal with.

He frowned slightly but nodded. "There's no way in hell I'll ever say no to having you in my bed, Emma."

The way that made his voice go lower got her all hot and bothered again. And the part of her that glommed on to the *ever* in his sentence, the one tiny word that made it sound like it could be a *for*ever thing, made her stomach hurt. He didn't mean that. It wasn't like this was going to last.

"Then I'll go," she said, trying to lighten her tone.

He hesitated, like there was something else to ask. But finally he said, "I'd better get Michael home."

She nodded. "Okay."

"I'll talk to you soon."

"I'll keep my phone on," she said, using the words he'd said to her so often.

He gave her one more intense look. "Do that."

She didn't reply and she hung back in the kitchen as Nate went to collect his son.

When she heard the front door shut, she let her shoulders slump.

Falling in love with Nate Sullivan was not a good idea.

Too bad she'd already done it.

"You didn't use condoms?" Isabelle asked Emma five days later.

Emma frowned at Isabelle. "Of course we used condoms. Eight of them."

There had been no warning. She hadn't felt sick, she hadn't lost her breakfast, she hadn't been so tired she could hardly function. These were all things she knew were common. She'd simply missed a period by a week. And then, yesterday and today, her jeans felt a little tight. She was bloated. What the hell was that?

But she knew what the hell could cause a missed period and bloating.

Nate Sullivan.

Emma slumped further into the couch and glared at the little pink line that had just changed her life.

There was a long pause. Isabelle sat forward on the couch. "You and Nate had sex *nine times* in one night?"

"Six times in one night," Emma told her. "And once at the studio. And one time in the kitchen. Eight times."

"But you're pregnant."

Emma squeezed her eyes shut and slid lower on the couch. "I know."

"Which means you used *seven* condoms."

Emma's eyes popped open. "I'm telling you that we used a condom *every* time, Iz. Every single time."

"Does he know how to put them on correctly?" Isabelle asked.

Emma snorted at that. "You kind of have to wonder, don't you? I'd give him a lesson, but it doesn't matter now."

Isabelle sat back. "Six times in one night is impressive."

It sure had been.

"You couldn't have missed once?"

"Nope."

"I can go get one more test."

Emma sat up and swung her legs over the side of the couch. She'd peed on three of the stupid sticks. They all showed the same damned thing.

"No. It's positive. I'm pregnant."

Isabelle stared at her. It was the first time Emma had said it out loud. "Wow," she said quietly.

Emma nodded. Wow was an understatement.

Isabelle got up and came to Emma. She took Emma's hands and pulled her to her feet, then wrapped her in a hug. "I'm happy for you, Em."

Emma laughed softly, hugging her back. "Happy? That's a nice word to use."

Isabelle squeezed her before stepping back. "It will be okay."

Emma nodded. "I know."

She did. She was financially stable. She was healthy. She had a great family. Of course, she was going to keep this from Conner for as long as possible. She might invite him to the kid's first birthday. By then he or she should be super cute and Conner wouldn't be able to be mad at her. But her sisters would be great and her mother would love being a grandma—as soon as she got over the shock of it being Emma that gave her the first grandchild. "Thank you."

"Are you going to tell him Saturday night?"

Saturday night was their date night. Their first date.

She hadn't seen him all week. He'd called her twice and texted once. One night on the phone she'd turned things around on him and talked *him* through an orgasm. That had been the sexiest thing she'd ever heard. Especially him groaning her name as he came. The next night they'd talked past midnight. It had started out as a sexy contest. He'd seemed determined to not get distracted like he had the night before. She was equally determined to do it all again. But they'd ended up laughing and talking about their first time and their first date and that led to talking about other firsts and other high school memories and then other memories in general.

Then there was his text. She'd opened it expecting an order. Or at least something hot. Instead he'd simply said, *I can't wait for Saturday night.*

She'd teared up.

That should have been her other indication that something was off with her hormones.

"I can't tell him Saturday. That's two days away. I can't keep it from him for two more days," she said to Isabelle. "And it's our first date. It's the first thing we've done together that's just sweet and romantic."

It might be silly, but she didn't want their first date to be accompanied by one of the biggest shocks of his life. And this baby would be, she had no doubt. She had wanted the date to be about…them dating. About maybe possibly seeing if they might want to start something more than a sex-only fling. Perhaps.

Becoming parents together was a bit beyond *maybe* getting serious.

"What are you going to do?"

"Tell him in a somewhat public place where he can't freak out but private enough that he can process it."

"You know I'm here for you. Whatever you need."

"How about carrying this baby for about nine months for me?"

"I would *help* with that if I could," Isabelle said.

"Or I'll handle the nine months and you do the labor and delivery part for me."

Isabelle grinned. "I might be busy that day."

"Uh-huh." Emma knew that Isabelle would absolutely be right by her bed throughout the whole thing, as would Amanda and Olivia. But Emma was going to have to do the hard work.

"And I think I'm also going to be busy the day you tell Conner," Isabelle added.

Emma groaned, then shook her head. "I can't even think about that right now. I have another guy to dread telling first."

Isabelle held out her phone. "Then do it."

Emma took the phone and punched speed dial four. "Hi, this is Emma Dixon. I need to make an appointment with Dr. Sullivan. Today. As late as possible."

CHAPTER
ELEVEN

"OUR LAST PATIENT is in exam room five."

Nate looked up from his computer to find Jeremy, the intern that was following him for the week while Dr. Miller was out, standing in his office doorway. "Last and patient are two of my favorite words right now."

It had been a hell of a week. He'd been slammed at work, at the office until late, in the OR early and trying to have dinner with Michael at least three of the nights since he'd returned from Chicago. He was pleased with how things had gone both at work and at home. Michael had opened up more about his relationship with Shannon and was still talking about college, and Nate felt confident that his son had his head on straight. Or as straight as it could be when there was a woman involved.

In fact, Michael was doing better than Nate.

Nate was a mess.

He missed Emma like crazy. He thought about her constantly. It was a completely anomaly. He never got too distracted over women. Ever.

He pushed back from his desk. The sooner he got this last

patient seen, the sooner he could get home. It was Thursday. One more day and it would finally be Saturday and he was taking Emma on a date.

He hadn't been this excited about a night out with someone since his high school prom. He was going to wine and dine her, take her out on the town, make her laugh and flirt with her, make her feel beautiful, spend an obscene amount of money on her and then take her home to bed and not let her leave until Monday morning.

And, though she didn't know it yet, the date was going to start early. He was picking her up for brunch Saturday morning. Screw waiting for Saturday. Who ever said a date had to be at night anyway?

"Who are we seeing?" he asked Jeremy as they turned toward room five. He knew this was a last minute call-in. He was supposed to be done by now, but he trusted Shelby, his receptionist and keeper of his schedule, to know when someone needed to get in quickly.

Jeremy flipped the top paper on his clipboard up to read what was underneath it. "Looks like a post-op pelvic fracture. Emma Dixon."

Nate's heart thumped hard in his chest and he tripped.

He stopped and looked at Jeremy. "Emma Dixon called in to see me today?"

Jeremy nodded. "Guess so."

Uh, huh. Nate felt a grin stretch his mouth. She couldn't wait to see him? That was awesome.

"Have you been in to talk to her yet?" Nate asked.

Jeremy had been doing some of the prep work on the follow-up patients, going through their post-op questionnaire, asking about their pain and therapy program and such.

"No, sorry. Mrs. Waverly took awhile. She had a lot of questions about her pain medications."

"No problem." Nate suspected that Emma was there in something skimpy with nothing underneath. Her hip was doing very well. He could attest to her improved range of motion and decreased pain levels personally. He knew what feel-good prescription she was after. What would she do when someone else sat in on this appointment? "After you," he told Jeremy, gesturing toward the door to room five.

"Miss Dixon?" Jeremy asked as he stepped through the door.

Nate was right behind him and saw her sit up straighter on the edge of the exam table in surprise. "Uh, yes."

Her eyes flickered to Nate. She gave him a questioning look and he simply smiled and leaned back against the counter across from where she sat. It was a challenge. Everything in him screamed to go to her. He'd missed her so much it shook him.

"I'm Dr. Jeremy Kelson. I'm working with Dr. Sullivan this week."

Emma raised an eyebrow. "How nice. A two for one deal for all of us *patients*, huh?"

Nate grinned behind Jeremy's back. The younger man didn't seem to pick up on her emphasis on patients. "Don't worry, Miss Dixon," Nate said. "Jeremy here is fully capable of handling any needs you have today."

Both of her eyebrows were up now. Then she looked back at Jeremy and got a calculating look on her face. Nate settled in to watch how she handled this. She would have fun punishing him for this, he was sure.

"Is that right, Dr. Kelson?" she asked. "You can do anything for me that Dr. Sullivan can do?"

"Certainly not everything," Jeremy said.

Nate smirked. The kid didn't even know all of the things Nate had done for Emma but Jeremy still knew he wasn't on the same level.

"But I'm happy to help however I can."

Emma gave a soft laugh and the devious look left her face. "That's great," she said. "Now that you mention it, Nate hasn't been as available as I'd like him to be. Can I have your personal number?"

Her words were flirtatious, but they lacked the usual playful tone and the mischievous twinkle in her eye was missing. Nate frowned. She didn't seem like herself.

She'd already surprised Nate. She was dressed in black silky yoga pants and a fitted hot pink T-shirt. She wore white tennis shoes and had her hair pulled back in a ponytail. It was the most dressed down she'd ever been in his office. When she came to see him she always dressed her signature look—short skirt or dress and heels with her hair down. To torture him, he knew.

But she looked amazing to him now. He wanted her. Badly.

And the idea that something was actually wrong, that something had taken the sass out of her, made his stomach clench.

"I, um—" Jeremy was patting his pockets like he'd lost something. "I don't have any...of my...uh, cards with me," he told her.

Emma's gaze met Nate's and she gave him a little smile that seemed almost sad. "That's okay, Dr. Kelson. I can't imagine needing anyone more than I need Dr. Sullivan right now."

Again, the words were sexy and Nate wanted there to be innuendo oozing from them—but it wasn't there. Something wasn't right. He loved hearing that she needed him, but he got the definite impression that the need wasn't a do-me-here-and-now-or-I'll-die need. It was a real, honest to goodness need.

And while his cock swelled at the idea of her needing him in the bedroom—or on the exam table in room five—something else welled up at the idea of her coming to him because something was really wrong.

"Jeremy," Nate said simply, his eyes locked on Emma.

"Yes, Dr. Sullivan?"

"Leave."

Jeremy turned and blinked at him. "What?"

"Leave. For the day. Go home." Nate had felt possessive toward Emma. Now a strong protective instinct reared up and he wanted to grab Jeremy by the back of his collar and physically remove him from the room so Nate could take care of her. Whatever she needed.

Jeremy looked incredibly confused, but he followed instructions. The door shut behind him five seconds later.

"What's wrong?" Nate went to her immediately.

"I'm—" Emma stopped and cleared her throat. "I—" She tried again. Then she pressed her lips together and shook her head.

Nate wrapped his arms around her and was relieved to feel hers slide around his waist. She rested her cheek against his chest. He lifted a hand, running it from the crown of her head down her back over and over.

Holding her felt good. She wasn't naked. She was more covered than usual when he was around, and it still felt damned good. Part of it was also because Emma was strong and confident and determined. Seeing her vulnerable tugged at his heart, but it also pleased him that she would let those walls down around him.

After several minutes, he said, "Tell me what's going on."

He hated that something might be upsetting her, but honestly? This was great. He wanted her to need him, to turn to him, to confide in him.

While he'd been in Chicago it had become clear to him that he wanted her, completely and exclusively. He'd called Rebecca and broken things off the first night he was away from Emma. Rebecca had taken it well. In fact, if he wasn't crazy about Emma he might have spent some time nursing a wounded ego over just how well Rebecca had taken it. But on their date he had planned to tell Emma that he wanted a relationship with her, all the bells and whistles, and that he wasn't about to share her with anyone else. Her days of changing guys like she changed shoes were over.

She pulled in a deep breath and sat back. She looked at him for a few seconds, as if debating how to say whatever it was.

"I have a question about my pelvis."

Nate straightened. She had a medical question? He'd been preparing to offer support for an emotional problem. Maybe a fight with a sister. Maybe something was up with her business. Maybe something that was going on with Dena. Hell, maybe even her brother finding out they'd slept together.

"What's up?"

"I'm healing well, right?"

"Yes. Things are progressing nicely."

"Is there anything that might...slow that down? Or even cause a problem? Set me back?"

He frowned. "Anything like what?"

"Anything," she repeated. "Is there *anything* that could happen to that part of my body that would cause a problem? Specifically to *that* part of my body?"

Nate crossed his arms. He had no idea what was going on, but he was her doctor. He'd answer her question. "At this point, other than another blow—a car accident, falling while skiing, something like that—there's nothing that's going to cause a problem."

"Nothing could happen *inside* of me in *that area* that would be problematic?"

"Emma, what the hell are you talking about?" Was she having an issue he should know about? His heart rate kicked up. There were, of course, things that could happen. There was an almost-zero chance of any of them being true for her, but she could have a cancerous tumor or an infection. "What's going on?"

"What if I gain weight?" she asked quickly. "If I put on some pounds, would that stress my pelvis? Cause pain or problems healing?"

He nodded, not sure if he felt relieved, but glad for a more specific concern he could address. "That could cause some pain. Depending on how much weight. A significant gain would stress all the bones and joints in your lower extremities. Why? Planning on going up a weight class?"

"I wasn't exactly *planning* on it, no," she muttered.

"Emma," he said, frustrated. "What's going on? You seem… off. And these are weird questions. Are you okay?"

She sighed. "Yes and no."

"Are you sick?"

"I'm pregnant."

Nate had no idea how long he stood there staring at her. Those two words rattled around in his brain but for several seconds he could have sworn she spoke them in Chinese, because his mind simply refused to make sense out of them. But eventually he'd replayed them so many times that the second one finally registered.

Pregnant.

He wet his lips, feeling the need to say *something* but completely unable to decide what it might be. He stepped back from her.

"Nate?" Emma finally asked. "Are you going to pass out? Because that will piss me off. *I* didn't get to pass out and I'm the one who is going to have to buy new jeans soon."

Finally he forced himself to speak. "You can't take your pain pills if you're pregnant."

She blinked at him. "*That's* going to be the first thing you say about this? That's your biggest concern?"

"As your doctor, that should be my concern."

"Uh, huh." She leaned closer from the edge of the table. "How about as the baby's father?"

He swallowed hard, feeling his throat threaten to close off. "You're sure?"

Her expression instantly changed to you've-got-to-be-fuck-ing-kidding-me. "Oh, good, I was hoping we'd get to have the you're-a-slut-so-how-can-you-be-sure-I'm-the-father conversation."

He looked at her, then sighed. She wasn't the type to not be sure. She also might enjoy men, but she enjoyed them one at a time. If she was sleeping with him—and she most definitely was —he was the only one.

Emma was pregnant. With his baby.

He shook his head, amazed. "Unbelievable. Three times. Three fucking times."

"What?"

"I've fallen for three women in my life and I got them all pregnant."

She stared at him "Seriously?"

"Yes. Stacie, Trisha, and now this baby."

Emma shook her head. "No, I mean…you've fallen for me?"

Not at all the way he'd planned to tell her. "Yes. And I got you pregnant." Maybe if he kept saying it eventually he'd believe it.

"I've fallen for you too," she said.

If his system was capable of any emotion beyond shock, he would have loved hearing that. "And you're pregnant."

"We used condoms," she said. "It's not like I planned this."

He nodded. "I know."

Her eyes narrowed. "And the condoms weren't from nineteen ninety-nine or something, right?"

He frowned. "Of course not." If nothing else, he had easily used up any condoms he'd bought fourteen years ago. He'd hardly been a monk.

"And you *do* know how to put them on correctly?"

She was such a smartass. He cocked one eyebrow. "Of course I know how to put them on."

"Well then, you could've told me that you have superhero sperm. Good Lord. That stuff should come with a warning label."

"What modern day, promiscuous woman doesn't have a birth control method?" he asked, the thought occurring to him.

"First of all, promiscuous is an exaggeration. So, thanks for that. Second of all, I have a birth control method. Condoms."

"Condoms are more effective when combined with another form of birth control."

She rolled her eyes. "No shit. That's like saying your locked door is more effective in not opening when you use three locks instead of just one. But guess what? Someone can still knock the damned thing down if they really want to."

"I don't have super strength sperm, Emma." Or did he? Hell, it sure seemed that way. "But why aren't you using something besides condoms?"

"Because I'm a modern woman who gets sick from every shot and pill she's ever tried and who recently had a bad incident with an IUD."

"You shouldn't have had sex with me then." Even as the words came out, he regretted them.

Her eyes narrowed. "I'm starting to think of some other reasons too." She slid off the exam table and pulled her purse strap up on her shoulder. "Tell you what. You process all of this —quietly and without saying stupid, insulting things to me— then give me a call when you've got your shit together and we'll talk." She started for the door.

"Emma—"

She turned. "Nate, stop," she said, holding her hand up. "I'm going to keep you from being an asshole right now by advising you to not talk. At all." She watched him carefully for a moment, then dropped her hand.

He made a decision right then and there. "You'll move in with me, behave, and take care of yourself."

"Not taking the not talking advice, huh?" she asked.

"We'll get married."

Her eyebrows rose. "Uh, no. And to the moving in thing."

She had to. It was that simple. He'd missed all of Michael's pregnancy, been robbed of two others. He *was* going to be there for this one. "You said you've fallen for me," he pointed out.

"But I didn't hit my head when I fell," she said. "Geez, Nate. You're overreacting. We've both known about this for about ten minutes. Let's just think. And talk. Later. Rationally." She was watching him with mild trepidation. "Maybe with other people around."

He could only imagine what he looked like. He could feel that his eyes were a little wild. He was definitely breathing fast. His heart was racing. He was very possibly having a panic attack.

A panic attack. Yes. That was exactly what this was. Panic was the perfect word.

"You *will* move in with me," he said firmly. "Your lifestyle and habits are unbecoming for a pregnant woman. *Any* woman but especially one pregnant with my child."

"Unbecoming? Could you sound more pompous?" she asked. "I'm going to go. Before you say something *really* stupid."

"But…" He struggled to find the right words to convince her that this was the right thing to do. He wanted this baby and he wanted *her*. He wouldn't lose them to her stupid pride. Her best friend had raised a daughter all on her own and he respected how difficult that must have been. But Emma didn't have to do it the hard way. "You don't know what you're doing," he said, hoping it sounded as reasonable out loud as it did in his head. "I'll help with everything. I'll *pay* for everything."

Emma's jaw clenched. Her cheeks were flushed and her breathing fast. Her eyes sparkled. She looked ready for battle.

But when she spoke, it was calm and even. "We're going to need to come up with a sign that I can give you when you need to chill the hell out. We'll call it the Asshole Alert, okay?" She turned and yanked the door open. "I will talk to you *later*."

Obviously it hadn't sounded as reasonable out loud. She was halfway down the hall when Nate finally snapped out of his I'm-totally-fucking-this-up daze. He stalked into the hallway. "Keep your phone on!" he called after her.

She held up one hand, with her middle finger extended. "Asshole alert!" she called back without turning.

💋

Emma managed to get to the parking garage before she started crying. And then she was pissed. She hadn't cried over a guy since Luke Carlson dumped her for Abi Potter in tenth grade. And Luke Carlson wasn't a jerk. He was a sweet guy who had taken her to see the second Harry Potter movie. She'd loved him for that alone.

Nate Sullivan, on the other hand, was a Grade-A jerk. And he had never taken her on a date.

He wanted to raise the baby with her because he didn't think she could *afford it*? Not because he wanted to be there, not because he had feelings for Emma, but because she didn't know what she was doing and didn't have as much money as he did.

He was so not worth crying over.

She turned the car for home, but had no intention of staying there long. She'd dressed down, way down, for the appointment with Nate. She'd wanted him to see that she was taking this seriously. But she was headed for home now—and her closet and her sexiest dress. She wasn't going to be serious about anything more tonight and, hell, she wasn't going to be able to wear the thing much longer. Better enjoy it while she could.

An hour later she was in a booth at Trudy's with her sisters, nursing a ginger ale.

Isabelle kept casting her worried looks. She didn't know how things had gone with Nate but Emma assumed it was easy to tell it had been a disaster. Olivia and Amanda were oblivious to anything being wrong. Amanda had been dancing with her fiancé, Ryan, and Olivia had been shooting pool with her buddy Cody and some of the other firemen she worked with every day.

Emma hadn't told them about the baby yet and she wasn't in the mood now.

She frowned at Isabelle and shook her head. Isabelle looked from Amanda to Olivia, then back to Emma. Emma frowned harder and shook her head again. Isabelle lifted an eyebrow and nodded. Emma slapped her hand down on the table. "Not now."

Amanda jumped in her seat and looked at Emma. "You okay?"

"Yes."

"No," Isabelle said at the same time.

"You're not okay?" Amanda asked Isabelle.

"I'm fine." Isabelle pinned Emma with a look. "How about you, Em?"

Emma shot back her drink. Ginger ale went down smoother than tequila. Which wasn't a point in its favor at the moment. "I'm going to dance."

She was not going to tell her sisters yet. She wasn't ready. She was still trying to process it all herself. She was *pregnant*. Something like that took some getting used to. Especially considering Amanda and Olivia didn't even know everything that had been going on with her and Nate.

She thought she should actually talk to Dena about it. Dena knew the panic, the disbelief and the pain that went along with being unexpectedly pregnant and the father being a dick.

But really, she just wanted to forget about it for a few minutes. Maybe an hour.

Her whole life was about to change. She got that on a cerebral level. It was taking time to sink in further than that.

She slid out of the booth and made a bee-line for the bunch of guys at the bar. They were doing shots and laughing and giving each other a hard time. Emma knew every single one of them. Had danced with nine out of ten of them. Had gone on an outside-of-Trudy's date with six of the ten. Had slept with two of the ten.

Fuck. Okay, the ways her life was going to change were starting to hit her.

She changed directions and headed instead for the only one of her brother's close friends who wasn't spoken for by one of her sisters.

Cody Madsen was a nice guy. A genuine, couldn't-be-a-dick if he tried, nice guy. He was not only her brother's best friend since college, he acted like an older brother to Olivia. He was also her boss. Emma knew Conner loved having Cody around to keep an eye on Olivia nearly twenty-four-seven and she had to admit that Cody treated Olivia very well.

She could use being treated well by a nice guy for an hour or so herself.

She walked up to the pool table where Ryan, Conner and Cody were playing.

Nate was noticeably absent.

She pushed that out of her mind. "Cody, dance with me."

All the guys turned to face her at once.

"We're in the middle of a game," Conner pointed out from where he was posed for his next shot.

Emma really wanted to dance with Cody. She looked around and spotted Kevin Campbell, another of the seemingly endless supply of hot paramedics that worked for St. Anthony's, sitting at a table nearby with Sam Bradford and Dooley Miller. She walked over to Kevin and put a hand on his shoulder.

"Kevin, would you take Cody's place at the pool table? I need him for a minute."

"Uh." Kevin glanced at the pool game. "I guess?"

"Thanks." She tugged him out of his seat—which was a feat considering the guy was an ex-NFL player. She pushed him toward the table and then took Cody's hand. "There you go, big brother," she said to Conner.

Cody didn't say anything as they made their way to the dance floor. He simply turned and took her in his arms, swaying with the music.

They danced for an entire song without talking. Emma felt her body relax and she rested her cheek against Cody's shoulder. He was like a big teddy bear. A good-looking, six-foot tall teddy bear with wide shoulders, a hard chest and a six-pack. Still, she felt content and comfortable and that was a huge thing at the moment. Content and comfortable were two things that seemed to be hard to find and she was afraid in the next several months —or eighteen years or so—they were going to be even more elusive. That much she did know about motherhood. And motherhood with Nate Sullivan in the picture? Comfortable wasn't going to be very common.

She made herself stop thinking about Nate and concentrated instead on the act of dancing with a guy she didn't want to sleep with. She didn't have to flirt or tease or act sexy. She also didn't have to worry about pulling back, looking into his eyes, and knowing that she was never going to get over him, no matter how much of ass he was.

Cody was safe.

The second song started and they kept swaying. Even though it was not a swaying-only song.

"You wanna talk about it?"

Cody's deep voice rumbled against her ear and she sighed. Did she? Kind of. But not with a sibling that would have all kinds of their own emotions about it. And not with Dena and not with any of the other guys and definitely not with Nate.

Cody was safe. She trusted that he would keep her confidence, and not try to give her any advice, and the first thing out of his mouth wouldn't be about Nate or Conner.

She looked up at him. "Something big has happened," she said as introduction.

He smiled. "Something good big or something bad big?"

Now that was a hell of a question. Her first instinct was to say "bad big" but she hesitated. Because it wasn't bad. It was complicated and inconvenient and confusing. But it wasn't bad. She felt her first real smile since seeing that initial pink line curl her lips. "Good big. Mostly. Maybe with a dash of this-is-going-to-get-messy."

Cody looked intrigued but he simply said, "Are you happy about it?"

Another good one. And this time her first instinct was to say yes. Which shocked her. Was she happy about it? It was a baby. A *baby*. With Nate. Things between them were messy but Nate was a fantastic father who could give her child everything. He needed a smack upside the head from time to time, but if she could have written down every trait she wanted in the father of her child, the list would have pointed right at Nate Sullivan.

And she was going to be a mom.

For a second, Emma couldn't take a deep breath. The idea of being someone's mother was…humbling. And terrifying. And exciting.

"I am happy about it," she finally said out loud. "I am."

"Then I'm happy for you," Cody said.

"Can I cut in?"

Emma turned to find Steve Jacobsen grinning at her. "Uh." She glanced up at Cody. "Not right now, Steve, okay?"

Steve shrugged. "I'll catch you later then."

He sauntered off and Emma tried to resume her conversation with Cody. "If I tell you my news can you keep it under wraps for awhile?"

Cody nodded. "Of course."

She needed to tell him about her and Nate spending time together first. Or maybe Olivia had mentioned that to him. "Did Olivia tell you that me and—"

"There you are!"

Emma looked at Mitch Bauman. "Hi, Mitch."

"You haven't been around lately. I've been waiting to tell you —I got tickets to see Maroon Five and I want to take you."

Emma stared at him. Mitch was asking her out. While she was dancing with another man. And pregnant with *another* man's baby. Of course, he didn't know that, but the strangeness of the situation hit her hard.

This was her life. She dated a lot, she flirted *a lot* and the men who knew her knew that she didn't get too serious and that she sometimes dated more than one guy at a time. If she was sleeping with someone, she was monogamous to that guy for the course of their relationship, however long or short it was, but if she was only dating someone, then she had no qualms about saying yes to more than one invitation at a time. That was more common than not. Her intimate relationships were not as extensive as everyone thought. There were a lot of assumptions out there and most of the guys she spent time with simply didn't bother to correct those assumptions. But she'd always been comfortable with knowing the truth about her relationships and not caring what everyone else thought.

Suddenly she cared.

A lot.

And just as suddenly, her stomach started to hurt. The "morning sickness" was hitting now?

Awesome.

"No, Mitch," she said, more forcefully than necessary. "I don't want to go to the concert with you."

Mitch looked surprised, then glanced at Cody.

She frowned. "And no I'm not dating Cody."

"I thought we had a good time when we went out last month," Mitch said.

That also hit her hard. They hadn't slept together, but they'd made out heavily. And Mitch hadn't asked her out again in a month. Sure, she hadn't been around as much the past two or three weeks, but she had a phone.

"Last month," she repeated. "Did it ever occur to you that I might have moved on since then? That things might have changed in that amount of time?"

Like everything. Everything had changed in the space of a few hours.

"I figured you were having fun," Mitch said. "I didn't realize there was a timeframe here."

And now she was officially sick. Sick of one guy after another, sick of none of them being quite right but ignoring the fact because what good would it do, sick of no one having any expectations of her or wanting more from her. She was capable of more, she was able to *be* more.

"Emma."

That deep firm voice made her suck in a quick breath as she pivoted.

Then there was this guy. The first one to have some expectations, to push her, to make her think, to make her work…the one who pissed her off the most.

"This is not a good time, Nate."

Except that it was. She wanted to be in *his* arms. She wanted him to tell her this was okay. She wanted him to not be a jerk and to *make* it okay. It was a very good time. She'd decided that she didn't want all these guys anymore, she didn't want to party anymore, she didn't want to be the last one anyone depended on. That was why she'd stayed friends with Dena. That was why she'd been there to watch Shannon grow up. Because they needed her.

She liked being needed, it turned out. She was even good at it some of the time.

All of that hit her as she stared at Nate. The guy who had gotten in too deep and too fast with her and had created a lasting bond with her whether he liked it or not.

"We need to talk," he told her.

Emotions rolled through her fast and hot. The kaleidoscope she felt when he was around seemed to be spinning too fast, the colors and sensations changing on top of one another, pushing each other out of the way, tumbling around until she felt dizzy and out of control.

"Not now. I need some time."

"Emma—"

Cody stepped forward, putting himself partway between them. "Everything okay?" He was looking at Nate as he said it, but there was a warning in his tone.

Cody was a nice guy, but he'd step in when needed and Emma knew he'd be on her side. At least initially.

"No, everything is not okay," Nate said, his frustration and tension clear. "I need Emma."

"She wants some time," Cody told him evenly, using her words.

"There is no time," Nate said, reaching for her. "Let's go."

"Hang on." This came from Mitch, who caught Nate's wrist before he touched Emma. "I think she said no."

Emma looked from Mitch to Nate to Cody to Nate. Cody was the nice guy who wanted nothing from her, Mitch was the guy who wanted almost nothing from her—a date to a concert and maybe a quickie before he dropped her off afterward—and Nate was the guy who wanted her to fricking marry him, move in with him and raise their baby as if they were a happy family rather than two people who just couldn't keep their mouths shut or their clothes on.

And that was worse than wanting nothing from her.

She wanted it to be real and it wasn't. It couldn't be. Not now. Yes, he'd said he'd fallen for her. Maybe that was even true. But this was the *start* of something. This was new. And now they were pregnant. And they'd never know if this start, this new thing, could have truly grown into something real and strong and lasting. Now they were bound together by their child, not by love or commitment to each other or a desire to be together no matter what.

She could have a life with Nate. *The* life with Nate. The one that would look, and maybe even feel, perfect. But deep down she would always wonder—was he there with her because he wanted to be or because he was a good guy who wanted to be a good father.

Nate jerked his hand away from Mitch. "This is between me and Emma." He focused that intense gaze on her and moved in closer. "We need to talk. We need to tell Conner. Together."

She moved back, stepping on Cody's foot but unable to even say she was sorry. "Conner? You're here because you're worried about Conner? You thought I was going to tell him without you and cause a huge problem for you?"

That was wonderful. Peachy even. Nate had come after her because he was afraid she was going to do something stupid. Not because he was concerned for her, not because he was excited—that was for sure—but because he didn't trust her.

"Aren't you going to smell my breath?" she asked. "I mean this is a bar, full of liquor and men, and I'm not exactly known for my pious ways. I've been here for over an hour, Nate. God knows what trouble I could have gotten into."

Nate's jaw clenched and his eyes narrowed.

"And how do you know I haven't already told Conner?" she asked, flinging her arms wide. Cody and Mitch both took a step back. "Everyone knows that I'm an open book. There's not much I think that doesn't come spilling out of my mouth. I think you've pointed that out a time or two."

"Emma," Nate said warningly. "Calm down."

And there was the bossy thing. It had been a turn on in the beginning but he'd been completely right—outside of the bedroom and over time, it got old.

"I'm tired of you telling me what to do," she said, planting her hands on her hips. "I don't want to talk, I'm not going to move in with you, I'm not going to marry you and I'm not going to tell my brother that I'm pregnant."

The last word, *the* word, hung in the air between them as she stared at Nate. She couldn't decipher the emotions in his eyes, but she could tell by the set of his mouth that he was pissed.

It was probably a good thing they were in public.

Public. Slowly she became aware that Nate was staring, with a combination of resignation and oh-fuck, at something behind her. She let her eyes close for a moment, bracing herself. It was a someone. When she opened them she made herself turn.

To face her brother.

"Emma," Conner said evenly, his expression hard, not revealing any specific emotion, "You need to go with Nate."

Dammit. Dammit, dammit, dammit.

She was causing a scene. The music was still loud and not *everyone* had noticed the little showdown in the middle of the dance floor but that also drove home an important realization—it wasn't uncommon for Emma to be in the midst of a scene at Trudy's. It was the shock-and-awe thing Nate had called her on. She liked the attention. She liked the spotlight. She liked stirring things up.

But she was twenty-eight years old. And on her way to being a mom.

She needed to grow up.

"Fine." She didn't know what else to say to Conner. She hadn't wanted him to find out yet. She wasn't ready for him to know. But…that was called a consequence.

Nate took her arm and steered her through the crowd before she could say or do anything else. She let him, only because she was suddenly tired. Tired of making the wrong call, tired of fighting with him, and tired of holding it together.

By the time they got to the hallway leading to the bathrooms, she'd decided to agree with whatever Nate said.

Until he actually said something.

"Is this why you won't marry me? Because you don't want to be monogamous?" He moved in close to her, pinning her against the wall with the tension emanating from his scowl. "Because like it or not, you will *not* be sleeping with anyone else."

Oh, he kept getting more and more charming with this. But the comment gave her a warm feeling at the same time. She was a mess. "Nate, on the list of four billion reasons I don't want to marry you, that's number two billion six hundred million and three."

"What's reason number one?"

She couldn't answer that. She would not admit that she couldn't look at a ring on her finger every day or hear someone call her Emma Sullivan and not think about how it wasn't real. And that if she had to live the life she wanted without the love she needed it would slowly eat her up inside. She had to face what *was* real. She and Nate could raise this baby into a wonderful human being. There would be love between the child and each of them and that would be enough.

It would have to be.

But she could not tell him that she didn't want to marry him because she only wanted him if he was truly in love with her. No. Hell, no.

"I don't like being bossed around."

He paused, searching her eyes. Then his gaze dropped to her mouth. "That's not entirely true."

The heat jumped up between them like a physical presence and she had to work to breathe normally.

"Knock it off." She squirmed, hoping he'd move back.

No luck.

He braced a hand on the wall near her ear. "I was an ass back at my office."

She breathed deep and nodded. "Yes, you were." He'd also been in shock, so she was inclined to give him some leeway.

"I'm sorry. And I'm very sorry if you think that my reaction had anything to do with Trisha. I know you won't do anything to hurt this baby."

She braved meeting his gaze directly and frowned. "That's not what I was thinking." She narrowed her eyes. "I know that you know I'm nothing like her."

That hadn't been her problem at all. Stacie and Trisha had both hurt him badly and with the jolt of hearing about another unplanned pregnancy, maybe she should have expected him to worry that she'd disappear on him...or something worse.

But she trusted that he knew her.

"I do know you're nothing like her. Like either of them." He stroked the back of his fingers down her cheek.

She fought to not turn her face into his touch. "I figure there would be a private investigator here right now if you thought I was going to do something stupid."

He smiled and everything in her went warmer and softer. Dammit.

"You're absolutely right about that."

"Nate?" she said softly.

"Yeah?"

"If I ever find out that you put a PI on me, I will slash his tires and put so many laxatives in his coffee he won't be able to leave the house for a week. Then I'll deal with *you*. Got it?"

He grinned. "Got it."

Her phone rang just in time to keep her from kissing him.

His did too.

They met each other's eyes as he stepped back and they both fumbled for their phones.

"Hello?" Emma answered.

"Michael?" she heard Nate say.

"Emma, you have to come down here." It was Shannon. "I'm at the police station."

"Again?" Emma asked already moving toward the door. She felt Nate right behind her.

"I'm sorry. It was stupid. There was this party and—"

"Dammit, Shannon," Emma cut in. "Enough already. Enough with the parties and crappy decisions. Cut Ashley and Carrie loose. You're better than this."

"No. It wasn't like that. There was this guy and…" The music in the main room of Trudy's was loud and Emma lost part of Shannon's story.

"Were Ashley and Carrie at the party?" Emma asked over the noise around her.

"Yes, but…"

Again she lost the rest of what Shannon was saying.

She hurried past her sisters and Conner, ignoring their concerned looks and attempts to get her to stop. She jammed a finger in her ear as she neared the door in time to hear, "Michael's in the hospital."

She shoved the door open, stepping out into the quiet night. "What?" she demanded, continuing to stalk toward her car.

"Michael's in the hospital."

"What for?"

"He got in a fight."

Emma swung around to find Nate. He was still near the door. His phone was against his ear, his other hand curled into a fist. "What are you talking about?" she hissed to Shannon. That didn't sound like Michael at all. "A fight? What happened?"

"No. It was this one guy. He was…acting weird and when we tried to leave he wouldn't let us. Me. He didn't want me to go."

"Do you know him?" Emma asked.

"No."

"Who's party?"

Shannon paused. "Brooke's."

Of course. Brooke had introduced Shannon to Ashley and Carrie. "You took Michael to this party too?" How did Shannon have so many party friends? Emma had known Brooke when she was still young enough to go to the park with them and beg Emma to push her higher in the swing. It had never been high enough for that kid. And it sounded like she was always pushing it now too.

Emma could relate.

It was so clear in that moment, that she had to stop and put a hand over her tight chest. Shannon was hanging out with girls like Emma. Like Emma had been. Like she still was in many ways.

"The party was my idea," Shannon confessed. "But I didn't know something like this would happen."

"What happened exactly?" She could freak out later. Right now she needed to help Shannon and Michael. And Nate.

He looked like he was about to break something. Or break in two himself.

She wanted to go to him, to help, to say something that

would make him feel better, but she had to get the whole story. And figure out what she could possibly say right now.

"This guy was hitting on me. He didn't care that I was with Michael. We tried to leave and he blocked the door. He shoved Michael back and said that I couldn't leave."

Shannon was talking too fast and it was obvious she was trying to talk past the tears and Emma wavered for a moment. Shannon reminded her of Isabelle in a lot of ways.

Emma had always been the leader, the first one to jump into something, the first one to say "let's do it". But Isabelle was always right beside her and often the one who first said "I have an idea". Isabelle was totally an instigator, but Emma was the action girl, the one to get it done, the one to take the risk. Isabelle went along because she trusted Emma. She knew that nothing bad would happen—or if it did, it would happen to Emma first and she'd clean up the mess.

She'd been doing that for Shannon her whole life. Emma was still the do-er. When Shannon wanted to try horseback riding, Emma found a stable and flirted her way into five free lessons for Shannon. When Shannon wanted a kitten for her birthday, Emma had found one and then proceeded to take care of it for the next ten years because Dena was horribly allergic. When Shannon had wanted to learn to drive a stick shift, Emma had taken her to an empty parking lot and when Shannon crashed through the fence by the building, Emma had taken the blame and flirted her way out of the ticket. That had led to four great dates with the cop.

Emma shook her head. The point was, Shannon had ideas and Emma made them happen...and cleaned up the messes that resulted. Shannon was now old enough to make some of her ideas happen on her own. But she wasn't good at cleaning up. Or even caring that she might make a mess in the first place.

Fuck. Emma had screwed this all up.

"What happened then?" Emma asked, feeling weighted down and very, very tired all of a sudden.

"The guy grabbed me and Michael lost it. He punched the guy but then three of his friends jumped in. Michael's really hurt, Emma."

She paused and Emma could hear her sniffling.

"He was unconscious when I last saw him, but they wouldn't let me go with him."

"Okay. I'll let you know what I find out about Michael," Emma told her.

"Wait. Are you coming to get me?"

"No, honey I'm not." Emma braced herself against the guilt. It wasn't as strong as she'd expected. "You're going to have to call your mom."

Dena wasn't great at cleaning up messes either, but why would she be? Emma had always done it.

"But Emma—"

"Sorry sweetie." Emma started to hang up, but she quickly added, "I love you." *Then* she hung up.

She went to Nate. He'd hung up a couple minutes before and was standing under the eaves of Trudy's, simply breathing.

"You okay?" she asked. Stupid question. Really, really stupid question.

"I assume you know what's going on?"

"How is he?"

"Still unconscious."

That wasn't good. "That wasn't him on the phone?"

"It was Shane."

She was relieved. Hearing the story from a friend and teammate might make it easier.

"He broke up the party?"

"Yes, and accompanied Michael to the hospital."

She reached out and gripped his arm. "Let's go."

Nate didn't say anything but let her take his hand and pull him off the sidewalk and into the parking lot. They were literally across the street from St. Anthony's, so she slipped her hand in his and headed across the loose gravel of the parking lot. At the curb, they paused, then ran across the four lanes of traffic and over the grassy lawn of the hospital until they got to the sliding doors of the emergency room.

Nate was, of course, well known in the department and the receptionist jumped from her seat the moment she saw him.

"In here, Dr. Sullivan."

He started after her, his hand slipping from Emma's. She missed his touch immediately. She crossed her arms and watched him go. When he disappeared through the inner sliding doors, she turned to the receptionist. Emma knew Lisa. She was a regular at Trudy's.

"How's Michael?"

Lisa knew that Emma wasn't family but she still said, "He'll be okay. He's waking up now."

Emma nearly wilted with relief. "I'll be..." She turned in a full circle. "Over here," she finally said, pointing at the benches along the far wall of the waiting room.

Lisa nodded. "I'll let him know."

CHAPTER
TWELVE

HE COULDN'T BELIEVE she was still here. Nate stopped in the doorway of the ER waiting room and studied her. Emma's head rested on the wall behind the bench, her eyes were shut and she was breathing steadily.

"How is he?"

But she wasn't asleep.

He crossed the room and sat next to her. He'd been in with Michael and the doctors for the past forty minutes. He was going to be sore and the black eye would last for awhile, but Michael was going to be fine. Still, having Emma here with him felt good. He leaned back, copying her posture, his head against the wall. He reached for her hand and linked their fingers.

"Fine. Resting. He can go home tomorrow."

"Thank God."

"Definitely."

They sat for a few seconds without talking.

"I've been thinking," Emma finally said.

"Uh, oh."

She opened her eyes and rolled her head to look at him. "No, you'll like this." She swallowed. "I'll move in. I'll live with you. We'll both be there for the baby."

He frowned and sat up. "What?"

"It's the right thing. And..." She swallowed again. "You should have full custody."

He felt like she'd slapped him. "If we're married, there's no question about custody. We share it."

"About that. I'll move in. But we need separate rooms and...I won't marry you."

He worked on not gripping her hand too tightly. This had been a long ass day. First work, then her news about the baby, then Michael and now this. He was going to crumble into about a thousand pieces. As soon as they got one thing straight. "There is no way that you are sleeping in my house and not sleeping in my bed."

"We can have sex," she said agreeably. "We just need our own space...and stuff."

That made complete sense. "No."

She sighed. "And we're back to this."

"As long as you're going to say ridiculous stuff, yes."

"Ah, a yes."

He worked on keeping cool. They couldn't both lose their minds and apparently right now was Emma's turn. "You're the one who should be saying yes. As in, 'yes Nate I will marry you'."

She didn't say anything at all.

Finally he sighed. "What's going on?"

"It's a bad reason to get married."

"Having a baby together?" he clarified. "Bringing a child into the world is a bad reason to get married?"

"Yes."

"Then marry me for my money."

"This isn't funny, Nate."

He turned to her. "I'm not joking. I don't care why you do it, as long as you do it."

She looked so sad, he wanted to pull her onto his lap and hug her. Finally she said quietly, "But I do care why."

"Em—"

"Look, Nate," she said, pulling her hand from his and pivoting on the bench and tucking her foot up underneath her. "I'll live with you because this baby needs you. The kid you raised all by yourself is amazing. He's smart and sweet and funny and now with Shannon…he takes care of her. He stepped in to save her tonight. He put himself in danger for her. The kid I helped raise, on the other hand," she said, regret clear in her tone, "got too big for her britches and got mouthy—don't know where she could have gotten *that* from—and because of it, her boyfriend is now in the hospital. Tough choice on who's the better parent."

They sat in silence for a long moment. A million thoughts tripped through his mind. He wanted her. He wanted this baby. He was excited—down underneath the fatigue and shock—that this woman was carrying his baby.

But Emma Dixon was one of the most stubborn people he'd ever met.

It was one of the things he loved about her.

"Would it make you feel better if I told you we could break up if it didn't work?" Because it *would* work. He'd make sure of it. "People have kids together but hate each other all the time."

She shook her head. "But we won't. No matter what happens, we'll be there for our kid and that means we'll get along and we'll figure things out."

He couldn't believe it. Talking about how they could reserve the right to break up made him more and more positive that he was in love with her. "You'd stay?"

"As long as it was what was best for my kid. And you'll always be what's best for my kid, Nate."

She was a fighter. Where Stacie had taken the easy way, Emma was assuring him she'd do whatever it took. And where

Trisha had done everything to *make* things easy, Emma was ready to tough it out.

Nate reached over and took her hand. "Emma, if this baby is a girl, I hope she's exactly like you and Shannon. Smart, strong, sure of herself, beautiful. I want her to say what she thinks. I know that it might get her into trouble sometimes, but if she's anything like you, then she'll have a ton of people who love her and who will back her up. So I won't have to worry." He paused. "I still will of course, but I won't need to."

Emma was staring at him like she'd never seen him before.

"What?"

"It's amazing," she said.

"What is?"

"Sometimes you open your mouth and it makes me nuts— like I want to smack you. Sometimes you open your mouth and it makes me hot—like I want to strip you down."

Nate felt heat and need streak through him. He started to lean in, but she kept going.

"But sometimes, like now, I don't know what I'm feeling or what I should do."

He freaking loved that. "Sorry."

"No you're not."

"No, I'm not."

She licked her lips and took a deep breath. "I have something to say and I have no idea what you're going to feel or do about it."

"I might be at my quota of hearing strange things from you today."

She nodded. "You might be right." She sat back. "You tell me when you're ready to hear this."

She stood and grabbed her purse.

"Hey, where are you going?"

"Home."

"I thought you had something to say."

"I thought you didn't want to hear it."

"I didn't say that."

She stood, watching him, her hand on her hip. "Well, yes or no? We both know which of those two words you like best."

He wasn't sure about this. Not much he'd heard today would be chalked up as good news.

Regarding the woman in front of him, he immediately adjusted that thought though. She was gorgeous. Trim, tight and sassy. And she was going to get big and round. With *his* baby.

And she would still be sassy.

The sudden urge to pull her into his lap gripped him hard.

She was going to make him a dad again. Boy or girl, this child was going to have a mom who was strong and independent and willing to do whatever was needed to make the kid happy and safe. Maybe not every choice with Shannon had been the right one, but Emma had been there, making choices. That mattered.

And he definitely wanted to pull her into his lap.

"Yes, Emma. I want to hear this."

She cocked an eyebrow. "You sure? It's big."

He dropped his gaze to her stomach, then moved it back to her eyes. Her cheeks got a little pink. He smiled a smile he knew would drive her crazy. It was a smile that said "I know you". He did too—what made her crazy in bed and what made her just plain crazy.

But all he said out loud was, "I think I can handle it."

She shrugged. "Here it is. You want to marry me because of the controlling thing you can't seem to help. If I'm married to you, everything mingled, then you get to make sure that I do things the way you think I should, and that I don't do anything stupid. But I can't do that, Nate. When it involves clits and cocks, I'm all about you getting bossy."

Nate shifted on the bench and glanced around. The room was empty and Lisa was the only one at the reception desk and guaranteed she'd heard more interesting things than this.

"But," Emma went on. "When it comes to my life and my

child, it's not gonna work. It made me nuts always biting my lip when Dena made decisions about Shannon and when you got all riled up about Shannon and Michael, I couldn't sit back. I jumped into the truck so that I could be involved in what happened. So, with my own son or daughter, I don't see me sitting back and letting you run the show."

Nate leaned forward, resting his forearms on his knees. "I don't intend to be a single parent again, Emma. I want you involved. I'll insist on it."

"See, there. That," she said pointing at him. "Insisting and stuff. No, Nate, I can't do it."

"But we are going to do this *together*," he said. "I am going to have a say."

"Yes, but if we're not married then I have…" She trailed off. Then shook her head and lifted her chin.

"An out," he filled in, his heart turning over. He'd known the controlling asshole thing was going to come back to bite him. "If we're not married and we have separate rooms, then you think you have an out. A way of keeping space between us and a way of exerting your own control over situations."

He rose from the bench and she took a step back.

"But you know what I think?" he asked her.

She swallowed hard.

"I think it's your way of keeping your distance. You're trying not to get too close because you're afraid you'll never want to leave." He took another step forward and caught her arm before she stepped back. "But, Emma, you never have to leave. And you're right about one thing—once you're mine, I'll never let you go."

She thought he was going to kiss her. He could see it in her eyes.

He loved surprising her.

So he kissed her on the forehead and headed for Michael's room.

Emma wasn't sure she'd ever actually trudged anywhere in her life. But she most definitely trudged up the front walk to her condo after the Longest. Day. Ever.

As she neared the steps she saw someone sitting at the top. For a moment she thought it was Nate and her heart leapt. Then she realized there was no way he was sitting on her front porch. For one, Michael wasn't being dismissed until tomorrow—which meant Nate wouldn't be leaving St. A's until tomorrow. For another, Nate was going to let her stew.

And it was probably going to work. He was going to wear her down. He was going to make her come to him. He was going to make her admit that she wanted him. Just like in Carl-Mart.

All thoughts of Nate were obliterated as she came to the bottom of the steps.

It was her brother.

Of course it was.

"Hey."

She sighed. "Hey."

"Michael okay?"

"Shane told you?"

"Yep."

"He's going to be fine. He's going home tomorrow."

"Great. How's Shannon?"

Emma climbed the steps and sat next to Conner. "I don't know. I told her to call her mom."

"Wow." Conner knew that was unusual.

"Yeah."

They sat quietly for a few minutes.

Eventually, though, Conner broke the silence. "You know that the best way to avoid getting pregnant with Nate is to not have sex with Nate."

"Oh, good. You're going to be supportive and comforting,"

she said dryly. "I was afraid you'd be sarcastic and nasty about this."

He sighed. "Sorry, okay. I can be supportive and comforting. Are *you* okay?"

And the tears started.

She felt Conner's arm go around her shoulders and he pulled her close. "Hey, now. Come on, Em. It's not so bad."

She sniffed. "You sure about that? You do realize this means I'm going to have a *baby*. I'll be in charge of someone else's life, *responsible*, and stuff."

He chuckled. "I'm not saying that it's not going to be amusing."

She elbowed him and he squeezed her.

"You're not mad?" she finally asked.

"I am," Conner said. "My friends don't listen worth a shit."

She snorted.

"But..." He trailed off like he wasn't sure he should go on.

"But what?" She looked over at him.

"Nate?" Conner asked. "I honestly never saw that one coming."

Because her brother was apparently stupid about undercurrents and foreplay.

"I mean, you're always at each other's throats."

"Well, we decided to go at each other's something else for a change."

There was a beat of silence before Conner groaned. "*Why* do you do that to me?"

"Come on, that was too easy." She was starting to feel better already.

"Now what?" Conner asked after a moment.

Great question. "I'm thinking cheddar cheese popcorn."

He nodded. "And what about Nate?"

"Nate can get his own popcorn."

"I knew you were going to stay that." Conner sighed. "What's happening with you and Nate?"

"He thinks we should get married."

"You don't agree?"

This was her brother. The last person on earth who wanted to know about her sex life. Yet, there was something about sitting with him in the dark, his arm around her, teasing and laughing —and *not* yelling, thank goodness—that made her want to spill her guts.

Or maybe she just couldn't keep it in anymore.

"I can't marry him, because I'm in love with him."

Conner seemed to think about her words, then groaned and dropped his forehead to her shoulder. "This is a girl thing, Em. Don't make me do girl things."

She shrugged, bumping his head. "This is not a girl thing. This is a…me thing."

He sighed. "I don't get it. If you're in love with him, why can't you marry him?"

"Because he doesn't love me."

"How could he not love you?"

She snorted again. "That gets you a few more supportive points. But…I think he might have been starting to."

Conner shook his head. "That's great. Right?"

She knew he had no idea if he was right or not. "No, it's not."

Conner sighed.

"He might have been starting to, but," she paused and swallowed. "I think he's going to be excited about this baby once it all sinks in."

"Which is…great?" Conner asked carefully.

She nodded, smiling in spite of herself. "That part is great. But now neither of us will ever know what could have happened. The baby will be the main reason he's with me and so I'll never know if he loves me or…if he loves his baby's mother."

Conner looked at her. "I'm getting a headache."

"You know, someday you might want to know a thing or two about being in love."

"I already love five women," he said. "That's more than enough."

Emma shook her head. He often said that. The five women in his life were his four sisters and his mom. He claimed they'd taught him all about living with women—and that he didn't want to ever do it again.

"Shut up."

Again a few minutes passed without words.

Finally, Conner asked, "You really love him?"

"I really do."

"You do realize that you won't get away with anything with Nate, right? I mean, the more I think about it, the more I like that you're going to be with Nate. But he's going to expect more from you than the other guys, I'd guess."

"What does that mean?" She felt offended but wasn't exactly sure why.

"You know what I mean. You have men wrapped around all of your fingers *and* your toes. And whenever you're feeling ignored or unappreciated, you reel one of them in, flirt him up, and bask in his attention for awhile. But they are content to buy you a drink or dinner, compliment you, make you laugh. And you're satisfied with that too."

She shifted on the step, wondering when her brother had gotten insightful. "And Nate won't compliment me?" she asked lightly. "You're right, I might have to rethink this."

"Nate's an intense guy," Conner said. "And he's got...depth. You know? He's going to expect you to share things with him, to talk to him about things that matter, to spend time with him in your sweatpants and bare feet instead of your short skirts and high heels."

Tears stung her eyes and she had to blink to keep them from rolling again. She wanted that. All of that. She wanted to be able to be un-put-together with Nate and know he'd still want her. It was scary to think about letting Nate that close, but she knew Conner was right—

Nate had layers and he was going to want to know all of hers. He was going to expect her to be vulnerable with him and to bare herself to him.

And she knew she'd be totally safe doing that.

Unlike all the guys in the past, the flirtations at Trudy's, even the ones that lasted a few weeks, no one had asked more of her. And she had more to give.

"He's demanding alright," she agreed with her brother.

"You love attention," Conner said. "You love being the Queen bee, the star, right?"

She nodded. That was no secret. "Settling down with one guy seems stupid, doesn't it?"

"Oh, I think you're going to find that being the center of Nate's attention is a fairly…potent place to be."

Potent was a weird word for her brother to use but, it fit. And it was an echo of what she'd thought a few days ago when she'd decided to follow the kids to the party at the river. Being the center of Nate's universe had been an intense—but safe and comforting—place for Michael to be. Emma wanted that for her child. That assurance that someone would do absolutely anything for him or her.

She wanted it for herself too.

"I won't miss my male harem?" she joked. She wouldn't. Nate was enough.

"I think you're going to feel like most of the receivers in the amateur football league."

Emma rolled her eyes, but couldn't help her smile. "How's that?"

"That once Nate's on you, that's where all your attention and energy is for the rest of the game."

Emma burst out laughing. "But those guys are trying to stay *away* from him. If those guys take their attention away from him, he'll knock them on their ass."

Conner grinned. "It's an analogy. When Nate's around and concentrating on *you*, I don't think you'll be able to put your attention anywhere else."

He, surprisingly, had a point. But she couldn't admit that to him. She elbowed him in the side. "Sounds like you're half in love with Nate yourself."

"I love having him on my side," Conner said sincerely.

"That means you're okay with me being in love with him?"

"Hell no. That's still weird."

She laughed and shook her head.

"But you're going to say yes to his proposal right?"

"You just don't want to have to be my Lamaze coach."

"I am *not* going to be your Lamaze coach. No matter what," he said firmly. "But, yeah, you won't need me. You're Nate's handful now."

"See, you act like you don't want your sisters hooking up with your friends, but they're taking us off your hands one by one. It's not all bad."

"Don't think I don't remind myself of that every time Ryan or Shane says something about getting lucky or being up all night or getting their off-the-field workouts."

Oh, she really hoped Nate would say inappropriate things about her that would drive Conner crazy too.

"Listen," Conner finally said. "Not that I'm surprised, but you're making this way more complicated than it needs to be. If you love him and want to be with him, then be with him."

"But I want…it all. I want him proposing because he can't live without me, not because I'm pregnant."

"Well, Em," Conner said, putting a hand on her knee and pushing himself up off the step. "You can't have it that way. There's no changing how this is going down. You have to decide what you're going to do now."

He was right.

"I just wish I could know what could have been."

Conner laughed. He stood on the front walk facing her. "You can never know what could have been. What if you'd turned right instead of left? What if you'd had chicken salad for lunch instead of a BLT? What if it rained today instead of being sunny? There are a billion what-ifs and could-have-beens every day, Em."

"So you think I should marry Nate."

"I think you should stop comparing your chicken salad to the BLT and make the chicken salad the best you've ever had."

She stared at her brother. "What?"

"There are choices every day and once you make one, you can't go back and see how the other one would have turned out instead. You're pregnant with Nate and he wants to marry you. You can't go back and see how it would have been without the baby. You're having the chicken salad, whether you now think the BLT would have been better or not."

She hadn't smelled liquor on his breath but... "Have you been drinking?"

"Nope."

"Hanging out with Dooley Miller?" Doug Miller—known to everyone as Dooley—was another paramedic Conner worked with at St. Anthony's. He was famous for his strange but surprisingly sage advice and analogies.

Conner grinned. "A little of that."

"It shows."

"Thanks."

She took a deep breath. He was right again. "The thing is, I think this might be the best chicken salad I've ever had already."

"Then who cares if the BLT might have been better. It's fucking awesome chicken salad. Enjoy it."

She looked at him, amazed that her brother was giving her relationship advice—good relationship advice—and that he was essentially telling her she should marry Nate.

"Okay, thanks."

"And," Conner said, digging his car keys out of his pocket. "I wouldn't worry too much about him loving you, Em,"

"Why's that?"

"Because if he doesn't now, it'll take him about ten minutes of living with you to wonder how he ever lived without you."

Emma's jaw dropped as she watched Conner saunter toward his car.

Her shock faded as he opened his door.

"When are you going to show this secret sweet, romantic side to a real girl?" she called after him.

"A real girl?"

"A non-sister girl?"

He laughed. "How about when Elvis can sing at my wedding?" He leaned over the top of the car. "And impersonators don't count."

Dammit. She knew a guy who did an awesome rendition of "Burning Love."

"You're missing out," she told him.

"On Elvis?"

"On love."

"What do you know about it? You had to get knocked up to get a guy to marry you."

"Hey!"

But he was laughing and slamming his door shut and starting the car by the time she thought about getting up off the step so she could smack him.

Oh, yeah. She couldn't wait to see Conner fall in love.

"Whoa."

Michael came into the kitchen to find takeout containers from not one, but three of his favorite restaurants.

"Hoping we could hang out for a while," Nate said as Michael took in the fact that his father was letting him eat hot wings, manicotti and eggrolls in the same meal.

"Did I do something wrong or did you?" Michael asked,

sliding up on one of the stools that lined the marble countertop between the kitchen and the informal eating area.

Nate handed Michael a root beer.

"Ah, you did," Michael concluded.

Nate routinely lectured his son about cutting back on the soda. So, yeah, it was clear that he was going to be the one confessing. But he didn't like thinking about it as something he'd done *wrong*.

He and Emma were going to have a baby. That just didn't feel wrong.

"I have something to tell you," Nate said.

"Is it about Emma?" Michael asked around a mouthful of spicy chicken.

Nate looked at him in surprise. "Yes."

"You're mad because Shannon keeps calling her to help us."

"I do wish you and I could have worked some of this out between us," Nate admitted. "But—" Was he mad about Emma's involvement? How could he be? Because of it, he was in love with an amazing woman and about to be a father again.

"I'm not mad," he finally said.

"Okay, what's up?"

Nate waited for Michael to dish his pasta up and worked on not wrinkling his nose as Michael added chicken wings to his plate and the buffalo sauce mixed with the marinara.

"Emma and I are…seeing each other."

Damn, that sounded stupid. And inaccurate. In fact, he hadn't seen her in two days.

"Really? That's awesome."

"Yeah?"

"Of course. Emma's great. Just a little surprised."

Nate nodded. "Us too."

"Well good. Were you worried about how I'd take it or something?"

"No," Nate said. He knew his son liked Emma. He wouldn't

have been concerned at all about Michael's reaction if that had been all the news. "Not that part."

"There's something else?" Michael looked at Nate with interest. "You okay?"

Nate took a deep breath. Things were great. But he hoped Michael would feel the same way. "Having you was the best thing that ever happened to me," Nate started. "I know it wasn't perfect, I know it was tough sometimes, but I wouldn't have traded it for anything."

Michael's eyes widened and Nate started to assure him that he wasn't dying or anything.

But before he could say anything, Michael asked, "Is Emma pregnant?"

Nate's eyes went wider than Michael's had. "How did you—"

Michael burst into laughter. He shoved his plate back and laughed. And laughed and laughed and laughed.

Nate scowled at his son, but when Michael had to wipe a tear away, Nate felt his mouth curve. And when Michael had to get off his stool and bend over, bracing his hands on his knees to catch his breath, Nate freely grinned.

Michael looked up, shaking his head.

"Dad, that is the best thing I've ever heard. And yes, you can raid my condom stash anytime."

Nate felt his face get hot and Michael looked at him quizzically.

"What?" Michael asked.

"We used condoms," Nate said sheepishly.

Michael snorted again. "Are you using them right?"

Nate Sullivan had *never* blushed in his life. Until his teenage son accused him of not knowing how to use condoms.

Michael climbed back onto his stool and took a huge bite of pasta, shaking his head. "This is the best thing ever."

"So you're okay with this?" Nate asked.

"Totally okay."

"And you know this isn't condoning—"

"Dad, I got it covered. I really do." Michael put his fork down and leaned in. "I don't want to be a dad yet and I want to go to college. My computer business might take off and it might not, but I do want to go."

"Because Shannon's going?" Nate asked. Though he wasn't as bothered by the girl's influence on his son as he had been a few weeks ago. Shannon made Michael happy and vice versa. That was really all Nate could have asked for.

"Partly," Michael admitted. "I do want to go where she goes. See where this relationship can go. And we both want to stay closer to home." He took a sip of root beer and gave his dad a smile. "Especially now that I'm going to have a little brother or sister."

The words hit Nate and he had to swallow hard past the sudden lump in his throat.

"I'm glad to hear that," he told Michael sincerely. Then he coughed and said lightly, "And I'll be sure you do plenty of two a.m. feedings, just to keep you sure that you're not ready for the dad thing."

Michael chuckled and chewed his pasta.

Nate chewed his bottom lip. Finally he said, "There's one more thing."

"Well, I'm loving this whole conversation so far," Michael said. "Bring it on."

"I need your advice."

"You need *my* advice? About what?"

"How to get Emma to marry me."

Michael's eyes went wide. "I assume you tried asking her?"

"Yes."

Michael whistled. "And she said no?"

"More or less." Okay, definitely more. "Can you help me?" he asked. "I need something big and over the top and public."

Michael nodded. "Shannon would also be helpful. She knows Emma really well."

Nate smiled. "As long as we're not talking about *your* proposal and wedding, Shannon is welcome."

"This is like Christmas and my birthday all rolled into one," Michael announced.

"How so?"

"You're in love and having a baby with the one person in the world who tells you no."

Yeah, it's fantastic, Nate thought dryly.

But…it really was fantastic.

She was going to stand him up for their date.

Emma so wanted to go on a romantic date with Nate. She wanted this first date.

But she also wanted candlelight and sweet talk…not talk about what flowers they should have at their wedding and how tall their white picket fence should be.

So, she was going to stand him up.

Which would also accomplish showing Nate that pregnant or not, he still wasn't the boss of her.

Emma turned her phone off, put her yoga pants on and settled onto the couch for a marathon of season one of *Hart of Dixie.*

Twenty-five minutes in, she turned her phone back on.

Reading sexy texts wouldn't hurt anything. And if his texts got a bit demanding and desperate—that wouldn't be so bad either. Besides, she wasn't intending to answer any of them.

Probably.

Fifty-two minutes later, she was through the first episode and was growing exceedingly irritated by the lack of texts from the man who said he wanted to marry her.

It was three p.m. Twenty-two and a half hours after she'd told Nate they were going to be joined by another life for the rest of *their* lives. And he wasn't even texting her?

She paced the living room through the first half of the second episode, then decided if she wasn't going to lounge or wallow she should try to be productive. She dusted the living room, including taking all the books off the shelf instead of running the dusting cloth around the books like usual.

Episode three started and she turned up the TV volume so she could hear it in the kitchen while she scrubbed the sink.

This sucked.

She hated cleaning.

She glanced at the clock. She still had plenty of time to get ready and show up at the restaurant.

First dates shouldn't involve picking out baby names. But she wanted to see Nate.

Dammit.

She threw the sponge down and started for the living room and her phone. She was going to text him. Something simple, something ambiguous. She wouldn't jump right into accusing him of ignoring her.

But if Nate thought he wanted to be married to her, he was going to have to figure out that she needed attention—even when she told him she didn't want his attention.

As she reached for her cell, it rang.

She grabbed it quickly without looking at the incoming number.

She was pathetic in her need to talk to him, to see him, but hell, she was willing to marry him without him loving her— what difference did it make if she didn't let the phone ring more than once when he called?

"Hello?"

"Emma, you have to come down here."

"Shannon?" She hadn't talked to the girl or Dena since Shannon's phone call from the police station. She knew the girl would forgive her and they would soon be shoe shopping together again—or maybe baby clothes shopping now. Shannon was going to love being a pseudo-aunt-big-sister to this baby. "You mad at me?" she asked Shannon.

"Only a little."

"You're going to get over it and realize it was tough love—for you and your mom."

"I know."

"Cool."

"You have to get down here. Please, Emma. He's making such a big deal about this and it's ridiculous. He's going to piss everyone off."

"Who? Michael?"

"Nate."

Her heart tripped even hearing his name. It was probably a good thing he wanted to marry her—no matter the reason—because she'd never feel like this about another guy again. "Where are you?" And what the hell was Nate doing?

"Carl-Mart."

Emma groaned. "What's he doing now?" Had her reluctance to marry him pushed him over the edge? She shouldn't like that idea as much as she did.

She grabbed her keys and headed for the door.

"He's having a meeting with the management staff. He wants them to put up this huge sign in the store."

Emma stopped walking. "*What?* A sign about what?"

"A warning sign in the condom aisle. So that everyone can be better informed that condoms are not one-hundred percent effective in preventing pregnancy."

Maybe he *wasn't* as thrilled with the baby news as she'd thought. That sucked.

She started for the car again. "Doesn't everyone already know that condoms aren't one-hundred percent effective?"

"He's got handouts, a Power Point presentation, everything. You're the only one who can calm him down," Shannon said.

"I'm on my way."

This was stupid. No way would Carl-Mart put up a big sign cautioning people *against* buying something they sold. What the hell? He was under a lot of pressure. Michael was growing up, Michael's girlfriend was a bit of a troublemaker, he was about to be a new dad…maybe he'd cracked.

Shannon met her by the doors at Carl-Mart.

"What are you wearing?" she asked when she saw Emma.

Emma looked down at her yoga pants and tank top. "I was…cleaning."

"You weren't getting ready for your date?"

"No." She'd been thinking about getting ready for her date, but she hadn't gotten even as far as taking her hair out of the bun.

Shannon smiled. "He was right."

"Who?"

"Nate said you were going to stand him up. That's why he's doing this."

He'd known? "Protesting the condoms?"

Shannon's smile turned sly. "Come with me."

Shannon took her hand and led her down the center aisle. Emma found herself almost jogging to keep up with the younger girl. They turned down the Play Doh aisle, then stepped out into the lawn and garden department.

And there was Nate.

No Power Point, no handouts. He was in a suit and tie and was standing next to the patio table where they'd sat together the day they'd followed Shannon and Michael.

If her heart tripped hearing his name, it swooped and looped and downright fluttered upon seeing him.

"What's going on?" Emma asked as Shannon dropped her hand and nudged her forward.

"Considering it's *you*, I knew this had to be big and bold," Nate told her.

She took a tentative step forward. "This?"

"My proposal."

She felt her mouth curl. "You mean, 'we'll get married' wasn't the proposal?"

"No. That was a reaction." He gave a self-deprecating smile. "*This* is the proposal."

He stepped back and she saw the patio table was covered with a multitude of items. She stepped closer, taking each thing in. There was a bowl of chocolate covered pretzels, a ticket stub, a blender and a box with a bow.

She picked up the ticket stub and realized it was from the Washburn Theater from the first night they'd hung out, spying on Shannon and Michael. The pretzels were certainly a key to her heart, and she couldn't help but grin at the blender—and the memory of the woman she'd confessed to about Nate's effect on her.

And then there was the box.

An engagement ring. If she opened that box and put that ring on her finger, it would be a sign to the world that she belonged to Nate. Most of all, it would be a sign to him that she was his. As her brother had pointed out, being the center of Nate's attention would be an intense place to be.

A place she wanted to be.

She picked up the box with a trembling hand, pulled the bow free, and opened it.

That was when it registered that the box was too big to be a ring box.

Inside was a set of nipple suckers.

She looked up at him, unable to keep from grinning. "You got me."

The look in his eyes was instantly hot and possessive and her mirth died.

He stepped forward. "I hope so. That's exactly what I want—to have you. All of you." Instead of reaching for her, he grabbed the blender and handed it to her. "This stuff represents our story. Crazy and unconventional and fun and nothing that I would have ever expected."

She took the blender and hugged it. "Unexpected. Good word."

"Falling in love with you wasn't unexpected, though," he said.

Her heart tripped. He'd fallen in love. He'd said it with witnesses. "Oh?"

"It took about ten minutes here in Carl-Mart to realize that I wanted to be with you every day for the rest of my life."

She felt her eyes sting. "Ten minutes? Have you been talking to my brother?"

Nate shook his head. "I'm staunchly avoiding your brother."

"Oh." She motioned for him to go on. "You were saying something about not being able to live without me." She especially liked that part. She wouldn't mind hearing it again and again. For fifty or sixty years.

He gave her a half grin. "Exactly. And most importantly, that happened here, in Carl-Mart in the midst of blenders and Play-Doh, instead of in the hotel room or the park or your kitchen."

That was nice. He hadn't fallen for her in the sexy times. It had been the silly, fun trip to Carl-Mart, of all places. That was very nice. Romantic even.

He turned and picked something else up from the table. He handed her the baby blanket.

Tears threatened and her throat felt tight. "This is beautiful."

"*This* is the most unexpected thing of all, obviously," Nate said. "But the blender came first. I don't want you to forget that."

She swallowed hard. "I know you said you were falling, but…you didn't finish."

Except that this seemed complete. It had been fast and a huge surprise, but *she'd* fallen totally in love in that amount of time. Maybe he could have fallen all the way too.

He stepped close, the blender the only thing separating their bodies, and took hold of her upper arms. "The way I see it," he said, low and husky. "I have the next eighteen years—give or take a few months—to prove to you that I was done falling long before that pregnancy test came back."

Looking into his eyes at that moment, she felt it—the satisfaction of her heart accepting that this was real.

She smiled. "Eighteen years? And then what?"

"If by the time our child graduates from high school, you don't believe that I'm head over heels, do-anything-to-have-you in love, then we'll get a divorce."

Her smile grew. Eighteen years of Nate proving how he felt? Laughing, fighting and playing?

That was a good start.

"I'll give you twenty years," she said, her voice thick. "You know, by the time our second graduates."

She couldn't have named the exact emotion in his eyes at that, but it was a combination of happiness, and heat, and love. Definitely love.

So that's what that looked like. She could get used to that.

And then there was the kissing.

He pushed the blender and blanket out of the way and pulled her up against him, kissing her long and hot and sweet. Until they heard two teenagers clearing their throats behind them. Emma pulled back and she had to ask, "Michael helped you come up with this whole Carl-Mart proposal thing?"

He nodded. "He's an expert on how to make a headstrong, mouthy girl fall in love with him."

"Hmm, good point." She stepped back slightly. "I hate to mention it, but…"

He gave her a grin. "Yes?"

"This is all very sweet and romantic."

"Yes it is."

"But…"

"Emma," he said in that delicious low voice.

"You haven't actually proposed."

His grin grew. "You sure about that?"

"What do you mean?"

He took her by the shoulders and turned her, then pointed up.

From the ceiling at Carl-Mart hung a huge, bright blue sign with yellow letters that said, "Emma Dixon, will you marry me?"

She laughed even as the tears started. Damned hormones. "There really was a big sign you wanted the management to put up?"

He wrapped his arms around her from behind, his hands resting on her belly.

"I love you, Em, and I promise you I can and will give you all the attention, all the spotlight, all the public spectacles you need."

Yes, he could. She laughed again. "It's been like one big spectacle since I got into your truck that night."

And then, before either of them could say anything, or do anything else, they were surrounded by people.

There were some random shoppers who had been drawn by the sign, but most importantly, her sisters were all there as were Dena and all the guys, Ryan, Shane, Cody and even Conner. Everyone was carrying drinks or snacks and they quickly pulled up additional patio and lawn furniture for the make-shift engagement party. They'd all been hanging out in other parts of the store, waiting for Shannon and Michael's signal that they could move in. Now everyone was hugging and laughing, asking questions, talking about wedding plans and what was coming up with the baby.

Emma felt more tears slip free. Nate Sullivan had proposed to her in public. He'd proclaimed his feelings and claimed her in front of an audience. She loved it. It was big and crazy and unconventional and she absolutely, freaking loved it.

Nate and Emma let everyone separate them for the moment. Emma found herself pushed into one of the patio chairs, Nate was a few feet away talking with Michael and Ryan.

But Isabelle and Olivia had barely started planning the baby shower and Amanda was in the midst of explaining why it was more appropriate to have a *bridal* shower first, when Emma felt her phone vibrate.

Everyone she knew was here with her. Confused, she pulled her phone out.

It was a text from Nate.

I'm in the mood to buy a sleeping bag.

She laughed and typed in, *I'll meet you in aisle sixteen. Bring the nipple suckers.*

In less than a minute, Nate was by her chair, pulling her to her feet. "See, how could I not be totally in love?"

She wrapped her arms around him and stepped into a hug. "Then you're going to be falling at my feet in another twenty-two years."

"Twenty-two?"

"Yeah, you know, after our third goes to college."

Heat flared between them and Nate said, low enough for only her to hear, "I'm thinking I'm gonna need more than a sleeping bag tonight."

"Oh, an air mattress at least."

He turned to the crowd of family and friends. "We're leaving now. And Michael and Shannon?"

The teens looked over from where they were talking with Cody and Shane.

"You need to go out tonight," he told them. "And stay out late." He looked down at Emma. "Really late."

Emma laughed as he swept her up into his arms and started for the front of the store. Over his shoulder, Emma gave Shannon a wink. "And don't call us for bail this time."

Thank you for reading Why You Should Never Kiss Your Enemy! I hope you loved Nate and Emma!

Cody and Olivia's hot friends to lovers story, *Why You Should Never Kiss Your Best Friend* **is up next!**

Cody Madsen has stayed away from Olivia Dixon for almost two years—technically. Even though he talks to her every day and sees her every weekend. But there's no kissing, touching, or telling her how he really feels.

Olivia wants what her three sisters have—true love. She could almost believe she's found it with Cody, if it weren't for the fact that he's her older brother's best friend and her brother won't have it.

She needs to move on. Fall in love with someone else once and for all.

Her solution? The "Perfect Pick" dating site where they can each finally find love.

But how will she handle someone else being his soul mate?

Or someone else being hers?

Grab *Why You Should Never Kiss Your Best Friend* **now! Or read on for an excerpt!**

ഗ

Find all of my books (including a printable book list) **at ErinNicholas.com**

ഗ

And join in on all the FAN FUN!

Join my **email list!**

bit.ly/Keep-In-Touch-Erin
(be sure you get those dashes and capital letters in there!)

And be the first to hear about my news, sales, freebies, behind-the-scenes, and more!

Or for even more fun, join my **Super Fan page** on Facebook and chat with me and other super fans every day! Just search Facebook for Erin Nicholas Super Fans!

ᶜ

Enjoy this excerpt from Why You Should Never Kiss Your Best Friend!

Cody Madsen had never seen Olivia Dixon naked. Until today.

And there was a very good reason for that.

Two, in fact.

She was his best friend. And her brother would kill him.

But damn, the sight was breathtaking.

Breathtaking enough that his entire system short-circuited and all he could think was *Every day for the rest of my life.*

"Cody! Oh my God! What are you doing here?"

She'd obviously just stepped from the bathroom. Her hair was wrapped in a towel, the scent of her favorite shower gel and lotion were strong in the air and, most significantly, she was as naked as the day she was born.

Which had to be why his brain and mouth would not connect.

Olivia crossed an arm over her breasts—her glorious, perky, perfect breasts—and put a hand over her even-more-private part—the mouthwatering, holy crap, light blond hair that was trimmed into a perfect *V* pointing the way home—and said louder, "What are you *doing*?"

But it wasn't until another voice hit his ears that Cody was able to pull himself out of the Olivia-is-even-hotter-than-I-thought daze.

"Cody! I'm heading to the fuse box!"

Olivia's eyebrows arched. "Is that Conner?"

It was. And Cody's first spoken word on the matter was, "Fuck."

He grabbed her upper arms, backed her into the bathroom and kicked the door shut.

That proved to be the biggest mistake of all. Her skin was silky and warm and he should *never* have touched her.

"What's Conner doing here?"

Cody was an idiot. When he'd first seen that she was naked, he should have turned around and gotten the hell out of here. Instead, what had he done? He'd touched her. Then he'd put himself in a closed room with her.

A tiny closed room.

"There's a good reason we instituted the conservative-clothing-at-all-times rule," he said gruffly.

She still had her arm and hand covering the most important parts, but that didn't matter one iota. He was never going to be able to forget what he'd seen.

"That rule is for when we're together," she said.

"We're together now." Wow, were they. Her scent was imprinted on his brain. Now, standing submerged in a cloud of it between her and the bottles on the shelf behind her, he found himself taking deeper and deeper breaths—and growing harder and harder.

The naked-breasts-and-other-parts thing wasn't helping.

"I didn't know we were going to be together now," she returned. "What are you—and *Conner*— doing here?"

"Fixing the outlet in the kitchen that's not working." He

breathed deeply and concentrated on keeping his eyes on hers. "I texted you."

"My battery died."

"Why are you naked?"

"I took a shower."

"You're not in the shower *now*. Do I need to buy you a robe?"

"I don't need a robe when I'm in my house, presumably alone."

"You always walk around the house naked when you're alone?"

"Yes."

He had nothing after that. He pressed his lips together and resolutely continued to focus on things *above* her shoulders. Like the two empty towel racks. "Where are your other towels?"

"In the dryer."

He pulled the towel from her head, handing it to her. "God. Cover up."

She wrapped the towel around her body, her wet hair falling past her shoulders, big blue eyes staring at him. "You okay?"

"Yeah, why?"

"You look…weird."

"This is, apparently, how I look when I'm trying with every fiber of my being not to kiss you."

Grab *Why You Should Never Kiss Your Best Friend* now!

WHY YOU SHOULD NEVER... THE SERIES

Why You Should Never...

MORE FROM ERIN

Want more hot protective guys who wear badges? Try my Badges of the Bayou series!

Badges of the Bayou
Gotta Be Bayou (Spencer & Max)
Bayou With Benefits (Michael & Ami)
Rocked Bayou (Colin & Hayden)

*

If you love steamy romance with big groups of family and friends, check out my Boys of the Bayou series!

Boys of the Bayou
My Best Friend's Mardi Gras Wedding (Josh & Tori)
Sweet Home Louisiana (Owen & Maddie)
Beauty and the Bayou (Sawyer & Juliet)
Crazy Rich Cajuns (Bennett & Kennedy)
Must Love Alligators (Chase & Bailey)
Four Weddings and a Swamp Boat Tour (Mitch & Paige)

*

ABOUT ERIN NICHOLAS

Erin Nicholas is the New York Times and USA Today bestselling author of over thirty sexy contemporary romances. Her stories have been described as toe-curling, enchanting, steamy and fun. She loves to write about reluctant heroes, imperfect heroines and happily ever afters. She lives in the Midwest with her husband who only wants to read the sex scenes in her books, her kids who will never read the sex scenes in her books, and family and friends who say they're shocked by the sex scenes in her books (yeah, right!).
Find her here:

facebook.com/ErinNicholasBooks
bookbub.com/authors/erin-nicholas
goodreads.com/author/show/3155383.Erin_Nicholas
tiktok.com/@erinnicholasbooks

Printed by BoD™ in Norderstedt, Germany